SILVERBROOK

SILVERBROOK

HISTORICAL EPIC ADVENTURE WITH STUDY GUIDE

Karen Petersen

Writers Club Press
San Jose New York Lincoln Shanghai

SILVERBROOK
HISTORICAL EPIC ADVENTURE WITH STUDY GUIDE

Writers Club Press
an imprint of iUniverse.com, Inc.

For information address:
iUniverse.com, Inc.
5220 S 16th, Ste. 200
Lincoln, NE 68512
www.iuniverse.com

ISBN: 0-595-19690-X

Printed in the United States of America

To my mother Gloria Anderson,
who led me on a journey into historical research.

Contents

Main Characters

Nicholas (Nic) Steubing—The main character of the book
Fritz Nagel—Nic's best friend
Herr Zeller—Captain of the immigrant group and Nic's mentor
Opa and Oma—Nic's grandparents
Tante Gretchen—Nic's aunt
MaMa and PaPa—Nic's parents
Dorothea—Nic's sister
The Gray—The gray house given to Nic by Herr Zeller
Herr Nagel and Frau Nagel—Fritz's parents
Captain Kerr—Captain of the "Angelina"
Baron von Musebach—Leader of the immigrants in Texas
Harry Knight—Nic's friend and business partner
Katherine—Fritz's wife
Matilda "Mati" Heskie—PaPa's second wife
Millard Lancaster—Captain in the U. S. Army
Anka—Indian scout
Wilhelm and Ella Steubing—Nic's half siblings
Anna—Anka's niece in Mexico
Ernst and Fritz Nagel Jr.—Fritz's sons

German Vocabulary

Opa—Grandpa
Oma—Grandma
Tante—Aunt
Aldesverine—A company which settled immigrants in Texas
Gutten Tag—Good day
Wilkomen zu Texas—Welcome to Texas
Shootzenfest—Shooting contest
Ya, das is gute—Yes, that is good
Ser gute—Very good
Ya—Yes
Danke—Thank you
Herr—Mr.
Frau—Mrs.
Verinskirche—Building used for school and church
Schnell—Fast or quick

CHAPTER I

THE JOURNEY

Rustling sounds stirred the lush green grass, and an explosion of brown and white feathers burst through the air in several directions. Fritz instantly grasped a rock, throwing it at the mass of flapping wings. Fritz was always throwing rocks, and it would seem that by now he could hit something. But the quail retreated to safety long before the rock became fully airborne. We were hungry for meat, but without the benefit of a gun, the prospects for a tasty supper grew dim. Corn meal boiled in water was not a real supper, and having it every morning, noon, and night was dreadful. I had always considered corn to be food only good enough for the animals, and now corn was all we had to eat. Herr Zeller had promised that we soon would be met with appropriate provisions to last until or arrival in New Braunfels. If the weather held, and we were not bogged down in the mud, we would arrive at that golden oasis of New Braunfels within 10 to 15 days, where we would be able to indulge on juicy sausages, potatoes, fresh bread, butter, and milk. It seemed so near in my mind, yet like so many more steps toward the horizon.

Our journey began over two months ago with our departure from Bicken, Germany, the town in which our family had resided for many generations. My father, Johann, his father, and his father before him, had been in the freighting business. Their oxen-drawn wagons traveled from the harbor cities hauling freight to many small towns that speckled the coast, and as far as Frankfort and even stretching to the mountains of the BlackForest.

Opa and Oma were old and there was no reason to spend their meager savings to travel this great distance with us. Tante Gretchen promised to take care of them, and my father would send money as soon as he could earn a wage in Texas. Papa would probably be a farmer there, for it seemed that the few wagons and oxen for sale were priced extremely high.

Many warned that traveling across this desolate land of Texas made us vulnerable to Indian or outlaw attacks. We therefore traveled in a group of approximately 30 families. Ten wagons hauled all of our possessions, as we walked. The uncomfortable ride was rarely missed as the hard wooden wheels jostled roughly over rocks and caused one's stomach to ache. MaMa teased that we children (I was not really a child) had walked twice as far already, because we ran and played, waiting for the slow wagons to catch us. MaMa warned us many times (too many times) to stay close to the wagons, for she had been told of the venomous snakes that lurked between the rocks. The noise stirred by this many people, oxen, and wagons seemed to warn all wild animals of our approach and it was unusual to see a covey of quail like we did today. Herr Zeller and three armed guards, mounted on horseback, accompanied our group. They refused to shoot wild animals for meat, conserving their bullets and gun powder for emergencies. If I had a rifle I knew I could have shot the wild deer that I saw bounding across the meadow near the creek this morning. I promised myself to save money until I could purchase my own rifle, and I would practice until I was the best shot in New Braunfels. I would lead people through the wilderness just as Herr Zeller did, but I would make sufficient bullets, and have enough gun powder to shoot animals for starving sojourners. The sojourners under my protection would not be required to eat corn mush.

*   *   *

Papa never thought about leaving our German homeland until he was stopped at a nearby town and asked to pay a toll fee, or tax, assessed according to the weight of the load he carried. The assessor looked at the load and then highly estimated the tax, saying that it was too time consuming to unload each box or bag and weigh it. When this same experience was repeated in several other towns and Papa protested, the authorities informed him that he could by-pass their town if he did not want to pay the tax. To bypass the town he would have to cross a river and ascend a mountain. The price to buy grain for the oxen doubled last year, and taxes on our old house, which once belonged to Oma and Opa, had tripled in the last five years. This was mandated by His Excellency, The Duke of Nasau.

My cousin Frederick asked His Excellency for permission to marry, but he was told that there were already too many families in Bicken. Frederick came to Papa and complained bitterly, for he was very much in love with a beautiful maiden. Frederick returned to our house one month later with a small book which he had purchased in Frankfort. He had attended a meeting of young men who were making plans to sail to America. Frederick purchased the book from one of the men who said he no longer needed it since his decision to go was firm. The book told about amazing amounts of land which were free to settlers in the United States. One must live on the land for three years to receive its ownership. Skeptical about such an adventure, Papa warned Frederick about gambling hard earned wages on such schemes. After that visit Papa seemed to sit outside almost every night thoughtfully smoking his pipe, staring into the darkness. When I told him about my plans to build a small wagon, he only nodded his head and later said, "Oh, ya that would be good". At the end of the week I found myself huddled on the stairway at the bedroom door, listening to PaPa and MaMa. MaMa said "no" to whatever PaPa had proposed. Six weeks later Frederick returned to inform us that he, his fiancee, and her brother would be departing for New York City in the United States. A friend would lead them to Pennsylvania where they would work on a dairy farm. As soon as money was saved, he would marry his beloved and then search for their own land in the Western United States. Frederick was convinced that he would become a rich landowner and his children would enjoy his wealth. Papa shook Frederick's hand and gave him a pouch of tobacco as a going-away gift. MaMa gave him a whole loaf of dark bread, which left us short of bread the next day. Frederick promised that he would write us a letter when he was settled in Pennsylvania.

PaPa was forced to sell the two yearling oxen in order to pay taxes. Because the winter was very harsh, we desperately gathered wood in the mountains to sell in Bicken for cash. The cold caused my sister Dorothea to become very ill in her chest, and MaMa nervously rocked her next to the fireplace for days before she felt better. Oma brought herbs and made a hot tea for Dorothea to sip. Just before Christmas PaPa came home with the first letter from Frederick and he read it silently to himself while MaMa was cooking supper. After we were in bed, I heard him reading it to MaMa. It said that Frederick was doing well at the dairy farm and that the United States was wonderful. He said that he would be married by Easter, and by next Christmas he hoped to be on his own land in the West. I fell asleep dreaming of Christmas at our house with Oma and Opa, my cousins, and my sister. I would get a new sled that was painted red with gold stripes on the edges.

At school the next day I told my friend Amol about the letter from Frederick. He said that his father was planning now for his family to embark on the same adventure. I felt sad that my friend was leaving. I soon began to wonder what the United States was like and why everyone there was so content.

Our neighbor's son, Gustof, got a letter delivered by an army private. The letter stated that Gustof was to report to Frankfort to become a soldier the next Monday. PaPa said that this was because Gustof was now 16 years old, and every 16 year old boy must become a soldier if he was called by His Excellency. Since I was 14 years old, I began to realize that the same thing could happen to me in the future. My Uncle Burton went to the army and never returned. Over three years later, PaPa found out that he had been killed, but did not know where or how. Soldiers had stopped PaPa's wagons and taken whatever they needed including turnips, blankets, and even two hogs. The men were very dirty, and one had his feet wrapped in rags. Once PaPa protested and a soldier struck him with his fist. PaPa fell to the ground and later his cheek turned black and blue, and then purple. PaPa lost all respect for the army.

Since Dorothea's birth ten years before, MaMa was sick much of the time with a severe cough. I learned to help her and could even knead the bread dough. I brought in the wood, kept the fire going in the kitchen hearth, and helped PaPa feed the oxen each morning and evening. PaPa even taught me to drive his older oxen team so that I could help him, but he also valued education and insisted that I continue in school.

*   *   *

Tonight the wagons were stopped along a lush green river called the Guadalupe. Herr Zeller called to me to take his horse to the river. I was sure to go downstream where the other animals were drinking so as not to muddy the water upstream where the people would drink. Herr Zeller promised me that I could one day learn to ride this powerful animal with black legs blended into an unusual gray coat. After the horse had his fill of water, I mounted him with PaPa's assistance, for the stirrup was too high for me to reach with my foot alone. We trailed behind PaPa back to the camp area where I dismounted and tied the horse to a rope which was strung between two trees. I untied the girth, the large leather belt that strapped around the horse's belly. Next I drug a log close to the horse, steadying myself on top to give me added height, and hoisted the bulky leather saddle off the horse. The unsure animal turned his head to watch this process with large dark eyes. I untied the horse, knotted a rope to his halter, and lead him to a clearing nearby, but not too close to the wagons. Enjoying this moment of rest, the horse lowered into the powdery dirt and rolled on his back, rubbing the ground beneath. Then, with a big heave, he sprang up onto his feet and shook every part of his body all at once. Dust thickened the air and felt rough against my face. The gray horse was eager to eat, so I led him slowly as he nibbled. Hunger and exhaustion masked his usual spirit, so he willingly followed me. He picked the tender shoots of new grass emerging from the soil, and even chose certain weeds that had a small flower at the top. After some time I saw an army of red ants progressing toward a hole in the ground. It was curious that the ants had cleared the grass from around the hole and the area was now filled with stickers. Herr Zeller once informed me that the stickers helped to keep predators from stepping on the ant bed, and that the red ants could sting or bite. I poked a stick into the ant hole and twenty or more red ants crawled onto the stick. The gray horse was chewing very slowly and seemed to be quite pleased with his meal. We wandered back to camp and I tied him to the rope between the trees. I rummaged for the curry comb and brush, working to get the dust from his hair. He lazily cocked one of his back feet and closed his eyes.

Next I filled the bucket from our family wagon with river water for washing and cleaning at the camp fire. MaMa and two other ladies carefully wiped the dust from a big black cooking pot and then put water in it to boil over the fire. Three other families watched reluctantly as MaMa added corn meal. There was an emptiness in our stomachs, but at the same time we were all very tired of corn mush. It seemed that the gray horse had a better meal than I, for a least he got to eat a variety of grasses and he seemed to be full and satisfied. My stomach still wished for more and my mind reminisced about sausages and applekuchen.

*   *   *

Last winter PaPa went with his cousin, Helmut, to the city of Frankfort for a load of fabrics, tobacco, flour and pickles. They would distribute the goods to several different towns en route back to Bicken. Upon his return PaPa was very happy and smiling like I had not seen since Christmas. He whistled as we unhitched the oxen and bedded them in the barn with hay. He kissed MaMa on the cheek and picked up Dorothea, giving her a hug. After our diner of potatoes and bread, PaPa presented a large piece of paper which he was given in Frankfort. At the top it said, "Land—Free Land", followed by many paragraphs telling about the United States and its free land in the west. PaPa said to all of us that he would like to consider immigrating to the United States. MaMa's face grew pale and she became very quiet.

PaPa said that he would wait to hear again from his nephew Frederick, who was still in Pennsylvania, before making his final decision.

The next night PaPa went to Tante Gretchen's house where he visited with Oma and Opa and told them of his plan. PaPa never told us what they said, but it seemed that PaPa was becoming more determined to immigrate. Two nights later I could hear MaMa and PaPa quietly discussing this wild idea of his, and I was happy that there seemed to be no arguing, just talking. PaPa assured MaMa that he would be very careful in his decision and would not act in haste.

*　　　*　　　*

I was dreaming of snow and the old sled I used to have to go down the hills around Bicken after school. But who was shouting? What were they saying? I pulled my eyelids open as far as my tired eyes allowed to see men running by my blanket. I tried to hear as I jumped up and followed them. "The horses, the horses!" they were shouting as they disappeared into the darkness. I rushed to the trees where I had left the gray horse tied, but the animal was gone! Herr Zeller came running with his rifle, and we followed to the top of the ridge in confusion.

Herr Gruene started hopping, yelling bad words in German.

When I reached him I realized that he had run into a cactus plant in his bare stocking feet. Cactus thorns embedded his long underwear and he tried to pull off his socks. I stopped to help him, he put his arm around my shoulder, and hopped on one foot back to the nearest camp fire. I ran to find his wife in the maze of people milling around by the fire staring out into the dark night. She went to him to help pull out the needle-like stickers which seemed an impossible task. Herr Gruene hobbled to the river and relieved his sore feet with the cold water. I was assigned to stay with him to watch for outlaws, Indians, ghosts, or whatever might have caused all of this trouble.

The younger children began playing by the fires and the women brewed coffee. Those who gave chase were now back in camp, yet no one returned to bed. Herr Zeller said we must wait until dawn to begin looking for the two missing horses. I helped Herr Gruene back beside his wife where he sat near the fire drinking coffee. PaPa and MaMa began boiling water in the big black pot so that soon we could eat more of that awful corn mush.

Gradually we saw the outline of trees, and then the eastern sky grew pink. Herr Zeller, and one other rifled man, searched for the horses. The other two men with rifles stayed in camp warning us to remain close to the wagons for fear that we could be attacked. The men discussed ways to defend the group in case this should happen. The men yoked the oxen and had the wagons in a ready position. Then the men found a variety of weapons including butcher knives, sticks, and pitch forks. The older boys picked up medium sized rocks with which we were sure that we could wound an enemy. As the sun rose higher, the tranquil countryside felt very peaceful and quiet and our emotions of concern gave way to boredom. There was no sign of anyone else as far as we could see. Around noon, as the pots boiled corn mush for dinner, Herr Zeller and the other man returned. They suspected that Mexican bandits had taken the horses, but there was no catching up with them. After we ate our corn mush we all began a new day's journey. Herr Zeller rode one of the other horses. I missed the gray and hoped that he would not be mistreated by his captors.

*   *   *

It was Sunday morning in Bicken, Germany and the bells of the Lutheran Church called us to worship. We stood very still, I by PaPa on the right side of the church, and Dorothea by MaMa on the left side of the church. The sermon seemed very long and I shifted from one foot to the other. If only I could sit I would not mind the cold, damp rock floor. Finally the service ended. We ritually went outside to play in the street while the adults talked to relatives and friends. As we walked home together, PaPa mentioned that a meeting was to be held that night in Luder, the next town. A new company was providing land in the state called Texas. PaPa met friends in the town square that afternoon, they boarded our oxen cart and rode to the nearby town. I anxiously waited for PaPa to return but MaMa insisted that Dorothea and I to go to bed, reminding us that if the meeting lasted very late that the men would camp in a friend's barn and start the journey back to Bicken in the morning.

Noises filled the street below. I rolled off my cot and peered out the window to see PaPa and several other men talking beside our barn. They shook PaPa's hand and departed. PaPa unhitched the oxen and led them inside the barn. I pulled on my pants, shirt, coat, and boots, and ran to the barn to help. PaPa whistled while he fed the animals, and I immediately asked what happened last night. PaPa said to wait until breakfast and he would tell us all at once. As we ate our day old bread with butter and jelly, and drank coffee, PaPa told about the meeting.

A group of rich German business men formed a company called Aldesverine that helped immigrants to settle the land called Texas. The company had purchased land suitable for farming. One price paid for everything, including the boat trip, food en route, transportation inland, 300 acres of land, a lot in town, a house, and farm equipment. When the immigrants arrived they would build schools and churches. It was all very well organized. The problem was that before boat passage could be booked, money had to be paid in full. This very high price, six hundred Florins, would require us to sell everything that we owned. PaPa went to the church to pray about this big decision. MaMa kept wiping her hands nervously with the dish towel and biting her bottom lip. This meant that she was worried, but would not say anything in front of us children. My sister and I rapidly asked questions such as, "What will happen to Oma and Opa?", "Can we take our sleds?", "Can we tell the kids at school?" PaPa promised to answer questions later, and asked us not to tell anyone yet.

As I walked through the school house door, Fritz anxiously announced he was going to Texas. When he asked if I would be going along, I admitted that I hoped to go, and then we talked about Texas. On the globe in Herr Schmidt's classroom we saw that the United States was very large, and we had no idea where to look for Texas. Then we remembered that Texas was reached by ship, so it must be on the ocean. We started at the right top of the United States shape on the globe, and kept searching down the coastline and then across. I spotted Texas first and jumped for joy in solving the problem. Fritz and I looked at the many rivers and streams shown on the map and agreed that it must be a very lush, green paradise. We hardly heard our lessons at all that day. After school we walked together imagining how we would help our families through this great adventure. We pictured ourselves as old men telling wonderful stories to our children and grand children about our younger years.

Arriving home, the house was quiet and empty. I began to bring in fire wood and pump water to be used for cleaning and cooking. Near dark PaPa, MaMa, and Dorothea arrived by wagon. I helped everyone get down and put the animals in the barn with plenty of hay and water. Then I walked into the house finding MaMa, PaPa, and Dorothea seated at the table. No food has been cooked yet, but this time had been chosen to discuss the situation. PaPa announced that, after contemplation and prayer, he had decided that we must begin a new life in Texas, a land offering freedom of choices and much opportunity. My sister and I clapped our hands and asked when we would leave. Our ship would depart from Baden on April 1, leaving only three weeks to quickly sell all that we had and pack. We would choose carefully what we took because, in the future, what was in the trunk would be our only possessions. Each family was limited to one trunk per person, which meant that we must leave room in each trunk for household items such as pots, pans, candles, dish towels, and utensils. We would wear our warmest clothes and our coats. MaMa said that I must wear my coat even though the sleeves were too short.

One week later PaPa brought a man to our house who specialized in purchasing property from those who were in a hurry to sell. PaPa showed him our old home and told him how good the barn was. PaPa hoped the man did not notice the holes in the barn roof. They were not so visible on a cloudy day, but that day the sun shone and little rays of light peeked through the holes on the hay below. The man returned the next day and offered PaPa 680 Florins for the house and barn. He would add 90 Florins more to also buy the house furnishings, which were sparse. PaPa agreed if he was paid within one week, for PaPa, and the buyer both knew that, because several families were leaving Bicken, there were many houses for sale. It would be difficult to find another buyer with a better offer.

I began to look at all of my belongings trying to decide what to take and what to leave behind forever. I would need my three pairs of pants. The best pair was for church, the next was for school and the third pair, which had holes in the knees, was used for working. I would also take my three shirts which were used in the same way as the pants. I had a coat (the sleeves were too short), and a cap with ear muffs that tied under the chin. I had two pair of underwear, the kind with long arms and long legs. I also had a night shirt made from one of PaPa's old shirts. I added my sheet and wool blanket. I would take two or three books to read along the way, but all of my books were special to me. Each day I would set aside three books to think about, and each evening I seemed to change my mind again.

On Sunday we got up before daylight and rode by wagon to the town of Heilmut, about five miles away, to visit MaMa's sister. She was surprised that we would embark on such an adventure and said that PaPa must have the "wanderlust". PaPa tried to tell her how wonderful our new life in Texas would be. She tried to understand, but cried when we departed. MaMa was very quiet.

* * *

As soon as we ungratefully finished the corn mush, Herr Zeller instructed everyone to pack, for we had to travel as far as possible due to loss of time hunting for the horses. We continued over the grasslands and at about mid-afternoon saw buzzards circling in front of us. Fritz and I asked Herr Zeller if we could run ahead to see what the buzzards were after. Herr Zeller said "no", and that we should fall back to our own wagons. Herr Zeller sent his assistant ahead on horseback to check. Fritz and I watched carefully for his return and ran to meet him. Herr Zeller signaled for the wagons to halt as he and his helper rode about 50 feet away from us and began to talk. Pulling their rifles from their saddle scabbards, they galloped in the direction of the buzzards. We stood by the wagons, all eyes on the vanishing horses as they rode over a small hill. Shortly they returned and called a meeting. Herr Zeller stood before us all to say that the buzzards lurked about two dead bodies. A gasp came from the crowd. The bodies appeared to be Mexican traders who probably had goods on pack mules or donkeys. They were attacked and killed by arrows. Even the young children seemed to shudder when the method of death was mentioned. Herr Zeller thought that perhaps the same Indians captured two of our horses, but were probably scared by the large number of men in our camp. Hopefully they did not realize that we had very few weapons. Five men volunteered to help bury the bodies. We camped there for the night in a tight circle and sparingly used the little water we had stored in barrels on the sides of the wagons. The children stayed very close to the wagons and no one left the wagon circle after dark without the permission of Herr Zeller. There was plenty of discussion around the camp fire that night. No one in this group had ever seen an Indian, but all had heard that they were fierce and likely to kill. Some stories warned that they had even stolen children. I put a pile of rocks beside me as I lay down in my blanket and tried to stay awake as long as possible to help PaPa protect our family.

Awakened by children running by my blanket, I jumped with a startle, rubbing my eyes and looking around. Another day had dawned and the men quickly hitched up the oxen and the women prepared to cook corn mush. We quickly ate and hurried along to reach the river as soon as possible. After eating the terrible corn mush, we began the journey once more. Kids hesitantly walked next to the wagons as we passed the place where the two men were killed, and we saw the fresh dirt on their graves. Everyone quietly paid their respects for the dead. Herr Zeller stopped the wagons for everyone to say the Lord's Prayer in unison.

At noon we stopped for a short rest and more corn mush. Just before dark we arrived at the Guadalupe River where we all rushed to get a filling drink of cool water. I helped Herr Zeller with his horse, and then hauled water to the camp. Just before dark there was much excitement as a wagon was spotted on the other side of the river. Herr Zeller shouted to the four men with the wagon and soon they crossed down stream from the camp. Everyone lined up and watched them arrive with great joy and excitement. To my amazement they lead the gray horse that was stolen from Herr Zeller. When the wagon stopped everyone clapped, including PaPa and MaMa. The men each carried a rifle, spoke German, and looked fit, handsome and healthy. We felt tired and dirty by comparison. The men told Herr Zeller that they found his horse the day before and became very worried when the wagon train did not arrive on time. The women served coffee as we gathered to hear the men talk. They arrived here yesterday from New Braunfels. When we did not arrive, they decided to wait another day before searching for us. They heard us coming to the river and then saw the water become muddy, so they started upstream looking for us. They brought food which would be evenly distributed between the ten wagons. They reported that there had been Indian raids in the area, and that they were well armed to defend us. A sigh of relief fell among us. Each group stood by their designated wagon in an orderly line as food was distributed. Our mouths watered at the sight of a flour bag filled with smoked sausages and a crock of sauerkraut. They also gave us a bag of flour and cans of lard. Several fathers put their hands on their children's shoulders to let them know that they must remain beside their parents and not run toward the food. Our group leader, Herr Schmidt, graciously thanked the men from New Braunfels and had our men divide the food into ten units, one unit for each remaining day of our journey. After this was done, the food for the day was prepared. Each person got a slice of hard smoked sausage and a large spoonful of sauerkraut. It was the best sausage and kraut that any of us had ever eaten. We were now sure that New Braunfels must be a paradise. In the morning the women made the flour into large round biscuits and cooked them in the heavy pot with a lid on it. Each child got two biscuits and each adult got three. We spread lard on the biscuits and ate them with coffee. Unfortunately I was considered a child and received only two biscuits. We continued our journey with renewed vigor and optimism.

* * *

It was a sad day for all of us when PaPa took the four oxen to the auction to be sold. The oxen were used by our family for several generations, and these oxen were descendants of the oxen owned by my great-grandfather. PaPa returned late in the afternoon and said that it was done and we were no longer in the freighting business. That night PaPa went to see Oma and Opa and gave them one-third of the money from the sale of the house and oxen. Hopefully this money would be enough for them to survive until PaPa made more money in Texas.

On Sunday there was a large crowd at church. There was a special sermon and prayers for those departing from Bicken to Texas. Nine families,

45 people in all, would leave this week. There were many handshakes, hugs, and some tears as everyone said farewell in the town square. I knew that I would never return to Bicken, and that what I saw here would soon be a memory. We shed more tears that afternoon as we told Oma, Opa, and Tante Gretchen farewell. We would probably never see them again. With a pat on the head Opa gave me his pocket knife as a gift. I would keep it forever to remember him. PaPa would take the photograph of Oma and Opa to Texas and we would pray for them.

Hired wagons took the group from Bicken to the port of Baden where we were to board the ship. We brought sausage, sweet potatoes, and several loaves of bread to sustain us until departure. It was a hard journey, but excitement overcame exhaustion. We felt joyous and sorrowful all at once. MaMa and PaPa stared straight ahead trying not to look at friends and family who were there to bid us farewell. I rode in the wagon with Fritz and we waved to everyone as we passed. We talked about how much money we would have when we were men—large farms with big barns and brick houses, surreys pulled by a pair of matching black horses that pranced when they trotted, many acres of fine fields of sweet potatoes, cabbage and hay. I would wear a new coat each winter, and my well educated children would marry Fritz's children.

The overwhelming town of Baden astonished us, for we had never seen such a large city. People swarmed the streets where many horses and oxen pulled wagons and carts. The cobblestone streets were dirty and the people looked grim. A wall of buildings and stores lined our path to the shipping dock, where we made camp in the large warehouse building. I could not sleep and spent night hours staring at the high ceiling, or watching the hundreds of people lying down around us also trying to sleep. There were crying babies all around. PaPa warned us to stay close or else we could get lost in this sea of humanity. The number of people leaving Germany surprised us. We thought that we were a part of a small group of adventurers. Most of these people seemed to be poor, but maybe we appeared that way too. All were anxious to get through the night, get on a ship, sail across the ocean, reach the United States, and establish new homes. Though uncertain about the future, they clung to hopes for a future brighter than their past.

Finally the morning came. We rolled up our blankets and ate the bread that we had brought from home. PaPa stood in a very long line for a single bucket of water. He said that we must learn to conserve water and use as little as possible because water would be at a premium on the ship. We poured some water into a metal pot to be used for washing our hands. The remainder of the water was for drinking. There was no coffee today since fires could not be built here.

PaPa stood in another line to get our boarding passes. He returned to say that we must wait until our ship "Angelina" was called, which could be within the hour or even several more days. Fritz and his family camped next to us, and soon I got permission from PaPa to visit them. PaPa asked me not to go anywhere except near our two camps, for when they called the ship "Angelina" we must quickly take our bags and trunks to the loading dock. It would take two of us to load each of the four trunks. MaMa and Dorothea could carry our bedrolls and small bags. Fritz and I discussed how life might be on the ship. Maybe we could get a job helping the sailors, and climbing up to the crow's nest to see fish, whales, and icebergs. Perhaps the captain would invite us to his quarters and show us maps of the ocean, the United States, and our landing spot in Texas. We asked many questions of Fritz's PaPa, but he did not seem to know any answers. Did the adults know what we were doing? It was scary, but also very exciting. It was difficult to sit and wait, and be excited at the same time. Maybe the sailors would teach us how to use their cannons and swords and we would even help them to fire the cannons at enemy ships filled with pirates!

* * *

As we traveled through the vast Texas grassland we were all anxious to stop for dinner because we craved the taste of more sausage. Soon the sun shone above us and Herr Zeller called the wagons to a halt. Fritz and I ran to our wagon and offered to help prepare the food, for we were in a hurry to eat. The rations for this meal were small and we would have liked to eat all of the sausage that the large sack in the wagon held. Each person got a small piece of sausage and a biscuit left over from breakfast. After we drank water, PaPa and I watered the oxen. The slow animals put their mouths into the bucket, sipping the water like coffee that was too hot to drink. Each oxen finished a whole bucket, then stared forward as though ready for the next leg of the journey.

In mid afternoon we passed several large clumps of trees standing in the sea of grass. Birds flew from the branches as our noisy crowd approached. Herr Zeller continuously urged the children to stay close to the wagons. To the left of the wagons Fritz and I spotted the remains of a camp fire, the grass around it trampled down by the hooves of animals. We called to Herr Zeller to come look. The coals were still warm so someone must have camped there last night. Tracks on the ground showed that there had been several horses. He showed us the tracks made by a man's boot and told us that Indians do not wear boots. He explained that Indians made their own shoes from tanned leather, and they were called moccasins. The moccasin made a very smooth track and was hard to detect unless the ground was muddy. Tracks leaving the camp showed that the people went west. This was good because we were traveling north. Herr Zeller explained that this was why we must stay close to the wagons. We felt very important that Herr Zeller has taught us these things about tracking, and we were sure that we knew more than most of the people in the group, for most of them did not even notice the camp site.

As night fell I went with PaPa to become acquainted with Herr Braun, one of the men from New Braunfels who met us with the supply wagon. He was a tall, friendly man with a red face and a large brimmed hat. He had been in New Braunfels for over 6 months, and had come here with Prince Karl to find the land for the town. He explained to us that New Braunfels lies where two rivers, the Comal and the Guadalupe, converge. These were Spanish names given by Spanish explorers many years ago. We would continue to follow the Guadalupe River to New Braunfels. Herr Braun said that each family would receive a one acre lot in town and ten acres outside of town for farming. We were shocked to hear that no houses had been built for us and that we would have to construct them ourselves. PaPa's face turned white when he heard this. As we walked back to our wagon I assured PaPa that I could help him build and that I knew we would do a good job. He put his hand on my shoulder and thanked me. He admitted that my help would be needed and that I should not yet mention the lack of housing to MaMa, or to anyone else. He did not want the news to disappoint them.

* * *

We became tired of waiting in the large warehouse for our ship to be called. Two other ships had boarded, but not ours. We ate cold sausage, bread and cold potatoes and then lay on our blankets waiting for sleep to come. About half of the families were now gone and it was not so noisy. I fell asleep very quickly. I awoke to PaPa shaking my shoulder. It was morning and our ship had been called. We quickly gathered our belongings, rolled up our blankets, and grabbed pieces of sausage to eat as we began to carry the four trunks out the large sliding doors by the dock. This was the first time that I got to see our ship "Angelina". She was about 50 feet long and had three masts rising very high into the air. Her sails were rolled up and thick ropes held her to the dock. PaPa and I made four trips with our trunks and placed them all together as MaMa and Dorothea joined us with our bed rolls and hand bags. Each family stood by their luggage, feeling very small with our small piles of possessions speckling the enormous ship next to the endless ocean. It seemed that we peered at the end of the world and would soon drop off of it, falling into eternity. Every heart beat faster as the captain of the ship, dressed in a blue uniform, approached the deck to address us standing below. He welcomed us aboard "Angelina", informing us that this would be her second journey to

Texas. He expected the crossing would take about 45 days if good weather prevailed. Each family would board when called by the ensign, taking all of their belongings with them below deck. He encouraged promptness to assure a noon departure and closed in prayer for a safe journey.

A quite hush fell and tears dampened many cheeks as the ensign motioned for the first family to board. We were the sixth family in line. PaPa and I lifted one trunk as MaMa and Dorothea grabbed our bed rolls and two carrying bags. We walked up the plank and then down very steep steps into the hold of the ship. It was dark and smelled like the warehouse did. We set our trunks against the left wall. MaMa and Dorothea saved this area for our family while PaPa and I made three more trips carrying the trunks. Fritz and his PaPa, Herr Nagel, put their trunks beside us, and the women began discussing how to arrange our quarters. As PaPa picked up the last trunk we turned and looked at the warehouse, mindful of the fact that this was our final walk on German soil. By noon all the families and luggage were loaded. The ensign rang a bell in our quarters and everyone became quiet. He announced that "Angelina" was now departing and invited us on deck for a farewell. There was to be no running and families were to stay together. We filed up the steep stairs and lined the right side of the ship. We stared at the city and, as the ship began to move, saw the mountains in the distance. The memory of the blue mountain peaks capped with white snow would be forever etched in my memory, and at any time I could close my eyes and see this picture of Germany, the land of my forefathers.

* * *

We must have looked like a group of gypsies moving over the grasslands. Our clothes were dirty, our hair had grown long, and the men were unshaven. We were lean and our faces had turned brown from the sun. A baby boy was born that night to the Knopf family. We all danced around the camp fire to welcome the first Texas-born German from our group.

We started the next day with new energy noticing more trees and brush. As we walked toward a small hill we were stunned by a group of about ten or more large cow-like creatures with brown hair. The oxen put their noses up and began to snort as they breathed this strange scent of the unfamiliar animals. Herr Zeller stopped the group and we all stared in amazement as the animals lumbered off to the west. Herr Zeller told us about the animals before we could ask. They were buffalo, the wild cattle of the western United States. The area used to have many of these creatures on it, but within the last fifty years they had become rare. Herr Zeller had never seen such a large group of buffalo. This also brought about new concern for our safety. Herr Zeller explained that the Indians usually follow the buffalo and we must be alert for an attack. If we had more time we would have killed the buffalo and butchered them for meat, but we left quickly in hopes not to be caught by Indians.

We had not seen the Guadalupe River all day, but sure enough, at about sundown, we met it again and made camp. Large trees grew along the banks of the Guadalupe. PaPa and I secretly agreed that they could be used to make a good house.

The next day we traveled within sight of the Guadalupe River and saw two homesteads. The owners and their barefoot children came out on their porches to wave at us. This was prime land since it was near the river and had an abundance of grass. PaPa feared that it would be very difficult to plow this hard ground and to raise crops needed for food. In winter the grass would be gone and the farmers would depend on hay set aside for their animals. PaPa and I discussed how to go to the prairie, cut hay, and haul it to our house where we could store it for winter consumption. This was a sort of "make believe" conversation because, right then, we did not have a home or animals.

* * *

Fritz and I tried talking to the sailors, but they seemed uninterested and were too busy for our questions. We stood watching what they did, how they climbed the masts and released the sails while men on the deck tightened the ropes. The ship moved fast through the water and the air felt crisp and cool on deck. This was not true in the hold below, which was dark and damp. Almost everyone tried to stay on the deck near an area where a fire brewed coffee, and potatoes baked. Potatoes were part of every meal along with hard sausage for supper. On Sunday we had a special meal of sauerkraut and strips of pork hams which had been packed in lard. The pork was cooked with lima beans the next day. I wished for bread, but there was no means to bake it. I found a piece of wood near the fire and passed time by using Opa's pocket knife to whittle. I could not make anything useful but a spear, and I pretended to throw it at the large fish in the sea. The men gathered mid ship to smoke their pipes and play chess. The women watched the children and kept them out of the way of the sailors.

Fritz and I wandered about the ship and even peaked inside the captain's quarters when a sailor came out the door. I desperately wanted to meet the captain and accompany him on his rounds if he would allow. Eventually he came out, nodding as he passed. I suddenly become embarrassed and could not speak. This was unusual because I normally had no problem in speaking to adults. Later that day I come upon the captain by accident, as he peered through his looking glass into the empty ocean. I stopped to say, "Guten tag" (good day), "My name is Nic". He was looking in the direction that the lookout thought he saw another ship, but he was unable to spot the ship through his looking glass. He handed me the glass and I gladly took the opportunity to view the blue and green. Was I looking at the sky or at the water? I could not tell for sure. I asked questions such as; "How do you know where you are going?", "How do you turn the ship?", "Can you slow down if you need to?", "Will we encounter pirates?". The captain admitted that he had never seen a pirate, and invited me to accompany him to see how the ship operated.

I spent many hours in the captain's shadow. I learned to use a sextant at night to measure the distance of the stars from the horizon which helped to determine our location. I learned to identify the North Star and the Big

Dipper, and assisted in navigation. I was even allowed to steer the ship. In return for these lessons, I often took the captain a cup of coffee, and read poetry to him as he stood at the helm. The captain was tall with dark black hair brushing his broad shoulders. He wore a long black beard. He had been on the sea since he was a young boy. He had few memories of his family, who was very poor. His mother died, and when his father whipped him for eating too much bread, he stowed away on a ship. When the ship was at sea he was discovered and was put to work swabbing the deck and killing chickens to be fried for the captain to eat. He had been all over the world, including the United States. He had been to New York City and to New Orleans. He had been to Galveston, Texas, but had never been inland. He planed to remain a sea captain until his hair turned gray. Then he would join the pioneers in Texas where he would build a grand hotel. His name was Captain Kerr. I had no desire to go to sea again, but I did want to have the qualities and strength of this captain.

It was our thirtieth day aboard ship when the sky turned dark and the sea grew rough. Soon many people were on deck with sick stomachs. I was too busy to be sick, for the captain had sent me on many errands to check with various crewmen, secure ropes holding the anchor, and to bring him a map and his coat. Water began to splash onto the deck and people were falling. The captain ordered all passengers below deck, including me. We spent a miserable night. MaMa was sick and our trunks kept sliding about. Fritz was laying on the floor groaning. I could not look at him for fear that I would also become sick. After several hours, the waves began to die down and we were able to sleep. But the next morning MaMa had a fever and was still on the floor wrapped in her blanket. I climbed on deck and welcomed the sunrise. I helped to make the coffee, and then took a cup to the captain who was still at the helm. He drank it quickly and then told a sailor to take over while he went to sleep in his quarters.

I spent much of my time trying to learn to speak English. Several of the crewmen from London were sometimes willing to help me. When I tried to say a complete sentence in English they all laughed at me and I became embarrassed. After a while I decided that it was more important to learn English than to be worried about my feelings. I went back to the Englishman and continued my lessons. Soon I began to teach the same words to Fritz, but he did not seem very interested in learning English, and he laughed a lot. The captain loaned me his English Bible and I began trying to say the words and to learn the alphabet.

The general daily routine on the ship seldom changed. Most of the men rose at daybreak and drank coffee around the fire.

They talked about farming in Texas, and what crops to plant.

Soon the women and younger children began to arrive, and oat gruel cooked in a large pot. Everyone finished their coffee and got a spoonful of gruel in the cup. We drank the gruel as we watched the sun and looked out to sea in search of other ships or land. Gradually the men pulled out their pipes and began to smoke. The women talked and watched the children play. Several children formed into groups for reading and mathematics lessons led by various mothers. Some of the men began their daily chess tournament. I usually read the English Bible and then tried to help the captain. In the afternoons people laid about the deck to nap in the cool breeze. At night several men played musical instruments including the violin and the flute. From time to time we tried to do German folk dances around the fire, but we were limited by the large number of people in a small space. At about 8:30 most families headed down to the hold and began to prepare for sleeping.

On the forty fifth day of our journey the ensign called a meeting of all the men to explain what would happen when we reached Galveston. The families would be called to disembark from the ship in the same order as before. We would stand in line and unload our trunks. Then a small boat would take us to land, and we would walk to a nearby camp where a sloop (a smaller sailing vessel) would take us to Carlshaven several miles down the coastline. This was a camp set up especially for the German immigrants. From here our guide would escort us to New Braunfels. Everyone became excited that afternoon as we spotted land in the distance. Even though we headed in its direction, it seemed that we never reached the shore. The captain explained that we were looking at New Orleans in the distance, and by tomorrow we would arrive in Galveston. I returned the English Bible to the Captain and tried to thank him for his many lessons. He promised to visit New Braunfels some day and look for me there. I then found one of the Englishmen and had my final English lesson aboard ship. That night everyone packed their trunks and prepared to disembark. I rolled over and over in my blanket but could not sleep, for tomorrow I would see Texas, my new home.

* * *

I was glad that Herr Braun found Herr Zeller's gray horse. I missed caring for him and was relieved that he had not been harmed by his captors. I wondered why they released him, or if maybe he was able to run away. Herr Zeller was very happy today because, after 32 days of travel, our journey was almost at an end. That morning I saddled the gray horse and handed Herr Zeller the reins. He immediately returned them to me and said that, if I promised to stay beside him at all times, I could ride the gray horse today and he would ride the brown mare. I was more experienced at riding oxen than horses, but I was sure that I could handle this horse because we had become good friends. Herr Zeller gave me a boast to mount and then we were off. I waved as we rode past PaPa and MaMa and they both smiled in return.

We saw more houses and even a herd of goats with a Mexican shepherd. His skin looked brown and he had black hair and dark eyes. He removed his large hat and waved it in the air. We all waved to him and the gray horse snorted as he began to smell the goats. Herr Zeller said that the Mexicans were our friends and we must do all that we could to keep our friendship pure. He insisted that we should never look down upon others as being inferior, even if they had a different religion and no schooling. Herr Zeller believed we could learn much from the people who had been in Texas for a long time, and we should take every opportunity to study their ways.

This was the final night in camp, for tomorrow we expected to arrive in New Braunfels. We kept to our regular routine although excitement filled the air. After supper we sat around the fire reminiscing about this great journey which we had experienced. There was much laughter, and a few tears, as we wondered about those we left behind in Bicken. We looked at the vast Texas sky and I saw the Big Dipper. I wondered about Captain Kerr and where he was now. He was probably on the ocean going back to Germany for another load of German settlers. I thought about the gray horse and how I would work hard to buy my own horse and gun. The women were excited about moving into their new houses. PaPa and I glanced at each other and continued to keep our grim secret about the lack of housing in New Braunfels.

The next morning, June 8, 1845, we arose quickly and began to pack and eat breakfast. Herr Zeller called everyone to a central meeting where he complimented us and told us that we were very good travelers who were not afraid of our future. He was sure that we would find wealth and satisfaction with our new home, but he cautioned that we must remain patient because the settlement of New Braunfels was new and still rather primitive. He promised that the land was plentiful with good soil, there was more than enough water, and if we all worked together in an organized way, we would be able to bring in a crop of food for storage before winter. He then lead the group in the Lord's Prayer. No one looked back to where we had been, we only looked forward to where we would be tomorrow.

At about four o'clock in the afternoon we could see houses, tents, cattle, horses, and people in the distance. When the people saw us, they all began to run to the town to greet us. I rode the gray horse proudly beside Herr Zeller as we led the wagon train to the crude homemade fortress called Zinkenburg. We dismounted as the wagons came to a halt, and the other German inhabitants shook our hands saying "Wilkomen su Texas" ("Welcome to Texas")! PaPa walked to the shade of a large oak tree and fell to his knees with his head bowed in prayer. MaMa wiped the tears running down her cheeks with her apron. I was elated with happiness just like on Christmas morning! Fritz and I jumped into the air, ran around in circles, and laughed out loud. We skipped toward all the other friends on the wagon train, grabbed their hands and twirled around in circles. MaMa did not seem to realize that there were only a few houses and buildings in this settlement. I gathered with my family and PaPa hugged each one of us telling us how proud he was of his family. Inside the Zinkenburg fort, which was made from logs stuck upright in the ground, the group of travelers built a fire. They boiled coffee and fresh eggs which had been brought as gifts from the other settlers. We camped there just as we had on the trail. As I laid in my blanket, I dreamed of cutting hay on the prairie and feeding the many cattle in the pen at our new home.

Chapter 2

A New Home

The next morning, after a breakfast of coffee and sliced ham, for we were still celebrating, the men met with Baron von Musebach outside the fort under a tree. He apologized for the absence of Prince Carl, saying that the Prince was not feeling well and returned to Germany. The men drew lots by pulling a numbered piece of paper from a hat. The one acre town lots and the ten acre farm plots had been previously numbered on a map. PaPa was the tenth man to draw, and he got lot number 81 and farm number 56. Each family was given a tent in which to live until their house was completed. The tents had to be returned within 30 days so that they could be used for settlers coming behind us. Oxen, wagons, axes, and other tools would be provided to assist with house building. As soon as the house was built, the fields must be plowed in order to make a fall crop for winter food. The men were very quiet, and Fritz and I were astonished at the amount of work that was before all of us. No more happy days of playing and throwing rocks at quail. From now on we would be hard laborers. Finally there was time for questions. Some of the men were very angry that they were not yet moving to their 350 acre farms that were promised. Herr Musbach explained that they would get the land later, but they would settle here first because the land was far away and was not yet ready for habitation. He explained that the threat of Indian attacks was great, and that each work crew must have a gun for protection. Some men were unhappy because they had to build their own house. One man asked how he might return to Germany because his family was unhappy.

When the meeting was over PaPa and I went to get the tent and set it up in the designated spot near the fort. We escorted MaMa and Dorothea to the tent as we carried one of our four trunks. PaPa was very quiet and was afraid of MaMa's reaction to having a tent instead of a house. But his fears were released when MaMa said that this was a welcome relief from sleeping outside in a group of people. She immediately began to unpack our few household items including a cooking pot, a bucket, four plates, four cups, four forks, knives and spoons, one long spoon for stirring, three cup towels and three wash cloths, two towels, a dish pan, and a coffee grinder.

All four of us then went to the warehouse to order some basic necessities. The warehouse was a large barn-like structure with wooden floors. We had not stepped on a wooden floor since we left the ship. The clerk was a thin, tall man who was not very friendly. He asked what we needed and then began to write a list which included: one bag flour, one bag corn meal, one side of bacon packed in lard, five links of hard smoked sausage, one bag of lima beans, one bag of coffee beans, one bag of potatoes, one bag of salt, one baking pan with a lid, one ax, one mallet, one pick, one shovel, one saw, one canteen, and five pounds of nails. The clerk called an assistant who began to gather the items. PaPa had to sign his name at the bottom of the list of items we had ordered. The clerk explained that we would be given credit on these items until the first crop was brought in and sold. At that time PaPa must pay the debt in cash. PaPa's hand shook when he signed for the supplies because never had we been in debt. Within a few minutes all of the items were brought to the front of the store and inspected by PaPa. We carried these precious belongings back to our tent. PaPa and I hung an old sheet in the corner of the tent so that we could have privacy in changing our clothes and washing. Before, when we were in a crowd of people, this type of activity had to be done under our blankets. MaMa and PaPa put their trunks on one side of the tent, and Dorothea and I put our trunks on the other side, making an aisle down the center. The small space between the wall of the tent and the trunks became our bedrooms. The front portion of the tent was to become our kitchen and eating area. We had to keep the tent door shut at all times to keep out the flies and mosquitoes.

I gathered large rocks, made a fire pit in front of our tent, and waved to Fritz who was doing the same thing next door.

PaPa took his new ax to the woods and came back with a three foot long piece of wood and several smaller sticks with which to make benches. With much difficulty he sliced the log down the center. First he made a small crack in the wood, and then pounded a small piece of wood into the crack to hold it open. He gradually made the log crack all the way through. He then bore holes on each corner with a boring drill which he borrowed from a neighbor, and in the holes he put smaller branches. These were the legs which held up the two benches. The benches were comfortable, although they rocked and we had to sit down gently in order for it not to turn over on us. That night MaMa cooked biscuits in our new pot and we ate them with a slice of bacon. It was delicious and we were very happy in our new home. At bedtime we all prayed together and thanked God for our safety and for our continued protection. We giggled with excitement as we laid down on the floor of the tent wrapped in our sheets.

The next morning we were awakened by roosters crowing which we had not heard since we left Germany. I pulled on my pants and began to build a fire while PaPa got fresh water from a nearby barrel. MaMa baked biscuits and we spread lard on them for a delicious bacon flavor. We drank a second cup of coffee and then wrapped left over biscuits in our handkerchief and put them in our pockets. I filled the canteen with water and carried it over my shoulder. PaPa and I found the street called Mill, and then we walked until we found a post with Lot number 81 written on it. We walked around on the lot and found the four corners marked with piles of rocks. PaPa was pleased to see that there was a grove of oak trees in the middle of the lot. We decided that the house would be built in front of the trees and the barn and cattle pens behind the trees. We stood under the trees for several minutes without speaking, thinking of our past and our future all in one moment.

We proceeded to Fort Zinkenburg where a meeting was held to organize the building of houses. The men and boys whose lots were on Mill Street gathered together. Each family was a team, and each team had a job to prepare for the day. Our team, PaPa and I, went with Fritz and Herr Nagel to borrow four wagons and four teams of oxen from the warehouse. Again PaPa had to sign his name, and he had to promise to bring back the wagons and oxen before sundown. We met the other men who brought food, equipment, and two rifles. We all rode in the carts for about three miles west of town to a small creek which ran into the Guadalupe River. There we unloaded and Fritz and I watered the oxen. The men made a quick survey of the available trees and began to saw and chopped the trees with the straightest trunks. The trees were not very tall in comparison to those in Germany. After the tree was chopped down, another team of workers began to chop the limbs from the trunk. By noon we had 23 large logs and 34 smaller logs.

We sat down and ate our biscuits and drank the water from our canteen. Fritz and I, and the other young men, sat with the fathers and listened to their conversations about how to build a house. PaPa had never built a house, but he had built our barn in Bicken. He seemed to be one of the more experienced builders in the group. After a short rest in the shade, we all helped to load the logs onto the wagons. In the afternoon we continued to cut and chop, and we loaded 39 more large logs and 42 small logs onto the wagons. We all walked back to town since the wagons were already heavy with the burden of the logs. My arms and shoulders ached and my knees felt a little weak as we walked the three miles. But most of all my stomach felt like it had a hole in it and I had to eat soon. We continued to Mill Street and unloaded logs in the first lot on the street, which would be the home of Herr Meyer. There were ten lots on the street, so I supposed we would continue this process for ten more days. PaPa and I, and Fritz and Herr Nagel, returned the oxen and wagons to the warehouse. PaPa made sure that the clerk signed his name beside PaPa's name in the book saying that the items that had been borrowed were returned. We walked home to our tent where MaMa and Dorothea were waiting for us with a delicious supper of potatoes, bacon, biscuits and coffee. As soon as we were finished eating we went to bed.

This same routine was repeated each day for ten days until we had delivered logs to all of the lots on Mill Street. With practice, all the cutting teams got faster, and we were able to cut more logs each day. Beginning the fourth day we took six wagons and filled them with logs. Each day we moved farther from town and the walk back in the afternoon was very tiresome. Herr Zeller came to our tent to visit on the tenth night. He complimented us because the Mill Street lot owners seemed to be working faster than any other group. He said that some of the men were so angry at the lack of provisions that they refused to work and were demanding that the Aldesverine reimburse them for any labor that they endured. Herr Zeller argued that everything cost more that the Aldesverine had imagined and that the group had spent most of its money before the settlers arrived. Baron Musebach struggled to salvage the operation and work out the financial difficulties.

On Sunday the whole logging operation was interrupted as everyone put on their best clothes to go to church under the big oak tree near the Fort. The Free Protestant pastor led the group in singing and reading from the Bible. The men and boys stood on the right side of the tree while the women and children stood on the left, just as we did in the church at our old home in Bicken. After the service ended everyone sat on blankets under the trees near the crystal clear Guadalupe River and had a picnic. We all pretended that was something special and tried not to remember that we had a picnic at almost every meal. We had not sat down to a table to eat since we left Bicken.

On Sunday afternoon PaPa and I escorted MaMa and Dorothea to our town lot where PaPa proudly pointed out the grove of oak trees in the middle. MaMa agreed that this would help to cool the house. The lot was only about a quarter mile from the Guadalupe River, convenient for the chore of hauling water to the homestead. The logs for our house were already lying at the front of our lot. We looked at them very closely and MaMa commended our job of cutting and hauling. We walked back to our tent and I sat under a tree to read one of my favorite books.

Two rifles were always carried on the log gathering expeditions, and there were twenty bullets for each gun. On the way back to town in the evenings, if a deer or other wild animal was spotted, the riflemen shot it and took it to the camp. The animal was butchered and meat was distributed to our group. This was a very pleasant addition to our diets, especially since we were using so much energy cutting the logs.

Finally the logs were all cut and delivered to each of the ten lots on Mill Street. The families began the task of building their own homes. PaPa and I went to our lot right after breakfast and measured each of our logs scratching their height and width on the bark of each. PaPa figured that we had enough logs to make a house twenty by twenty feet. We began to lay the foundation of our house by digging a trench six inches wide and one foot deep, twenty feet wide by twenty feet long. We found the ground to be very rocky and the digging difficult. The digging took one whole day, in which MaMa and Dorothea brought us lunch and helped by piling rocks beside the house to be used later to make a fireplace. By the end of the day our arms and shoulders were burning. In the evening we went to the Comal River and took a long soak in the cold water.

The next day we began to lay the logs side by side along the trench. We picked up each log and dropped it into the trench side by side, just as though we were building a very high fence. PaPa held each log as straight as possible while MaMa, Dorothea and I put small rocks into the trench around the log to hold it tightly in an upright position. The logs on the sides were taller than the logs in the front and back. In the front we left a space which would be used as the door, on one side we left a space for the fireplace, and on the other side we put three shorter logs where we would make a window. When completed this part of our project looked like a small fortress.

The next day we sawed the logs on the sides so that they would be sloping for the roof. We went to the warehouse and borrowed a froe, a knife with a handle on one side. PaPa used this to drive into the top of the log using a heavy mallet. He would twist the blade to split the wood to form a shingle. The shingles were 1/4 inch thick and measured approximately 4 inches by 6 inches. These were used to fill in the spaces between the logs. We started at the bottom, as close to the ground as possible, and nailed a row of shingles. We then nailed another row of shingles above that row which slightly overlapped the row below. When we finished, the outside of the house looked like shingles on a roof. This process took two days with PaPa cutting the shingles, MaMa bringing them to me, Dorothea handing me the nails, and I nailing the shingles onto the logs.

Next, PaPa tied short pieces of wood between two tall poles to make ladders. We put the ladders against the walls and, with the help of ropes, lifted our longest poles on top to form the outline of the roof. We tied smaller poles to the larger ones so that we could nail shingles to them to make the roof. Herr Zeller visited us almost every day to look at the project and to give us advise.

Finally PaPa used the rocks we had dug from the trench, as well as large rocks that we hauled from the creek bed, to make a fireplace. It was not very wide or very deep, but just big enough to place our large black pot over the fire. PaPa had never built a fireplace, but he had repaired the fireplace in our old house many times. The difficulty was to find flat rocks which could be stacked one upon another. I worked very hard to make a door and a window shutter tying small poles together in the shape of the door and window openings. I nailed small poles as close together as possible and then covered the poles with row after row of shingles. MaMa and Dorothea helped PaPa and I, clearing all of the rocks and grass from inside the house, smoothing the dirt floor, and then walking back and forth on it to pack the dirt. They sprinkled water on the dirt to settle the dust.

After six days of working from daylight until dark we were able to move into our house and returned the tent to the warehouse. Our new house was not yet ready for winter since it had many cracks which would let the cold air come in. When winter drew near we would put shingles on the inner walls as well, and we would fill the cracks with mud to help keep out the cold. But for now this house was very comfortable to us. We had slept in a warehouse, in the hold of a ship, on the ground, and in a tent. To sleep in our own house, even though we were still on the ground, was a great blessing. PaPa acquired some paper and wrote a letter to Oma and Opa. He did not have enough paper to describe our trip and our new home in detail, but he was able to tell them that we had arrived safely in our new country called Texas.

The next important building was the privy, or outdoor toilet. PaPa and I took turns digging in the rocky ground until we had completed and 4 foot by 4 foot pit which was 5 feet deep. We built the privy on top of the pit using the same methods as when we built the house. This was very convenient and we were delighted to once again feel that we had privacy.

PaPa and I wanted to find our ten acre farm which was located approximately three miles from town. We went to the Aldesverine headquarters to study the map and to ask if a surveyor could accompany us to the site. An appointment was made for 12:00 o'clock noon. PaPa and I ate a quick dinner and then met the surveyor. He walked with us and discussed the weather, it was getting very hot, and then we talked about plowing and planting a crop. He suggested that we plant corn, potatoes, and cabbage for a fall crop. We could store the corn and potatoes to eat that winter and we could make sauerkraut from the cabbage. He suggested that we try to buy a pig so that, in the winter, we could make sausage. The surveyor carried a pistol on his belt and suggested that PaPa purchase a rifle for our protection when we were at our farm. I hoped that PaPa heeded the man's warning and bought a rifle, for I was anxious to learn to shoot. If I could shoot, then our family would have plenty of wild game to eat that winter.

We walked on rocks over a creek, called Seco, and then the surveyor pulled a small book from his pocket and began to look for our farm. We saw one plot of land that had been cleared and part of it had been plowed. We went over a hill and the surveyor pointed to a group of trees and said that he thought that was our land. We walked down the hill and looked for metal stakes in the ground. When one was found the surveyor tried to identify it on his map. After an hour of searching he was finally sure that he had found our ten acre plot. We found each corner and erected a pile of large rocks to mark the spot. We put smaller piles of rocks at intervals of approximately every twelve feet to mark the boundaries. After much sweat and hard work, the surveyor was satisfied and so was PaPa. PaPa signed the surveyors book taking possession of his farm. The surveyor left us, and PaPa and I stood there in awe. We looked at the bright Texas sun, the green grass, the beautiful trees at the back of the property, the creek which was approximately a half-mile away. PaPa walked back and forth across the land and occasionally stooped to pick up a handful of soil. He picked up a stick and tried to dig a small hole in several different places. The ground was hard and we would have to bring our pick and shovel to inspect the soil. Ten acres seemed to be a very large piece of property to PaPa, for he had never owned any land except for a house and a barn. In Germany only the wealthy people owned land. We had been told that ten acres was not enough, but at that moment, we were stunned by the vastness of this land. PaPa said that some day it would be covered with fields.

When we arrived home MaMa proudly displayed the new mattresses which she had fashioned from old cloth. She sewed the cloth into sacks and then filled each sack with tree moss. They certainly felt soft after having slept on the hard ground for so long.

Our primary concern was to begin to plow and plant a field. We went to the warehouse and PaPa signed for a plow. We borrowed a cart and oxen to deliver the plow to the farm. Holes were dug in several different areas with the pick to try to find the best place to plow, where there were the least rocks and brush. Finally we hitched the two oxen to the plow and PaPa began to plow a field for the first time in his life. I led the oxen and PaPa told me to slow down because the plow could hardly break through the hard crusted earth. We tied a heavy rock to the top of the plow to make it heavier and we continued to plow and pick up rocks all afternoon. By evening we had plowed one row approximately fifty feet in length and had a tall pile of rocks. We hitched the oxen to the cart and slowly made our way back to town.

PaPa was very tired and said that this work was harder than cutting logs and building houses. Fritz and his PaPa, Herr Nagel, were now finished with their house across the street from our house. The four of us talked about how we could plow the field faster. Herr Nagel would take possession of his land the next day, and we would work together.

The four of us set out with the oxen the next day and met the surveyor at our property. He had already found Herr Nagel's land and it was one quarter mile from our farm. We could see it nearby. Herr Nagel and PaPa took turns holding the plow while Fritz and I led the oxen slowly to plow another furrow for fifty feet. There were many rocks to pick up to make piles on the property line.

The next day we got two pairs of oxen to pull the plow and we began to make real progress. By the end of the week we had plowed and seeded a sixty by one hundred foot field with potatoes, and corn. The next week we plowed and seeded a field of the same dimensions for Fritz's family. On Saturday, when we were finished with the field, we started the slow trek back to town. When we got over Seco Creek we heard shouting in the distance and then saw a man on horseback running towards us. We had no weapons and there we were with four slow oxen which did not even belong to us. We tied the oxen teams to a tree and ran behind some large trees picking up rocks as we ran. We ducked down behind the tree trunks and peered around to look for the man. We could still hear him shouting but we could not see him.

His voice faded as though he continued to ride away. Why was he shouting? Why was he running? Where was he going? We were all very scared. We quickly untied the oxen and took them into thick brush where we all stood for half an hour, quietly listening for any movement nearby. Finally PaPa slowly sneaked away from the brush and climbed a tall sycamore tree to look around. When he saw nothing he called quietly to us to come out and bring the oxen. It was nearly dark and we had to hurry to get back to town and not become lost. We returned the oxen to the warehouse just after dark. As we walked towards our house PaPa said that we needed to buy a rifle. That was just what I wanted to hear, because I wanted to learn to shoot.

The next day we walked to the warehouse where PaPa once again signed his name for a rifle, a bullet press, lead, a bag of bullets, and gun powder. We went to the woods, far away from town, with Fritz and Herr Nagel, and we all took turns loading the rifle, and shooting at cactus. We used all of the bullets we bought and half of the gun powder and that night we learned to make more bullets with the bullet press.

The next week was devoted to making three bed frames, and a table. PaPa wanted to do a good job so that the furniture would endure. We took our gun and walked approximately five miles from town until we came to a stand of cedar trees. We chopped the cedar trees and carried back ten logs approximately three inches in diameter. We peeled the bark from the cedar and found beautiful wood. Then, with a very sharp knife, PaPa began to carve out notches near the ends of the logs. He fit the notches together and tied the logs together to form a bed frame. We tied ropes from one side of the frame to the other, crossing back and forth. We put our mattresses on the ropes and tested the beds. They were sturdy and when we turned from side to side the ropes would bend and give. This was much better than sleeping on the ground. Sleeping on a bed became more important when it rained because the water came under the walls of our house and covered the dirt floor. We loaded flat rocks from the creek bed and put them around the bottom of the exterior of our house to try to keep the water and bugs out. This worked well, but some day we would have a real wooden floor.

PaPa also built a kitchen table from cedar logs and it was a fine feeling to sit at the table to eat dinner, just as we used to do in Bicken. We now called Bicken and Germany "the old country".

Herr Schneider saw PaPa and I stripping the bark from the cedar logs and became interested in our project. He said that he would like to inspect the beds that PaPa made. After he laid on PaPa and MaMa's bed for a minute or two, Herr Schneider told PaPa that he needed five beds for his family. If PaPa made the bed frames he would give PaPa a baby pig. PaPa and I borrowed a cart and a team of oxen to bring in a large load of cedar logs to be used for building the furniture. Within five days we had made the five beds and delivered them to Herr Schneider. PaPa chose a baby pig from Herr Schneider's back yard and he carried it home in his arms as it squealed for its' mama. When we got home we did not know where to put it. We put a small rope around the pig's leg and tied it to a tree while we quickly began to make a rock pen for the animal. The pig squealed so loudly that Dorothea began to cry for fear that the pig was hurt. Several neighbors stopped their building chores and came to look. Herr Nagel helped us build a ten foot by ten foot pen with rocks stacked three feet high. We put the pig in the pen and it ran from side to side still squealing. We used our bucket to give it water and then we went to the warehouse and PaPa signed his name for another bucket and a 25 pound bag of corn. By the time we arrived back home the pig was wallowing in mud which it had made by turning over the bucket. We put corn in the bucket and the pig ate it with great relish. After he was full of corn, the pig laid down in the mud and seemed to be content.

The next morning PaPa told me to go feed the pig before breakfast. As I walked to the pen I heard no noise, and when I looked in the pen there was no pig. One side of the rock fence had tumbled down and the pig had escaped. Immediately PaPa and I started searching for the pig, and finally found it back at Herr Schneider's house. We immediately went home and rebuilt the pig pen with heavier rocks and several logs supporting the rock walls. I retrieved the pig from Herr Schneider and hopefully the pig would never be able to escape again.

After finishing the pig pen, Herr Nagel, Fritz, PaPa and I walked to our fields to inspect the crops. We took or new rifle, lunch, and a hoe for cutting weeds. Both fields had corn growing about one inch in height. But we discovered cow tracks up and down the rows, and parts of the fields were trampled so that the corn was completely gone. We were all disappointed and very angry. Whose cows did this? We had not even seen a cow in this area. PaPa kicked at the dirt with his foot and said that we must fence the property. As we walked back to town, plans were made for the fence building. It was decided that the "four farmers" (as we the referred to ourselves) would borrow a cart with two oxen, and a tent. We would camp at our farm until we had the fences completed. This way the fields could be guarded against further damage. MaMa was against this idea, but PaPa reassured her that she and Dorothea would be safe while we were away. Herr Zeller and several other guards continually patrolled New Braunfels to prevent invasion by Indians. We would take the rifle with us for our own safety while camping.

The next morning the "four farmers" set out on our adventure. We borrowed the cart and team of oxen for a five day period, and took hard sausage, biscuits, potatoes, and coffee. The sun was hot and the sweat poured from our brow as we loaded large flat rocks from the Seco creek bed onto the cart. We took five loads to Herr Nagel's farm and dropped them off the back of the cart as the oxen moved slowly along the edge of the field. Soon the foundation of large rocks was completed, and we made more trips to the creek to gather flat rocks to stack three feet high.

On one of the trips to the creek we saw a small herd of large cattle that seemed to be wandering aimless over the grassland. They were probably the culprits who raided our corn field. We steered the oxen cart in their direction and, when the animals saw us, we yelled as loudly as we could and started throwing small rocks at them. After several rocks hit their target, the cattle began to trot away from us. We continued to yell as they passed over a hill and out of sight. Maybe if we kept up this tactic they would stay clear of our fields. We discussed the possibility of trying to catch the cattle to sell, but they must have belonged to someone and that would be considered stealing.

Each day we worked until dark and then sat beside the fire cooking coffee and eating our sausage. Fritz and I asked permission to go hunting with the rifle the next morning. After discussions about gun safety and how to shoot an animal (try to hit it in the head so that it would not suffer and the good part of the meat would not be spoiled) we gained permission for the adventure. I had difficulty going to sleep and kept waking up. Finally I could see a faint dawn approaching in the eastern sky. I pulled on my boots and shook Fritz from his bed. We grabbed the gun and quietly tiptoed out of our camp walking quietly towards the creek. We saw three deer, two rabbits, and a squirrel, but they always ran before we were able to shoot. We went back to camp disappointed in our efforts. PaPa and Herr Nagel knew nothing about hunting either, since in Germany it was against the law to kill game which all belonged to the Duke.

By the fifth day we had completed the fences around both fields and we had to return the cart and oxen. It was a relief to get back home to MaMa's good cooking and she rewarded us with a bowl of noodles. The pig had grown at least 3 inches since last week at this time and he was always looking up at me with hungry grunts.

Herr Zeller came by our house for a visit and I asked him to teach me how to hunt. He said that he would take me on a hunting expedition the next day. I must have bullets, gun powder, and a canteen of water. I spent some time cleaning and polishing the rifle and getting ready for the trip. I traded fifteen cedar logs with their bark stripped for a straw hat. My boots were beginning to wear thin on the bottom, and occasionally dirt came in through a small hole. I had to find a way to make money so that I could buy a pair of sturdy boots before winter.

I met Herr Zeller and four other men at the fort at five o'clock in the morning. We started walking quietly along the Guadalupe River and Herr Zeller carried a candle to help light the way. I blindly followed the man ahead of me. After a long walk Herr Zeller told one of the men to stay at a certain spot, to sit in the bushes, and watch for game coming to the river. Likewise the other two men took up different positions each about a half mile apart. Herr Zeller and I continued another half mile where we saw a game trail leading to the river. Herr Zeller pointed out the tracks on the trail and showed me which ones were deer tracks. We also saw the tracks of a raccoon, as well as tracks that looked like a dog. Herr Zeller whispered that this was probably the track of a coyote, a small animal similar to a wolf. We crouched behind bushes near the trail and Herr Zeller extinguished the candle flame. We sat very still and there was no talking. After a while we heard something walking through the grass and Herr Zeller began to search for the animal. A small deer walked past us to the river where it began to drink. Herr Zeller slowly lifted his gun and tried to aim at the deer through the bushes. Suddenly the deer was spooked and ran away. Herr Zeller motioned to be quiet and to get down. We sat for a long time and finally another deer crept toward the water. This time Herr Zeller raised his rifle and shot at the deer who jumped and ran away. The sun was about to rise above the distant hills as we saw a large rabbit with very long ears. Herr Zeller helped me lift my rifle. I took careful aim and shot at the animal. My eyes squinted shut as the rifle boomed and smoke weld up in my face. When I opened my eyes I saw the rabbit lying on the ground very still and very dead. Herr Zeller patted me on the shoulder and showed me how to cut open the dead animal and take out its insides. We washed the body in the cool creek water until there was no more blood coming from it. The sun was now up and we started back to town. We stopped where we left each of the other four men and found that one of them shot a squirrel, and one shot a deer. We all helped to carry the deer back to town. Behind the fort was a place where the dead animals were hung on a tree limb and the skin was taken off with a knife. Herr Zeller illustrated this and then I used Opa's pocket knife to skin the rabbit. I was sure that Opa would be proud of me for using the knife in this way to help feed our family. Herr Zeller gave me the rabbit to take home to my family and said that, when I killed a deer, I should immediately share the meat with my neighbors. In the summer months when it is hot, the meat would only be safe to eat for two days. Herr Zeller gave me the rabbit skin and showed me how to put salt on it, roll it up, and tie it with a string. He said that once a month a fur buyer came from the city of Victoria, and he would buy the fur. As I walked towards home I felt the same excitement as when Captain Kerr taught me how to navigate by using the stars. I walked into the house holding up the rabbit for my family to see. Dorothea shrieked and turned away, but MaMa and PaPa smiled and complimented me on having a successful hunt. Later that morning we cut the rabbit into pieces and fried it in pork lard. All of us ate it for dinner with biscuits, and it was delicious. I cleaned the gun and hung it over the fireplace. That night I thought about future hunting expeditions as I slowly drifted off to sleep.

PaPa had orders for three more bed frames. After helping him all day, he gave me permission to go hunting that evening with Fritz. I was not allowed to go out alone because of the threat of Indian attacks. Fritz wanted to learn how to hunt and I was now the teacher. We followed the Comal River approximately two miles and looked for animals trails. Eventually we found a trail and then sat in the bushes beside it. Fritz became very tired of waiting and could not sit still. I jabbed him with my elbow and whispered that he must be still or else the animals would see us and would not come. Soon we heard the noise of animal feet coming towards us. I lifted my gun in the ready position and, as I took aim, I realized that I was looking directly into the eyes of a large cow. She snorted at me as she lumbered on down to the river for a drink. She had a calf and there were two other cows following her. Fritz laughed at me and I was embarrassed. As we walked back home we saw nothing to shoot at so we shot at the cactus. I was getting better each time. But soon we would be out of gun powder and it would be difficult to buy more.

PaPa traded the three bed frames for more corn to feed the pig. PaPa said that the correct terminology for this animal in English was "hog". We all laughed and tried to repeat the strange word. I was reminded that I had not been able to practice my English because no one seemed to be able to speak the language.

I asked permission from PaPa to go hunting morning and evening the next day. He said that as soon as I saw the sun come up I had to start back home. We had to get more cedar posts to make more bed frames. I got up when it was still dark and looked at PaPa's watch lying on the kitchen table. It was 4:00 o'clock. I took a piece of sausage and my boots and went outside to put the boots on. I went to Fritz's house and waited by the door. I listened for any movement inside, but it was quiet. I looked through the cracks in the side wall and I could see Fritz's feet still lying on the ground sticking out from the blanket. If I made noise I would waken Herr Nagel and that would be a mistake, for Herr Nagel was not very happy in the mornings until he smoked his pipe on the front porch and drank his coffee. I stood by the house and considered what to do. After a few minutes of waiting I decided to go on hunting alone. PaPa would never know because I would make sure that Fritz did not tell him. I walked along the Comal River and continued past where we saw the cows the day before. I came to a trail that made a steep descent to the river. There were bushes nearby so I sat down and listened intently for animals to come. After quite a long time of waiting I heard a sniffing noise. I raised to my knees and lifted my rifle to my shoulder. I tried to be very still and ready to shoot. After two or three minutes I was about to drop the gun because it had become very heavy in my arms. About that time I saw a deer directly in front of me. I moved the gun slightly, aimed directly for the deer's chest and pulled the trigger. When I opened my eyes, and the smoke was clear, I saw the deer lying on the ground and kicking. I turned my head and looked away. When I turned back the deer was still, and I realized that it was a buck with four points on its antlers. The antlers were fuzzy because in the summer the antlers were still growing and they had a fuzzy texture. As I knelt beside the dead animal something deep within me remembered seeing my PaPa fall to his knees below the oak tree thanking God for the trip to Texas. I said a silent prayer of thanks to God for giving me this deer. I would use it wisely to feed my family and I would never kill for sport only. I dressed the deer (took out its insides) and tried to carry it. It was very heavy for one person to handle and I could walk only a short distance before resting. The sun was rising and I was still making my way slowly back to our house. When I finally arrived PaPa was in the yard talking to Fritz. I saw them spot me and they both stared at me silently. I was ashamed that I did not follow PaPa's orders not to go hunting alone. I was also very proud of the deer I was carrying, and my legs were about to give way under the weight. I walked up to PaPa and then fell to my knees. He helped me get up and asked what happened. I tried to tell him how Fritz was sleeping and I went hunting anyway. I then said that I was sorry and I asked for his forgiveness. PaPa was quiet for a moment and then he looked at the deer. He asked how I got it, and I told PaPa and Fritz my first deer story. The three of us took the deer to the back yard and there I illustrated how to skin the animal. I salted the hide and rolled it, and we used the ax to butcher the deer. We gave several choice pieces to Fritz to take to his family and we took pieces of meat to several other neighbors. We cut the meat from the spine, called the back strap, into small pieces which MaMa fried in lard. We ate it with potatoes and it was delicious. That evening, as PaPa and I fed the hog, he told me that he was proud that I was able to kill the deer, but that he was also angry with me for going hunting alone. I apologized once again and we were both very quiet. That night at bedtime PaPa said that if I could not go hunting with Fritz then I should try to go with Herr Zeller.

PaPa spent most of his time making bed frames and trading them for a variety of items such as corn meal, sausage, potatoes, and even sometimes cash. One of the most welcomed trades was five hens, called White

Leghorns. They were large white chickens who constantly clucked and wagged their heads as they walked. They searched our yard for bugs and seeds. We built a chicken coop which was a small house similar to the privy, or outhouse. We made a window with slats crisscrossing the opening so that predators could not get in and we hung a pole inside where the chickens roosted at night. We would make nests in the coop and urge the hens to lay eggs there so that they could be protected.

PaPa and I went to our farm land one day per week, pulled weeds and hoed to keep the soil soft. We enjoyed the opportunity to view our growing crop of corn, potatoes, sweet potatoes, and cabbage. Several other farmers were working in the area and they all came by to admire our rock fence. The cows were still getting into the farmers fields and tearing up the crops. We had carefully piled pieces of thorny cactus on the outside of our rock fence to help control the cattle. The cactus had taken root and was beginning to grow there. We also encountered a rattlesnake by the rock fence and I was able to crush its' head with a rock. I proudly skinned it and we ate the meat for supper. No one in "the old country" has eaten snake, but Herr Zeller explained to us that it was just as good as eating chicken or rabbit. I saved the skin and had several hides to sell when the opportunity arose.

August 21 was my 15th birthday! I got up and went hunting as usual, and when I returned I was greeted with Happy Birthday wishes from my family. They told me to look in my trunk where I found a new pair of pants. This was a wonderful gift since my old pants were too short and it was embarrassing to wear them to church on Sunday. I had grown two inches or more since I left "the old country". Most of the day was spent gathering acorns from under the oak trees and beans from under the mesquite trees to feed the hog who had doubled in size and would be ready to butcher in a few months.

The "four farmers" borrowed two wagons and two teams of oxen and began to cut hay from the prairie, just as PaPa and I dreamed about several months ago. We did not have animals to eat the hay, but we could trade it to pay off our debts owed at the warehouse. To cut the hay we traveled past all the farms until we came to the open prairie. We kept the loaded rifle nearby at all times in case of attack. We cut as much hay as possible before lunch and let it lay on the ground to dry. In the afternoon we loaded it onto the cart and drove back to New Braunfels. Eventually half of PaPa's debt at the warehouse was paid and we had not even had our harvest yet. Because we were very quick to build our house and work our farm we now had time to pursue other means of making money.

Fritz and I devised a scheme whereby I could wake him in the early mornings for hunting. Fritz tied a small string to his big toe and put the other end of the string through the crack in the wall beside his bed. When I was ready to hunt I looked through the crack and pulled on the string to awaken Fritz. Fritz has also become a good shot with PaPa's rifle and had killed a deer and two squirrels. We were hunting partners and it seemed that everyone who lived nearby appreciated the meat we provided free of charge.

The summer was passing and "the four farmers" began to harvest our crops. We hauled load after load of corn from our field to the warehouse where we sold it for 50 cents per bushel. We kept 18 bushels and sold 23 bushels. Our debt to the warehouse was completely paid and we were ready to begin to make money. In a discussion with Herr Zeller we found out that, if a cow did not have a brand on its side, it was probably wild and it was not against the law to capture it. Of course after I found this out I did not see any wild cattle.

Herr Zeller came riding by our house to tell me that the fur buyer would be at the warehouse the next morning. I gathered all of my furs which I had been saving including three deer, eight rabbits, five squirrel, and one rattlesnake. The next morning Fritz and I had our first encounter with the American from Victoria. He was a tall man with very wide shoulders and he wore a dark suit, white shirt, and a bow tie. He had shinny black boots and his hat was rounded on top. He had a long mustache and a stick-like brown item protruded from his mouth from which he puffed smoke. Later we found out that this was called a cigar which was made of rolled tobacco and was smoked like a pipe. The man was very friendly and he was delighted when I spoke in my limited English. I got a total of $1.25 cents in American money, the first cash I had in Texas. I peered intently at the bill which was green and white with a picture of a man on it, and then I tossed the silver coin into the air and caught it. Immediately I went to the warehouse, looked at the boots, and unfortunately they started at $2.00. I would have to wait a little while longer.

I spent the next three days trying to raise more money. Fritz assisted me in borrowing a cart and team of oxen. We took our rifle for protection and went approximately four miles from New Braunfels to the hills in the west. There we cut thirty cedar posts and went to a farm located near our farm and tried to sell them to Herr Mumme who was building a wooden fence around his property. He said that he would purchase the posts if we helped dig post holes. We returned to New Braunfels just before dark. The next morning I had to pull the string on Fritz's toe to get him up. We took our lunch, a canteen of water, and our rifle and worked for Herr Mumme. We dug post holes all day in the hot sun, and finally, near sundown Herr Mumme awarded us with a total of $1.50 for the posts and labor. I gave half the money to Fritz and my 75 cents now would make it possible for me to buy a pair of boots. It was a good thing, because on our walk back to New Braunfels the entire front sole of my boot came apart and the sole flapped as I walked.

The next morning PaPa accompanied me to the warehouse where we looked at all the boots. I tried on several pair until I found some that fit and paid the clerk $2.00. This was my first expensive purchase and I was very proud. The boots seemed a little heavy and tight as we walked back to the house, but I could hardly feel the rocks under my feet. Fritz and Herr Nagel were working in their yard and I immediately walked over there to talk. We talked about the weather and when we might harvest our potatoes. Finally Fritz noticed my new boots and Herr Nagel said that they looked fine to him. I said "Thank you" and continued on with the conversation about the potatoes. I did not want to appear overly proud of my new boots because PaPa said that too much pride was a sin.

I woke up several times during the night and looked around. I saw my new boots beside my bed. I rolled over and dozed off again, but soon I was awake. Just then I heard the chickens screaming loudly from the back yard. I pulled on my boots, lit a candle, loaded the rifle as quickly as possible, and ran out the door into the darkness. By this time PaPa had jumped from his bed and followed after me. I sneaked around the side of the house and peered into the dark at the chicken coop. In a few seconds my eyes adjusted and I was able to see a large dog-like creature trying to dig a hole to get under the wall of the chicken coop. The creature was so busy with his task that he did not notice me as I sneaked behind the woodpile, aimed and pulled the trigger. After the puff of smoke cleared I saw the animal lying still on the ground, heard the chickens still screaming, and PaPa running up behind me. By this time Herr Nagel was coming out his door while pulling on his pants. PaPa brought the candle and we inspected the dead animal. It looked very much like a dog, but we determined that it was a coyote. These animals are often heard during the night howling loudly in the nearby hills. I put my clothes on and then began to skin the animal by candlelight. I salted the skin and rolled it carefully including the fluffy tail. The next morning I dragged the body far away from town and buried it. PaPa said that this was one wild animal that we refused to eat. The chickens were very nervous and were reluctant to come out of the coop. We gathered large rocks and put them around the bottom of the chicken coop to help stop an animal, such as a coyote, from digging under the walls. It would be several days before the chickens settled down and began to lay eggs again.

It was time for me to try to make my own way in life. Of course I was still a part of "the four farmers", but there were many days when I went hunting and found odd jobs while PaPa was busy making bed frames. I spent some time with Herr Zeller who let me shoot his rifle and hand gun which were both very fine weapons. I also practiced with the local militia men, a small army trained to protect New Braunfels. They helped in times of emergency, for example, in case of fire. I attended their meeting where they organized a fire plan. A large wagon holding ten large barrels of water and sixteen buckets would be kept ready at all times. It would be parked under the tree next to the warehouse which was close to the oxen and horse pens. A large bell had been placed at the nearby fort to be rung only in emergencies. If the bell rang, day or night, the militia men made their way to the fort as quickly as possible. There they would be told what the emergency was and would then act accordingly. If the emergency was a fire, the first men to arrive would begin to hitch up the horses and get to the fire. The others would be sent directly to the fire. I was in the crew who would bring a secondary wagon filled with barrels of water. The crew would have to work quickly since the wagon would not always be at the ready. We would take a wagon from the warehouse, load it with buckets and barrels, drive to the Comal River, fill the barrels, and then go to the fire.

The militia men all rode horseback and wore fancy uniforms when they were on duty including dark pants, a gray wool coat which had a black collar, tall black boots, and a black cap. Each had a rifle and a pistol and there was regular target practice. These men all had regular jobs, but they were also paid a monthly fee of $3.00. They took turns patrolling New Braunfels day and night. I could not join the militia until I turned 16 years old, but I could be a volunteer who helped the militia. I helped care for the horses and made bullets once a week. In return I got to participate in target practice and ride along on patrols if I was needed. This was valuable experience and I improved my accuracy with our rifle.

At the end of the church service on Sunday, Herr Zeller announced that next Saturday there would be a Shootzenfest and all were welcome to participate. This would be a contest to determine who was the best shot. The contestants would shoot at targets and the winner would be given a prize. I immediately entered the contest.

All week I practiced shooting at cactus and kept our rifle clean and shiny. Even as we were digging potatoes out of the field, I fond myself day dreaming about winning the shooting contest. We dug many bushels of potatoes and hauled them to our houses. We dug a hole under the backside of our house and lined the sides with rocks. A door closed over the top of the hole and that is where we put our potatoes. If they were kept cool, dark, and dry they would last throughout the winter. After Herr Nagel has his cellar filled with potatoes, we sold the remainder to the warehouse where we got 30 cents per bushel. MaMa, PaPa, Herr Nagel and his wife went to the warehouse and traded potatoes for staples such as flour, coffee, corn meal, fabric and tobacco.

The weather was getting cooler and the trees along the banks of the Comal and Guadalupe Rivers were turning yellow and gold. Since almost everyone in town had bought a bed from PaPa, he was making tables and benches. I assisted him each Monday in gathering enough wood for him to work with all week. I went hunting every day and we nearly always had fresh meat on the table.

Finally Saturday had come and it was time for the shooting contest. The entrants lined up and drew a number from a hat. I drew number 12. Each entrant got two shots at a target of tin cans about 50 yards away. If the shooter missed he was out of the contest. When it came my turn, I hit the can on my first try. When everyone was finished shooting, the target cans were moved out to 60 yards. Those who had hit the target the first time around got to shoot again. There were only 6 shooters left in the running after this, and I was one of them. Then the target was moved to 70 yards. Only two men were able to hit the target and I was not one of them. The two men then shot again. One missed and one hit the target and was declared the winner. The prize was a bag of gun powder. We were very impressed and each of us shook the hand of the winner, Herr Brandt. I asked Herr Brandt if I might go hunting with him and he suggested that we go on Tuesday morning.

After the excitement of the day, Fritz and I stayed near the fort and talked to several other young people whom we had known in Bicken and there was a special bond between us. Most were glad that they no longer had to go to school, but none of us realized how much work would be involved in making our new homes. I wore my new pants and boots, and felt more like a grownup than ever before. Ella Brockoff seemed to think that I was handsome in my new outfit and I talked to her more than anyone else.

On the next Tuesday I got up before dawn and met Herr Brandt for a two day hunting trip. He signed for two saddle horses and a mule at the warehouse and loaded our bedroll, sausage, canteen and rifles on the saddle and led the mule. We went north of New Braunfels and in the afternoon we were farther from town in this direction than I had ever been. The hills were covered with tees and there were beautiful springs bubbling up out of the ground. As we rode we jumped several deer, but Herr Brandt was not yet ready to begin hunting. We found a camp fire from several days ago, and saw the tracks of several horses. Herr Brandt explained the ways of the Indians saying that they wandered about on the northern plains and from time to time sent out parties of braves to steal and rob. They especially liked horses and they used horses like we used money. The Lipan Apache and Comanche Indians were likely to kill whoever got into their way and without warning. He explained that we must be as quiet as possible and must be looking around us and be on guard. I was getting a little nervous and wishing that I was back in New Braunfels. We continued to a very high hill where we tied our animals half way up and then walked to the summit with our rifles. We could see for a great distance and the scenery was beautiful. Herr Brandt pointed to the direction of New Braunfels where we could see the Guadalupe River. When we looked to the north and west we saw more hills and trees. Herr Brandt showed me how to ride in the river for a while and then come out on the other side. In this way if someone had followed our tracks they would probably loose the way where we entered the water. He said that if we saw Indians from a great distance we could try to outrun them and make our way to New Braunfels. If we saw Indians nearby, the best thing to do would be to dismount with rifle, ammunition and canteen and shew the animals away. We would then hide in rocks or in thick brush, and hope that the Indians would go after the animals and not us. Herr Brandt warned me to always know which direction to go to return to New Braunfels and every half hour he would stop and ask me the direction to get home. This was a test, and I kept watching the sun and landmarks along the way. Usually I was able to tell the direction correctly and Herr Brandt said I was doing well. That evening we climbed a high hill and searched from there for a good place to camp. We saw a rock overhang across a canyon and decided to try that area. Herr Brandt suggested that we not camp on a waterway, because Indians liked to follow waterways at night. We stopped and gave our animals a drink and filled our canteens, and then went up higher to the rock overhang. We saw that others had camped there before. We looked for boot tracks and any trash which might have been left behind. When we found none, Herr Brandt said that this was a possible Indian camp. He asked if I thought we should stay there. I said, "No, because if Indians had been there before, they might come back". Herr Brandt smiled for the first time and said "Ya, das ist gute". We continued to another area which had large rocks and a grove of trees. We made camp there and slept behind the rocks and near the animals so that if they were disturbed we would hear them. We made a fire to cook coffee and warmed our sausage, but after that we let the fire burn down. We had a candle which we lit to check on the horses.

We climbed a nearby hill by candle light and looked around. The stars were bright and there was a half moon. I told Herr Brandt about my experience on the "Angelina" and how I had learned to navigate. We looked for the North Star and then I told Herr Brandt in which direction I thought New Braunfels was located. He say, "Ya das ist gute".

Herr Brandt shook my shoulder to waken me. It was still dark but the stars were not as bright and I knew that morning was near. We ate cold sausage, took our rifles, and walked quietly down to the creek. We sat behind bushes where we saw a trail crossing the creek and within a few minutes three deer came by. We both raised our rifles and shot quickly, each killing a deer. I started to walk over to the deer, but Herr Brandt held my sleeve and motioned to stay in place. We sat still and quiet for another half hour before he motioned to go ahead to the deer. As we cut open the carcasses and gutted the deer, Herr Brandt quietly told me that if someone heard our shooting they might come to look for us. We had stayed in the bushes for our own safety. If we had gone out and started gutting the deer, someone could sneak upon us and we would not be prepared. If we stayed hidden and someone came to see what happened, hopefully we would see them first before they saw us. Herr Brandt said to always reload the rifle immediately and be prepared.

We drug the two deer to the mule and tied them on to the pack saddle, mounted our horses just before dawn and turned toward New Braunfels. We came upon a small creek with an animal trail very visible, tied our horses a half mile away, and sat at the creek to wait. After about an hour I shot a large buck that had six points on its antlers. We gutted it, put it on the mule, and continued on back to New Braunfels. When we arrived at the fort several people gathered around to see what we had killed and helped us skin the deer and cut the meat into pieces. I kept the hides of the two deer I killed and the antlers from the buck. I thanked Herr Brandt as we returned the horses and mule to their pen, took meat to Herr Nagel and to MaMa, and then nailed the deer antlers above the back door of the house. I was very tired and went to bed immediately after supper.

We spent the rest of the week harvesting our sweet potatoes which were just enough to completely fill our cellar. "The four farmers" were very satisfied with our harvest. The Nagel family came to our house for supper and we discussed all that we had done at the farms and we even talked about our days in "The Old Country". Everyone agreed that the physical labor was more than we had expected, but that life here in Texas was very abundant. Our parents complimented Fritz and I for our help in building houses, establishing the farms, and putting fresh meat on our tables. PaPa announced that he was taking a regular job with Herr Kueger who made furniture and had his own shop on Main Street in New Braunfels. Herr Kueger had many tools which he brought from Germany and he would teach PaPa how to use them to make fine furniture. Herr Nagel said that, if the job worked out for PaPa, he would like to purchase PaPa's farm.

Herr Zeller came to our house early the next morning and we invited him in for fried eggs, bacon and coffee. He said that a large number of German immigrants would be landing in Galveston within two to three weeks, and somehow he would have to bring them to New Braunfels. Herr Zeller then surprised us by asking me to accompany him on this trip to hunt and take care of the animals. Many of the people who were arriving were from the city and were not familiar with oxen and horses. He said that I would be paid $1.00 per week for the trip and that I would be provided with a rifle and ammunition. PaPa said that we must have time to think about this offer and that we would let Herr Zeller know tomorrow.

After Herr Zeller departed PaPa, MaMa, Dorothea and I sat quietly at the table and drank more coffee. MaMa kept wiping her hands on her apron and Dorothea was anxious to go outside and play. PaPa finally asked if I would like to take this job. I immediately replied "Ya, this is what I want to do, these people will need help and I can now teach them what I know". PaPa said that this would not be an easy trip because winter was coming. MaMa said that I must have a coat and a good warm hat before I leave. So it was decided, I would take the job. PaPa and I went to the warehouse where he signed for a new coat, a pair of pants, and a winter hat. We walked to Herr Zeller's house near the fort and told him that I could take the job. He handed me a fine rifle with ammunition and said to meet him Monday morning at 5:00 o'clock to depart.

I spent the weekend preparing by polishing my boots and then putting oil on them to help repel moisture. When I awoke on Monday morning I put an extra pair of pants, underwear, socks, and a shirt on my bed and rolled up the sheet and blanket around them, tying the bedroll with a leather string. In a small bag, made from a flour sack, I packed a ring of smoked sausage, two cooked potatoes, and five biscuits. My parents were just beginning to awaken when I was about to depart. I paused and told them goodbye. MaMa got up from bed and gave me a hug, and PaPa shock my hand and patted me on the shoulder. They both said "be careful" as I glanced at the sleeping Dorothea and walked out the door with all my gear. On the way to the fort I stopped and filled by canteen at the Comal River.

Chapter 3

Harsh Reality

As soon as I arrived at the fort Herr Zeller came and we walked down to the stables near the warehouse. Herr Zeller pointed to the gray horse and said for me to ride him. I smiled at Herr Zeller and shock his hand. The gray has always been my favorite since I cared for him on our trip to New Braunfels. The horses all stood and looked at us as I quietly entered the pen with a halter and lead rope. I walked directly to the gray and he didn't move at all, it was as if he remembered that we were friends. Occasionally I had stopped by the stables with a handful of green grass. When he saw me, he came to the fence and ate from my hand. We saddled the horses and, because I had grown taller, I was able to mount the horse without a helping hand. We began or trip by following the Guadalupe River south.

The sky was cloudy but it was not yet cold. Herr Zeller had sent four other men on ahead to Galveston where they would try to purchase wagons and oxen or horses. We would stop at every house we see and ask if they had any wagons or oxen for sale. Herr Zeller asked if I could convey that message in English. I had been practicing my English with the fur buyer and with several salesmen who came to New Braunfels.

After an hours ride we saw a man in a field digging potatoes. I called "Hello" so that we did not frighten him, and he jumped to his feet. He grabbed a nearby rifle and pointed it in our direction. I looked at Herr Zeller and saw that he was holding his hands up in the air, so I did the same. "Guten Tag" said Herr Zeller. I said "Hello". The man lowered the gun but still held it in his hand. I said "we from New Braunfels". "Ah ha" said the man. "Das is Herr Zeller und I am Nicholas" I said. Then I tried to tell him about our need for transportation. He first laughed at me and then said "no", he had no wagons, oxen or horses for sale. He did know a Mr. Talbert, about three miles to the west, who might be able to help. We thanked him and continued to Mr. Talbert's place, which turned out to be a store.

We dismounted and walked through the door where several men were standing. When we entered they all become quiet. Then Mr. Talbert, I assumed, said "Can I help you?". "Ya" I said. I introduced us and then told them we needed transportation. Mr. Talbert said that the Texas army had bought almost everything he had. One of the men standing nearby said that he had a wagon and two horses for sale for $200 including harness. Herr Zeller and I followed the man to his farm.

He had a house made of finished wood with a large front porch. There was also a large barn with several horses in a nearby pen. He pointed to two dark brown horses and said that they would pull. We dismounted and looked at a wagon which was inside the barn. The wagon was in fair condition and the wheels and axle were still good. The harness had been repaired several times but was still usable. Herr Zeller told me in German that $200 was too much. I said to the man, "no $200". He shrugged his shoulders and said that the army offered him $175 and he turned them down. He would stay with his price of $200. I told Herr Zeller who took coins from his saddlebags. He told me that we would give the man $200 but we wanted a Bill of Sale with the man's signature. When I told the man he began to laugh but, when he saw our serious faces, he stopped laughing and said he would do it. He walked into his house and soon returned with a note on which I watched as he signed his name. I looked at the paper and understood the words “sell”, “two horses”, “two harness”, “one wagon” and his name was Mr. Mitchell. We both shook his hand and he helped us catch the horses and hitch them to the wagon. I tied the gray to the back of the wagon, took my rifle and ammunition with me, and drove the team. There was no cover on the wagon and I could look back to see if anyone was following us. Herr Zeller rode a little ahead and scouted the way for me. We went as fast as we could and stopped in the afternoon for a short rest. I ate some biscuits and drank from my canteen. Herr Zeller said that $200 was very expensive. The next time we wanted to get a better deal.

That night we gave the animals a long drink at the Guadalupe River and then held them on ropes while they grazed in the lush grass. When they were full, we re-hitched the team and drove to some nearby brush where we hid the wagon and animals. It was getting dark. I ate a cold potato and then put my bedroll in the back of the wagon. I laid down and looked up at the stars. I woke up several times in the night and checked the horses and then dreamed that I was once again aboard the “Angelina”.

The next day we continued and ate sausage while the horses had some grass for breakfast. We made very good time, probably going about 28 miles. We followed the same procedure that night.

On the third day we went to a German friend of Herr Zeller, Herr Voltz, and picked up a wagon and two horses which he had acquired for us. Herr Zeller had to give him $200 in cash. Herr Voltz told us that the army had been buying all the animals they could find to mount a war against Mexico. He tried to explain to us that Texas had broken away from Mexico ten years ago, and now that Texas was a state, Mexico was making war with the United States to try to get Texas back. This was a scary situation, but Herr Voltz assured us that the United States had a very powerful army and Mexico could not win. Herr Voltz introduced us to a delicious meal called pinto beans. He showed us the brown and white spotted beans and then explained that they grew like peas. They were very hard and must be boiled in water for about two hours to cook. They were easily grown here and the Mexicans ate them at almost every meal. Another good food which he got from the Mexicans was tortillas, made from ground corn and cooked like a pancake. We spent the night on Herr Voltz's porch and our horses were in a pen.

We were very grateful for Herr Voltz's hospitality and were reluctant to depart. By 5:00 o'clock in the morning we were continuing our journey. About mid-day we got to the city of Victoria. This was the first city that I had visited in Texas. The streets were muddy and the buildings were all made of wood. There were many soldiers in the town wearing blue uniforms. I talked to one of them, and he said that he was on his way to the Mexican border to fight. He invited me to have a beer but I declined the offer and thanked him. I also got a newspaper for one penny which I intended to read when I had time. Herr Zeller bought 20 large pots and 20 bags of corn meal. I knew what that would be used for, and I hoped I did not have to eat it very often.

We left Victoria and continued about eight more miles. We saw several other wagons with soldiers and supplies departing from Victoria, or passing us on their way from Galveston to Victoria. We waved to the people and they smiled and waved back.

We followed the same procedure of feeding and watering the horses and then hiding out in the bushes away from the river.

The fifth day we ended up on the Guadalupe just before sundown. The horses were drinking water when we saw them all raise their heads and look to the East. Herr Zeller was holding his rifle and I quickly picked up my rifle and had it ready for something. Approximately ten Indians ran towards us on horseback. We dove behind the nearest log and dropped the horses ropes. Just as we aimed and were ready to fire, the Indians seemed to run past our camp. Right behind them was a company of soldiers in blue uniforms. Neither the Indians nor the soldiers seemed to notice us or our horses. Herr Zeller and I stood up and watched as the army company disappeared out of sight. Well, Herr Zeller stood, but as for me, as soon as I stood my knees buckled under me and I fell to the ground. Herr Zeller was talking gently to the horses and trying to grab their ropes. I quickly got up and walked toward the gray. Though his eyes were wider than usual he stood still for me to grab his rope. Two other horses had run about twenty yards. I mounted the gray and walked toward to other horses. They were standing with their heads up and their ears forward listening carefully. I walked the gray and talked very softly telling them that it was all over and we were all safe and sound. Eventually they were still and I slowly took each rope and led the horses back to the wagons. Herr Zeller had already hitched the two other horses to a wagon and we quickly drove to a heavy wooded area away from the creek. We tied all the horses and then put brush around the wagons to conceal them. We got our food, water and rifles and sat behind a tree watching for anything that moved. We stayed very still for an hour until it was completely dark. Hopefully the soldiers chased the Indians far away, but we would take turns sleeping tonight. I slept first for three hours, and then Herr Zeller woke me and I took my turn at watch for three hours. We rotated until just before dawn when we harnessed the horses and began our journey.

By the next afternoon, when we had covered twelve miles, we stopped for a rest and drink. We saw a house about a quarter mile away. I stayed with the horses while Herr Zeller crept closer to the house to observe who was there. He saw a man with a cow and then saw a child on the front porch. Herr Zeller came back to me and we drove the wagons toward the house. When the man saw us he immediately picked up his rifle and held it loosely beside him. We stopped and both said "hello". We introduced ourselves and he said that his name was Mr. Brock. He did not see Indians or soldiers and he thanked us for warning him that Indians may be nearby. He gave us a drink of fresh milk and a loaf of homemade bread. We ate it hungrily as the little girl stood and watched us. After thanking him for his hospitality we continued and made camp in a tall grassy area. We took turns sleeping again.

The next day we knew we were near the coast because we saw fewer trees and sea birds were in the air. By that night, after dark, we arrived at Carlshaven. There were two other men there who had each gotten two wagons. They were cooking venison from a deer they killed. We ate with them and felt more secure with our animals in a pen near the building. We slept on the floor in the small warehouse. I had thoughts of home, and then I realized that when I thought of home, I was thinking of our house in New Braunfels. I no longer regarded Bicken, Germany as my home.

Herr Zeller and I boarded a small sloop headed for Galveston which was a big and rich city. The buildings were all new and the streets were made of sand and sea shells. We went to the dock and talked to several people there to find out if anyone had seen our ship, "The Viking". No one remembered having seen it. We stared at the ships in the harbor and then we stared out to sea in hopes of finding "The Viking". One sailor told us that "The Viking" was an old ship and he hoped they were able to make it across the ocean. Herr Zeller had a frown on his face as we sat on the dock and I passed the time by throwing shells into the sea. We decided to go shopping at several of the big stores. I was excited even though I had only $2.00 which had to last me until I returned to New Braunfels. Herr Zeller bought cans of lard, as well as several 50 pound bags of flour, and 20 pans in which to cook biscuits. He told me that I would have to teach the new immigrants how to make biscuits. We loaded all of our goods onto the sloop and, while we waited for its departure, we each ate a piece of hard candy which we bought for one cent. It was the first sweet food that I had since last Christmas. Herr Zeller said that this was something that you should not eat very often because it was bad for your heart and teeth. Because we had no place to stay in Galveston, Herr Zeller made an understanding with Captain Noble, the Captain of the sloop, that when the immigrants arrived he would provide several sloops to transport the immigrants to Carlshaven. "The Viking" could not land in Carlshaven because the harbor was too shallow. We returned to our warehouse in Carlshaven in time for a dinner of dry sausage.

We spent the next several days repairing the harnesses and greasing the wagon wheels. We packed the food and cooking utensils into the wagons along with large spoons, several bowls, a large number of tin cups, and 30 buckets. I spent my spare time in reading the local newspaper and talking to the few people who live in Carlshaven. They were mostly fisherman and some of them owned cattle which fed on the nearby grasslands.

In Carlshaven I met my first real Texan friend, Harry Knight. Harry was 17 years old and he lived there with his uncle. They raised cattle and also fished from their small boat. Harry's uncle used to be a sailor, but when Harry's parents were killed in a storm which sent large waves into Carlshaven, his uncle decided to stay and help Harry. Harry was born there and had never attended school. He could neither read nor write and he was very excited when I began to read the newspaper to him. We went hunting in the marshes and I shot two ducks which we roasted that night. They were delicious. Harry took me on my very first fishing expedition. We caught tiny fish, called minnows, with a small net and put them on hooks and threw them into the water. After a while we began to catch large fish called Drum. We cut large thin slices of meat from the fish and then laid them over a piece of rope that had been strung between two trees. In this way the fish would dry and could be kept for several months. The fish could also be put into a barrel and salted in order to keep them from spoiling. Harry was dirty, and he chewed tobacco and spit the dark brown juice. He offered me tobacco, but I declined. I knew that I could not afford to buy tobacco, so there was no use getting into that habit. Harry taught me to dip the fresh fish into corn meal and fry it in lard. It was delicious. I took several fish to the warehouse and prepared a feast of fried fish for the men there. Harry also taught me how to cook the pinto beans which were so readily available there. After I cooked them for Herr Zeller he bought three 50 pound bags of the pinto beans to take back to New Braunfels. I enjoyed speaking English to Harry and I was becoming more proficient each day. I also went to the local stores and spoke to the people there and read the catalogues from which the store owner could order a variety of goods from the eastern United States. Many goods were available for those with money.

The catalogues offered fascinating items such as fancy ladies dresses and hats, many different types of guns, canoes, and even fur coats made from buffalo hides. In Carlshaven there was no church, so on Sunday morning Herr Zeller read aloud from his small Bible and we had silent prayer.

After six days of waiting, there was much excitement when Captain Noble arrived with his first load of German immigrants. The immigrants, who were mostly from Berlin, complained bitterly about "The Viking" which was so old and dilapidated that they feared it would break into pieces when they hit a terrible storm. Water came into their living quarters and they had to form a bucket brigade to get the water out. It soaked many of their clothes and all of their bedding, and after the storm was over they hung their wet possessions on the deck to dry. The old captain was very stubborn and he did not care about the hardships of the immigrants. As Herr Zeller assured them that all would now be well, I wondered how these new immigrants would be able to handle the future hardships which they must endure. We all hoped that no one would ask how far it was to New Braunfels, but sure enough that was one of the first questions from Herr Bickle, who seemed to have taken over the leadership of the group. Herr Zeller said that the trip would take approximately 20 days if we had good weather. This was enough to quiet the group, and all 80 people bedded down in the small warehouse for the night. Even though it was crowded, many people expressed their happiness at sleeping on the still earth which did not toss up and down all night.

We got up very early and began to boil water in the big pots to make corn meal gruel. We fed the horses, and began to harness them and hitch them to the wagons. The immigrants seemed to awaken with new vigor and they were all anxious to begin their journey to their new homeland of New Braunfels. Herr Zeller gave a good speech about the journey. He explained that, because the guards had experience living in Texas, they would have authority over the immigrants and would do their best to protect the group. The families were divided into four groups of approximately 20 people. Each group elected their own leader and any problems would be told to that leader who would then speak to Herr Zeller. Each group would have two wagons in which to carry their possessions, and most people would be expected to walk. Each group would appoint a two man team who would be in charge of the animals for their group. Each group would appoint cooks, fire builders, and water carriers. Each parent would be responsible for their own children and must keep them near the wagons. Herr Zeller explained that we would follow the Guadalupe River and try to camp beside it each night, and that each group would provide men to keep a lookout through the night. Finally Herr Zeller introduced each of us guards and told the immigrants that they must follow our directions and learn from us. And so we set out on our journey with hopes for safety, good weather, enough food, health of people and animals, and that dreams be fulfilled.

The first days of travel were good and the sun shone on the brown and golden sea of grass. The birds sang and the immigrants were happy and robust. They were happy to be walking and they were amazed at the sights which lay before them. They asked many questions and I was suddenly elevated to the position of leadership because of my experience. That evening we stopped along the Guadalupe and I gave instructions on how to cook pinto beans and how to make biscuits. I quickly moved to those who were caring for the horses and gave instructions to them. After we all ate the corn mush, we boiled pinto beans until it was bedtime. The immigrants liked sleeping in the fresh air after having slept in the hold of the ship for so many nights. I was on watch from 10:00 p.m. until 2:00 a.m. and then I rolled myself up in my blanket to sleep.

I awoke early as usual, picked up my gun and told Herr Zeller that I was going up stream to hunt. I took a candle to light my way and soon I was alone, in this vast, dark countryside. I searched for animal trails and finally was able to kill one deer. A gutted it and drug it back to camp. Several men were awake and watched as I carefully skinned the deer and cut it into pieces. We put the meat into tow sacks and would cook it at noon.

Because of the war conditions, and the fact that we had actually seen Indians on our trip to Carlshaven, Herr Zeller decided that two men would be sent ahead of the group to act as scouts. I joined Herr Kempf for the first scouting trip. We stayed approximately one mile ahead of the wagons and watched very carefully for any movements nearby and on the horizon. We looked carefully at the terrain to make sure that the wagons could move easily over the trail. Several times I stopped to move large rocks or logs which were in the wagon path. The path was now almost a road because so many people were using it on their trip from Victoria to Galveston.

At noon we went back to the wagons and set up for cooking the deer meat and corn meal gruel. We skewered the small pieces of deer meat on sticks and cooked them close to the fire. Almost everyone tried the new meat and said that it was delicious. They had no meat on their ocean journey and subsided mainly on potatoes. That night we ate the pinto beans and biscuits and after supper we began cooking pinto beans for the next day. I was very tired and went to bed as soon as possible. Herr Brandt awakened me at 2:00 a.m. to take his watch. I took my gun and stood on an outcropping of rocks which gave me a good view of the countryside around us. After a while I sat down and then realized that I was beginning to get cold and went back to camp and put on my coat. Within one hour the wind began to blow very hard and it was a cold wind. Then rain began to fall. The whole camp seemed to come awake all at once when the rain came. People picked up their children, spread their blankets over each other, and some got under the wagons for protection. It continued to rain for a half hour and it was very cold. I immediately began to pick up sticks just as the rain started, and others helped me so that we had a fire going with dry wood. We made a tent-like structure over the fire using one of the wagon covers. We continued to gather wood and sat the logs beside the fire in order to dry them before adding them to the blaze. After a while we cooked coffee and people stayed under the wagons and tent. As soon as daylight came we began to cook corn meal gruel and got the animals ready for departure. As we started out the ground was mushy and everyone was very cold. Most people had coats and they also wrapped themselves in blankets. We were walking towards the wind and it made my eyes water and my nose run. I got permission to ride ahead with the scouts and to hunt. Soon I saw a buck chasing a doe through a meadow. I galloped the gray after them, dismounted on a ridge, kneeled to the ground, aimed, and killed the buck. The two scouts came and took care of that buck while I continued to hunt. The wind and cold made the gray frisky and hard to handle. He seemed to want to run and he put up his nose to smell the wind. After a few miles I saw three does standing at a distance. I dismounted and tied the gray to a stump. I crawled through the tall grass and got close enough to shoot one of the does. As soon as I finished gutting the doe it began to rain. I drug the doe back to the gray and then motioned to one of the scouts to come pick up the doe. When he arrived we decided to take the two deer back to the wagons. It was raining quiet heavily and the wagons were stopped. We were quite a distance from the Guadalupe River and there was very little wood in this vicinity to build a fire. After about one hour of waiting Herr Zeller said that we must continue in order to get to the Guadalupe River by nightfall. There was no dinner that day. Everyone walked in the cold rain. Before long most everyone's shoes were leaking and water was sloshing every time they took a step. We used all of our wagon covers to protect the corn meal and flour to keep the food dry. Just before dark we finally made it to the Guadalupe River for the night. We pulled small pieces of wood from under the leaves and found them to be dry enough to start several fires. We gradually dried enough wood to keep the fires burning all night and cooked all of the deer meat. I never went to bead that night.

The next morning the sky was cloudy but dry. We made biscuits and coffee. Herr Zeller decided that three of us should take a wagon and go as quickly as possible to Victoria to buy tents, or anything that could be used for shelter. We also needed blankets because a wet blanket did not keep a person warm. I put gun powder and bullets under my shirt and coat to keep them dry and covered my gun with my blanket. We set out with me driving the wagon and leading the gray horse. The other two men were on horseback. After we had traveled for two hours or more we came to a stream of water which was rushing by, and we were afraid to cross it. We followed it upstream and finally found a shallow place where we could cross. That night we took turns sleeping in the wagon with the horses tied to the wagon as well. By the next morning the rain was gone but it was still cold. We finally arrived in Victoria that afternoon and began to search for tents or some other shelter. I had to do most of the conversing in English and it was a great burden to be responsible. I knew that more than 80 people needed these supplies as soon as possible. We went to several stores and finally found a man who had three large tents which had once been used by the army. We tried to negotiate a fair price, but in the end we paid $50 for tents. We spent the remainder of our money to purchase ropes and 25 blankets. We packed them in the wagon and started back that very afternoon. The next day at noon we arrived back at the camp on the Guadalupe River. The immigrants had made several lean-toes where they had stacked logs and covered them with branches. This helped to block the wind. We tied the tents from the trees over these shelters and made fires under the tents. Eventually people gathered around the fires and began to dry their clothes. Four of us rode onto the prairie to try to find animals for meat. The cold weather and wind made the animals very active and in one hour we killed three deer which everyone enjoyed eating that night. Thank goodness for pinto beans, because all of the corn meal and flour got wet and had gotten rotten. We cooked large pots of pinto beans and made it into a stew with deer meat.

By the fourth day the weather cleared and the wind had died down. It was still cold but everyone was ready to continue our journey. We built many fires and almost everyone was able to sleep in the tents. By that night I was so tired that I could hardly wake up when it was my turn to take guard duty.

We continued on the journey making good time and soon we were near Victoria. We took a wagon to town and bought more flour and corn meal so that everyone got to eat biscuits the next morning. The immigrants said that biscuits and pinto beans were some of the best food they had ever eaten. Almost everyone was trying to learn as much as they could from us "old timers", and I could hardly get any sleep or rest because someone always needed me to do something. Herr Zeller's eyes were red and his shoulder's were slumped. I could tell that he was in the same condition as I. The gray horse turned his head when he saw me coming, which was his way of saying that he really wanted to rest and did not want to hunt. I was even elected to give English lessons. Only nine months ago I was an immigrant on this same journey, and now I was one of the leaders and a teacher to the immigrants on this journey. A little experience was very valuable here, for it could make the difference between life and death, success or failure.

On the twentieth day of the journey the day dawned bright and sunny. It was still winter, but not so cold during the daylight hours. I started to help make the fires and to get the horses to grass when one of the men came running to me saying that his child was ill. I called to Herr Zeller and we ran to the tent were they had been sleeping. The ten year old girl was very sick with a fever and her parents were worried. After breakfast we packed the wagons and made space in one wagon for the girl to lie down. By supper time that night, two women also had a fever, and the next morning three more children were ill. We put them all in the back of one wagon and continued the journey. By that night they were much worse. Herr Zeller sent Herr Tezel and I to the nearby town of Gonzales to ask for help. We set out with a few biscuits, our canteens full of water, our guns, and four candles. There was a half moon and, after our eyes became adapted to the darkness, we could see enough to travel slowly. We knew that the horses could see in the dark better than we, so we pointed them in a northward direction and let them decide where they should walk. We knew that if we continued north we would eventually come upon the Guadalupe River again and if we followed it we would begin to see houses. We also knew that the town of Gonzales was slightly west of the Guadalupe River. I was thankful that this was a clear night and I was able to follow the north star. As we rode I fell asleep several times and then suddenly awoke when the horse's foot hit a rock or a limb. Herr Tezel did the same and several times we woke each other. By morning we could see a house straight ahead. We walked our horses slowly and then dismounted at the gate which was about 20 yards from the house. I said "Hello" twice. A man came from the house while pulling up his suspenders. He had a revolver in his hand. I asked him how to get to Gonzales. He pointed to the left and then turned around and went back into the house. He never said one word to us. Herr Tezel and I continued to the left and found a well worn road which we followed to Gonzales. This was a very nice town which had many new buildings. We went to the stable and asked how to find the doctor. The man told us where the doctor's house was located and we went there. We tied our horses in front and I knocked on the door. A woman wearing a pink apron opened the door and I could feel the warmth of their fireplace. I asked for the Doctor and she said he would come right out. Soon he invited us to come in and have some breakfast. We were more than happy to eat there for they had bacon, eggs, biscuits, milk and coffee. I tried not to eat too much because I knew it was bad manners, but I could not help but eat two plates of food, two cups of coffee and three glasses of milk. The Doctor was a fine middle aged man who had come to Texas 15 years ago from New Orleans. His wife was very pretty in her pink apron and she was a good cook. I explained who we were, where we had come from, and what a problem we had with the sick. I also explained that we were willing to pay him in cash if he would go to treat our sick. He agreed and began to pack a large saddlebag with medicines. He put on a heavy coat and a big black hat and we saddled up his horse. Our horses had been eating grass in the yard. So the three of us set out to get back to the immigrants. It was much quicker in the daylight and we were back there by mid afternoon. All of the sick were in one tent and the Doctor began to speak to each one and to give them medicine. After he had done this he had a meeting with Herr Zeller, Herr Tezel and myself. He said that at least three of the immigrants had "red fever" which they probably were exposed to on the ship, or in Galveston. Being wet and cold then made them get sick. He suggested that the families who had the sick should go on to the town of Castell, which was not far from Gonzales, and would be one days journey in the wagons. There they could stay and he would tend to them. They could continue their trip to New Braunfels after they got well. Once again Herr Tezel and I were sent on a mission with no time to rest. Herr Zeller gave us money and we rode ahead to the town of Castell to find accommodations for the sick. The Doctor stayed with the immigrants throughout the day as they made their way to Castell. Herr Tezel and I first went to the stable and asked where we might find the leader of the town. He sent is to the store, the only store in town. The store owner sent us to the preacher from the only church. We knocked on the preacher's door and he came out and talked to us on the porch. He could see that we were very tired. He told us to put our horses in the small pen with some hay and to come into the house to eat. He had pinto beans with chunks of pork cooking on the stove. We drank milk and then ate beans and cornbread. The preacher said that he knew of an old barn about a mile from town that did not have a house or owner. After we ate, the three of us rode to the old barn and inspected it. It had a good roof and was clean inside. It looked like someone had camped there. The preacher said that no one would object if our sick stayed there in the barn. We went to the store and bought a wood heater which the stable man delivered by wagon. We gathered fire wood and built a fire in the heater. We then went to the store and bought a slab of bacon, all the ingredients for biscuits, and pinto beans, as well as ten blankets. Herr Tezel and I laid down in the warm barn and went to sleep. By late afternoon we woke up and rode out to find the wagons. We found them about three miles from town and led them to the barn. The Doctor was pleased with the accommodations for the sick.

The Doctor was given payment by Herr Zeller and promised to continue treating the sick. The next day the rest of us departed and waved goodbye to those brave people. They were sick, in a strange land, and they spoke very little English. There were four families who stayed in Castell. Of these 18 people, 4 died. Those who survived found work in town and none of those families ever moved to New Braunfels.

After many days of being cold, tired and hungry we finally began to recognize landmarks which indicated that we were nearing our destination of New Braunfels. We were very excited and I could hardly sleep the last night even though I was very tired. The next morning we continued and, as we got to the top of the hill, we looked down at the settlement of New Braunfels and saw where the Comal and Guadalupe Rivers unite. Everyone quickened their pace and we arrived there by 3:00 p.m. As the town guards saw us in the distance they alerted the people of New Braunfels who met us at the fort with milk and eggs. PaPa was there to greet me with a handshake. He looked at me as though he barely recognized me. All I could say was I want to go home. I put the gray into the horse pen with a bucket of oats and brushed his back. When he was content I hurried home where I could smell dinner cooking before I got there. MaMa and Dorothea hugged me and we sat down to eat a pork roast, for the day before PaPa had slaughtered the pig and made sausage. We had pork, sweet potatoes, cooked cabbage, and homemade bread. I went to bed right after dinner and slept until noon the next day. MaMa asked me how my clothes got so dirty. I smiled and then began to tell the story of our trip and hardships we endured. PaPa informed me that all was not well here in New Braunfels. Over 75 people had "red fever" and the doctor was having a difficult time trying to save them. Each man had to volunteer to dig graves because 2 or 3 people had been dying each day. The old house which had been used for a school was now the hospital, and the lean-to in the back was now the morgue where PaPa and Herr Keuger were making caskets as quickly as possible to bury the dead. PaPa said that I should not drink any water in the settlement or down stream from the settlement. As

PaPa went off to his job, I scouted to the North where I remembered finding a spring of water. I took two buckets and filled them with water for our house use. I then went to the graveyard and volunteered to dig graves the rest of the day. That night I saw Fritz as I was coming home. He informed me that he was now working at the warehouse for 20 cents per day wage. He also informed me that our friend Ella Brockoff had died from the "red fever". When I arrived home I sat on a stump in the yard. I thought about the days in Bicken, Germany where I had gone to school with Ella. I put my face in my handkerchief and cried.

The next few weeks were still very hard. The new immigrants were building houses in the winter cold and rain. They had very little food and I volunteered to hunt as much as possible to provide meat. Every morning I awoke and rode the gray horse away from town. I tied the him with a stout rope and walked another mile until I found a trail to the river. I sat behind the bushes and waited for deer. One morning I was able to shoot a large buck. After I had dressed (or gutted) the deer, I began to drag the carcass back towards the gray horse. I was having a difficult time since the deer was heavy and I also had my rifle, bullets and powder. As I walked through a dense wooded area near the river, I was shaken by a loud roar coming from behind me. I dropped the deer and ran for the first large tree. I got behind the tree and, while pulling my rifle to my shoulder, began to search in the direction from which I heard the roar. I blinked my eyes several times before I realized that I was staring at a large brown bear who was coming towards the dead deer. I carefully aimed at the bear's head and fired. He fell to the ground with a thud. At the same moment I saw the gray horse running to the left. I suppose he had been scared by the bear and had broken loose from the tree. I reloaded my rifle quickly and began to follow the gray. When he stopped and turned to look back at me, I also stopped and talked to him in a calming voice telling him that the bear was dead and he did not have to fear it any longer. He continued to walk away and finally, after about a half mile, he got tired and stopped. I was able to mount him and return to the dead deer and bear. I loaded the deer onto the back of the gray, but he would not come close to the bear. I finally put a rope around the bear's neck and tied it to the saddle to drag the bear all the way back to New Braunfels. This took some time, for I wanted to keep the bear skin from being torn and I carefully picked grassy areas in which to drag the body. When I got a mile from New Braunfels I dropped the bear and rode to the fort. Three men accompanied me with a wagon to pick up the bear and bring it to town. It almost became a parade as everyone saw us coming and ran towards the wagon to view the dead creature who was about four feet tall and weighed approximately 200 pounds when dressed. It took me some time to skin the bear with Opa's knife, for I knew that I could sell the fur for a great deal of money. I salted, rolled it, and placed it in the rafters of our smokehouse to be sold later to the fur buyer.

I walked into the house hoping to eat and rest, and there I found Dorothea kneeling beside the bed putting wet rags on MaMa's forehead. They said that MaMa had been ill with fever and shivering since that morning. I ran to town to tell PaPa and then went to the hospital to tell the Doctor to come. The Doctor said that he could not leave the hospital and that we would have to bring MaMa there to see him. PaPa and I ran to the warehouse and got a cart with oxen, put MaMa in the cart, and took her to the Doctor. After a quick examination the Doctor suggested that MaMa remain there where she could be observed. PaPa and I stayed until bedtime and then MaMa insisted that we go home and get some sleep. I awoke at dawn and PaPa and I went directly to the hospital. Ma Ma was no better than the day before. PaPa had to continue his work of building caskets. I stayed with MaMa, trying to make her comfortable, running errands, and helping to distribute soup to the sick. By that afternoon MaMa seemed to only sleep and would not wake up to talk to me. I then thought of Dorothea at home alone and went to check on her. I found her at the Nagel's house playing with their daughter Nelda. I told Frau Nagel about MaMa's condition and she said that she would keep Dorothea for the next several days until MaMa got better. I went back to the hospital and ended up staying there for three more days without going home. When I awoke on the third day I realized that MaMa was no longer breathing and her body was cold. I knelt beside her and prayed and wept, just as I had seen other families do the last several weeks. I stumbled out the door and went to where PaPa was working. As soon as he saw me he knew that MaMa was dead, for my face was red and covered with tears. He ran ahead to the hospital to see for himself, while I just sat down under an oak tree and cried. Later I walked to the river, washed my face, and dried it with my handkerchief. The dead bodies had to be moved to the morgue and buried as quickly as possible, because the hospital was full of sick and dying people and the morgue was always full. There was no time for dressing the dead in their finest church dress, or calling together family and friends, or having an elaborate church service. PaPa and I walked back to the Nagel's house and called Frau Nagel and Dorothea outside. PaPa told Dorothea that we tried to save MaMa, but she was too weak to survive and had gone on to be with her MaMa and PaPa and the angels in heaven. Then we all cried again and the Nagels went with us to bury MaMa in the new graveyard which already had 53 graves in it. The pastor came and said the 23 Psalm and then we all said the Lord's Prayer as the casket, that PaPa had built for someone else, was lowered into the deep, dark hole. PaPa and I shoveled the dirt onto the grave as Dorothea wailed in loud cries which echoed from the trees and nearby barn. When we finished, I happened to glance past the barn, and there was the gray horse staring at me from the pen. I walked to him, put my arms around his neck, buried my face in his thick black mane, and wept again.

Chapter 4

Into the Hills

In the next few weeks PaPa worked from daylight until dark, and I went hunting twice a day. Dorothea stayed with the Nagel's and only came home to cry herself to sleep at night. Gradually the pall of sickness over New Braunfels seemed to lift, and there were actually vacant beds in the hospital. PaPa went back to making furniture instead of caskets, and I continued to hunt twice a day. Each afternoon I helped with the building of the new schoolhouse. Though it was a very sad Christmas, for nearly every family had lost someone, I wanted to help as many families as possible to have special food for Christmas. Beginning four days before Christmas, Herr Zeller, Herr Brandt and I made an effort to shoot as many wild turkeys as possible for Christmas dinners. On Christmas Eve PaPa gave me a pair of leather gloves, and Dorothea a doll. The doll wore a dress that MaMa had made for it last month. I gave PaPa a pouch of tobacco, and Dorothea a small blanket in which to wrap her doll. Dorothea was between us holding our hands, as we walked to church at midnight. The stars shone brightly, and the air was crisp and clear. For just a brief moment I thought that I was back in Bicken, Germany walking to our church there on Christmas Eve. But then I realized that there was no snow, there was now only three of us, and my mind came back to reality. The pastor had a fine sermon about the Grace of God and then we all sang the hymn "Silent Night". As we sang each verse there were fewer and fewer singers, for most of us could no longer make sounds come from our taut throats. At the end of the service, Herr Musbach and Herr Zeller distributed small bags of goodies to each person. The bag included an apple, an orange, three pecans, and a piece of hard candy. We ate the candy as we walked back to our house and PaPa said to save the other goodies for another time. On Christmas morning I took the fresh turkey from our smokehouse to Frau Nagel so that she could cook it for dinner. We stayed there all day and ate, and then had a long chess tournament in the afternoon. We were able to laugh and have fun most of the day, and that night as I laid in bed I said many prayers. First of all I thanked God for leading us to Texas, for teaching me to get along on my own, for the bountiful first crops, for my new friends, and for this opportunity in life. I also thanked him for giving me a fine and noble MaMa, and I prayed that she was safe and warm in heaven. Tonight I decided that, in the future when I thought of MaMa, I would no longer think of her cold, white body lying in the hospital bed. In the future I would always picture her under the sheltering wing of an angel, still wearing her white apron.

During the cold of winter there was not much game for me to hunt. I worked with the local militia and spent two nights per week guarding the settlement. Herr Zeller and I had long talks about the future of New Braunfels and he informed me that, in the spring, a new settlement would be established in the Hill Country so that the immigrants could begin claiming their 350 acres.

I sold the bear hide for $18. In order to celebrate, I shot and then roasted a turkey, and served it to PaPa and Dorothea with sweet potatoes and pinto beans. For dessert we had an apple pie which I purchased from Frau Bipert.

PaPa and I put our money together to buy enough smooth cut boards to install a floor in our cabin. I did the work while PaPa was at his regular job. We were very proud of this addition and Dorothea said that she wished MaMa could see it. The wood floor helped to keep the house warmer and drier. I also gathered thick, wet mud from a creek that flowed into the Comal River, and chinked the inside walls of the house, which helped to fill in the many cracks between the posts and the shingles. I smoothed the mud on the inside walls so that the walls looked flat.

PaPa received a letter from his nephew, Frederick, who married, left Pennsylvania, and had homesteaded in Illinois where he had a 100 acre farm with a small house. They would have their first child in the spring.

Fritz was working for a new store in town called Schulenberg's. I stopped in to visit quite often and told Herr Schulenberg about the many items which were for sale in the stores in Galveston. It was decided that Fritz and I would take Herr Schulenberg's horses and wagon to Galveston, buy a load of goods, and transport them back to his store in order to broaden his merchandise. PaPa said that this was a risky business, for what if we were robbed, or attacked by Indians. Because I had just purchased a new rifle, I was sure that Fritz and I would be able to defend ourselves if we needed to. PaPa said that, because he considered me to be a grown man, he no longer must give me permission to do things. I thanked him for his trust, and I promised that I would inform him before I proceeded with any new ideas or trips. Dorothea was in school all day and when she arrived home she stayed at the Nagel's house. Quite often she stayed with the Nagels for several days without coming to our house. This was good, because she had lots of companionship with the Nagel's children. I kept the Nagel family well supplied with meat, eggs and firewood in return for their hospitality.

On Friday morning Fritz and I departed on our journey to Galveston. We took a small tent which we could use in case of rain, and we both had plenty of sausage, biscuits, and a pot for boiling pinto beans. We were blessed with fine weather and spent one night with Herr Voltz, Herr

Zeller's friend. We had no trouble at all, and saw no Indians or robbers. We went to Carlshaven and stayed in the warehouse there, and the next morning went to see my friend Harry Knight. He was glad to see us, and immediately we went duck hunting. My new rifle made it easy to kill a flying duck. We roasted the ducks and had a full meal. Fritz said it was the best duck that he had ever eaten. This was funny since this was the first duck that Fritz had ever eaten. We took a sloop to Galveston, visited all of the stores in town, and looked at all of their catalogues. We ate beef which had been smoked for many hours to make it tender. Then we bought hard candy and sat on the dock to eat. Harry knew many people in town and we found out where we could buy goods at wholesale prices. We went there and ordered many items including shovels, hoes, rakes, several bolts of fabric that we thought the ladies would like, five kegs of pickled herring, five kegs of pickles, man's work pants made from heavy fabric, and four cases of apples. We returned to Carlshaven, and the next day we drove the wagon to Galveston, crossing the boat channel on a ferry. Since Galveston was on an island, this was the only way to get to the city. It was expensive, and we had to wait in a line with 9 wagons ahead of us. After loading all the supplies and covering them with a heavy tarp we again crossed by ferry and set out on our journey back to New Braunfels. We had a safe journey and it rained only one day. Herr Schulenberg was happy with our purchases and he gave each of us $5.00 plus 5 apples.

I met with Herr Zeller regarding accompanying him to the hill country where Herr Musbach would establish a town called Fredericksburg. Herr Zeller and I would depart Monday morning at 5:00 o'clock. I took Dorothea to the home of Frau Broader, a seamstress, who was making Dorothea two new dresses, one for school and one for church. I also took her to a store and purchased a pair of shoes. I told PaPa that I would be gone with Herr Zeller for up to four weeks. PaPa told me to take all of our dirty clothes to Frau Schmidt to be washed and ironed. PaPa came home only to sleep, and seemed to work all the time. I worried that he was sad and had no fun. He took Dorothea to school every morning and went to church on Sundays. Our life had changed since MaMa died. We were no longer as close in our everyday lives. PaPa and I used to work together in the field, but now he leased the field to Herr Nagel. Fritz seldom had time to go hunting with me because he worked from daylight until dark at the store. I was glad that I would be going on another trip, for there was not much for me to do in New Braunfels.

On Monday morning I awoke early as usual and packed my food into a bag with a drawstring, including: 2 links of sausage, 5 raw potatoes, 3 cooked potatoes, 5 biscuits, 2 apples, a tin of salt, a tin containing matches, and my canteen of fresh water. I also put a pair of pants, a shirt, underwear and socks in my blanket and rolled it up. I would not take my coat. If it became cold I would wear two shirts. I also took my new gun with powder and shells, and my hat. I awoke PaPa and quickly told him goodbye. He said to be careful and to always watch for Indians.

It was March 15, 1846 and Herr Zeller, Herr Brandt and I met at the corral where we saddled up our horses and packed camping equipment on a donkey. Herr Zeller said that I could ride the gray horse, which put a smile on my face. It was a beautiful and sunny morning and the roosters were crowing as we rode out of town. We rode to the north and soon the hills began to grow higher and higher. We followed a creek bed through the hills until the brush got very thick and we had to move away from the creek. We saw lots of beautiful birds and even an eagle. We rode in silence with one person slightly ahead of the others, and we were all quite aware of our surroundings. We were on the lookout for Indians and hoped to see them before they saw us. At noon we stopped and I ate a potato with salt. That night we camped in a rock overhang at the foot of a large hill. When riding over and through these hills they felt like mountains, but in comparison to the mountains of Germany, they were merely hills. There were large oak trees, dark green cedar trees in the meadows, and lots of fresh water running between the hills. It was a very beautiful countryside. We saw many deer but did not shoot any since we had plenty of food with us. On the third day we met with the crystal clear Blanco River which we had seen on Herr Zeller's map. We followed the river in a northwesterly direction and soon came to beautiful waterfalls going over very smooth rocks. We ate our dinner there so that we could admire the view. The next day the Blanco River seemed to get smaller and smaller, and by noon it was merely a small creek. Now there were broad meadows with scattered clumps of oak trees. We found the foundation and broken down walls of an adobe hut which probably belonged to a Spaniard at one time. Herr Zeller explained that adobe was made of sun dried mud bricks and it would not withstand abundant rain. Perhaps that was merely a way-station for Spanish explorers who came to Texas in the 1700's, or perhaps it belonged to cattle or sheep herders. That evening we made camp beside some very large cypress trees near the creek. As I brushed the gray horse I noticed bees going into a nearby tree trunk. Herr Zeller instructed me in how to rob my very first bee hive. I put on three shirts, and tied rope around the bottom of my pants to keep the bees from climbing up my legs. I put my handkerchief over my head and put my hat on over it so that the handkerchief hung down over my ears. I buttoned the top button of the shirts and pulled up the collars to help cover my neck. Herr Zeller loaned me his handkerchief to tie around my face so that only my eyes were visible. I took a burning stick from the fire and a bucket and slowly walked toward the hive. When the bees saw me they started swarming, but the smoke from the burning stick seemed to make them fly less. I walked up to the tree trunk, put my hand in the hole, and brought out a scoop of honey comb dripping with honey. Soon the bucket was half full of honey. I slowly walked away from the bee hive, and gradually the thirty or so bees who were sitting on my clothes decided to fly away. As soon as the bees left me, Herr Zeller and Herr Brandt began to laugh loudly. I sat down on the ground and began to lick the honey from my hand. I had a feeling of exhilaration from the excitement of it all and I jumped in the air and turned in circles until I became dizzy and fell to the ground. I then washed my hands and face in the creek. We all sat in the shade and ate as much honey as we could hold. The next morning I put honey on my apple for breakfast. I thought that I should become a honey robber and sell honey for a living. Herr Zeller said that eating too much honey would cause your teeth will fall out.

By the fourth day we were nearing the site of the large land grant purchased by the Aldesverine and Prince Solms Braunfels. We crossed the Perednales River and camped. That night we studied the stars and, with the help of a sextant, we were able to find where we were located on the map. We continued the next day to look for a large mountain with a rounded domed top which was made of granite. This domed rock, with no trees growing on it, would verify that we had found the land grant. We continued in a northwesterly direction all morning and saw no mountain as described. However, that afternoon Herr Zeller, who was riding out front, began to point ahead. As soon as we came out from under a large oak tree, there it was, looming before us. An isolated huge rock, as big as a mountain. We came close to the monument and ascertained that it was made out of pure granite with no dirt and no trees. It was just a very large rock protruding from the ground which covered over 30 acres at its base. The map called it the Rock of Enchantment. We spent the entire afternoon climbing to the top of the rock to view the fantastic land which was part of the grant. We then walked around the bottom of the Rock of Enchantment which took the rest of the day. As usual, that night we looked for a hidden place to make our camp. I could hardly go to sleep because of the excitement of finding the domed rock in this truly enchanted land. Some day my father and I would own 350 acres of this beautiful land and there I would build my own home of rock.

Herr Zeller said that the town should be located near the Perednales River, so the next day we reluctantly departed and made our way back there. We observed that the river had steep banks and there was evidence of driftwood indicating that the river had recently been much deeper than it was now. If the town was built beside the river there would be danger of flooding. We eventually found a nice small creek draining into the Perednales River, which came from a spring about three miles from the river. The three of us decided that this would be the perfect place for a town, on this broad meadow which covered over 100 acres beside this creek. That night I dreamed that I was sleeping right in the middle of the main street of the town of Fredericksburg and that oxen carts and horses had to carefully walk around me.

We studied our map and tried to find the shortest route back to New Braunfels. This route would be used by the larger party coming next week. We saw no other persons on this entire trip and there seemed to be no Indians in the area. We arrived back in New Braunfels after 9 days.

Dorothea was delighted with her new dresses, and we spent some time together visiting with Fritz at the store. We walked home with PaPa and ate sweet potatoes and sausage for supper, along with delicious bread we had bought at the new bakery. About midnight I was awakened by the bell at the Fort which was ringing very loudly and not stopping. I put on my clothes and boots as quickly as possible and ran to the Fort along with almost every man in town. Right away we saw smoke and realized that the new bakery was on fire. The bakery was new, but it was located in an old building which had been poorly and quickly constructed. I immediately followed my training and ran to the stock pens where we loaded empty barrels on a wagon while others hitched the horses. We grabbed all the buckets we could find and ran to the river where we formed a line and loaded water from the river into the barrels. Then the horses raced with the wagon and we ran along beside the wagon to the burning bakery. The first crew of fireman had already used all of their water and were waiting for us to arrive. We immediately began to form a line and remove the water from the barrels to the buckets to the flames. The flames were very high now and it seemed impossible to save the bakery. A nearby tree caught fire up in its limbs and we immediately began to chop down the tree as fast as we could. We poured many buckets of water on the downed tree and then used all of our energy keeping the fire from spreading to other buildings. We were able to contain the fire to the one building and tree and, after working for over 3 hours, we were all exhausted. We were covered with mud and soot. We removed our boots and all walked into the Comal River with our clothes on to wash ourselves and our clothes all at the same time. I supposed it would be a while before I was able to buy good, fresh made bread again. We were thankful that no one was injured, but we also realized that it was almost impossible to put out the fire. We decided that, the next time, our main objective will be to keep the fire from spreading to other buildings.

The next day I attended a meeting with Herr Zeller, and Herr Brandt where we reported to Herr Musbach about our trip and showed him where we went on the map. We described the town site which we had chosen and it met with his approval. We would spend the rest of the week organizing the first party of settlers to go to Fredericksburg and establish the town. Herr Zeller, Herr Brandt, and myself would act as guides and provide meat. Herr Musbach would be the leader of the group, and Herr Zink would be the surveyor. 20 wagons pulled by oxen, and 85 volunteer settlers, would be guarded by 10 mounted, armed horsemen. Herr Musbach handed us each a list of items to be taken from the storehouse and loaded into the wagons. This was back breaking work, loading heavy stoves, plows, tents, and barrels of flour, lard, sausages, kraut, and other items. By Sunday I was ready to take a day off and attend church with PaPa, Dorothea and the Nagel family. After church we had fried chicken, green beans, kraut, fresh bread, and apple pie at the Nagel's house. In the afternoon we enjoyed a new game, learned from the Americans, which was pitching horseshoes towards a small stick in the ground. Whoever got the horseshoe to stay on the stick was the winner. I came close a few times, but Herr Nagel was the champion. PaPa laughed and told funny stories. That evening we sat on the stumps in the yard and enjoyed a long talk while PaPa smoked his pipe. PaPa told me that he was very proud of my actions and that Herr Zeller spoke very highly of my abilities. PaPa told me to claim our 350 acres near Fredericksburg and to build a small house on it as soon as possible. He had no intention of moving there, but he wanted me to have it. PaPa said to continue my good work and to always remain honest and truthful.

On April 23, 1846 the wagon train departed New Braunfels for settlement of the new town of Fredericksburg. (This began another new chapter in my life, for I was never a full time resident of New Braunfels after that, even though I returned from time to time to visit.)

Making the trip through the hills was much more difficult with the wagons and so many people. It was the duty of the 3 guides to ride ahead each day, and to scout out the best route for the wagons to follow. We moved logs and large rocks, cut brush, and looked for water. We kept an eye out for Indians and tried to kill at least two or three deer each day. At noon the settlers stopped and usually ate leftovers from the night before. I tried to meet them with the deer, or other animals, which they could then prepare for supper that night. I did not have to cook, or watch the animals, or pick cactus stickers out of feet, or build fires, or haul buckets of water. I was now a guide and my duties had changed. After supper I went to bed and did not have guard duty. I was up by 5:00 o'clock each morning to find something to eat for breakfast, and then to start another day. When we reached the Blanco River I found my favorite bee hive and, with Herr Zeller's help, I was able to rob three buckets of honey which was gratefully received by the settlers. These settlers were mostly experienced in the ways of the wild and had been in New Braunfels for some time. They were easy to work with, and no one questioned the authority of Herr Musbach. We were thankful that he was a man of great intelligence and vigor, and we all trusted him to make the right decisions.

We introduced the settlers to the beautiful water falls on the Blanco River, and camped there even though it was early in the afternoon when we arrived. Most everyone got in the water, in their clothes, and took a bath. The children ran and played on the slippery rocks near the falls. I was able to catch five large catfish with my fishing hook, which I had gotten in Galveston and always carried in my saddlebags. We cut up the fish and fried them in lard. It was a great feast, and then we all danced around the fire. This was truly a land of opportunity which would produce great wealth.

The next day we arrived at the proposed town site, near the Perednales River, where we all kneeled to pray for God's protection and assistance. Herr Zink quickly made some calculations to determine the approximate location of the center of the town, and that was where we made a large encampment of tents, kitchens and animal pens. We spent the next week helping Herr Zink survey the town lots and streets. Every morning and evening I went hunting and very easily found deer to shoot for meat. In one week the main streets, as well as 40 town lots, had been measured. A meeting was called and each man drew a number from a hat for his town lot. PaPa had given a letter to Herr Musbach authorizing me to draw a number for him. I drew number 17 which was located on Pecan Street near Main Street. The town lot was only one acre, just enough room for a house and pens. Tomorrow we would begin the hard task of cutting logs to build houses and a fort.

I worked as a hunter and guard for the men who were cutting logs. Four guards surrounded the men at all times with rifles in hand. The workers also had loaded rifles leaning against the wagons nearby. We had not yet seen Indians, but we had seen horse tracks and we knew that they may come at any time. The logs were hauled to town and dropped off at each lot. A crew will began to work on a fort in the center of town, where the townspeople could take shelter in case of Indian attack. The building projects continued without many serious problems because all of these men were experienced, having built houses and buildings in New Braunfels. The women cooked in the large kitchen tent and the food was good and abundant. I was too busy with guarding and hunting duties to build my own house, but I was in no hurry. I wanted to get the 350 acre farm and there build my first house. In the meantime I would live in a tent which I had put on my lot.

We had been in Fredericksburg for 40 days and still had not seen an Indian. It began to rain and continued all day so that we were unable to work. I spent the time reading the two new books that I borrowed from Herr Weir. They were both written in English and told about the history of the United States. I later ran to the cook tent to eat a hearty meal of kraut and sausage with bread and milk. This was a luxury which would soon disappear, for when the people moved into their new houses the cook tent would be torn down and each family would be responsible for their own meals. The rain continued all afternoon and all night. The next morning I decided to walk around town in the rain to see how things were going. Herr Zeller was working on his house and had mud all over his clothes. Herr Zink saw me and asked me to accompany him on a walk to inspect the creek and the nearby Perednales River. I got my gun and covered it with a blanket, and covered myself and the ammunition with another blanket. We walked to the nearby creek which had risen at least five feet since yesterday. Before we got to the Perednales we could hear the water roaring. It was a site to behold with logs and brush rushing past at a very rapid rate, and the water probably ten feet higher than yesterday. Herr Zink said that he would watch the creek carefully and not measure any town lots too close to it. We went back to town and I continued my reading. It continued to rain the entire day and all night for the second night. The flood came into my tent and I had to abandon it in the middle of the night. I went to the large kitchen tent where I laid on a table. Very soon there were many other people there who were also flooded out. We made a fire and cooked coffee. By the next morning the rain had let up and we could look around to see lots of mud and destruction along the creek. The Perednales was about 50 feet deep and was over 100 feet wide. We cut wet grass and put it on the muddy floor of the kitchen tent. Some of the new houses were damaged by water soaking into the trenches which held up the walls. No one yet had a wooden floor in their house, and water came in most of the houses through the cracks between the logs. Herr Zeller and I went to count the horses and cattle and realized that one of the pens holding cattle had become so soggy that the cattle were standing knee deep in mud. We immediately began to build a new cattle pen on higher ground. We could not dig holes, so we tied long poles between tree trunks and ended up with a long, strangely shaped, cattle pen. At least we were able to move the cattle out of the thick mud, for if they stayed in the mud for too long it could ruin their feet. I donated my house logs to anyone who needed them for repairs. Almost every family began to construct a loft in which they could put their household goods in case their houses were flooded again.

Herr Musbach called Herr Zeller, Herr Brandt and I to a meeting where he expressed his concern about the flooding. We all noticed that the rain had come from the South, and this meant that it probably had flooded in New Braunfels as well. Herr Musbach asked us to travel to New Braunfels to let them know that the people of Fredericksburg survived the flood, to offer assistance if New Braunfels was flooded, and then to bring two wagons of supplies back to Fredericksburg upon our return.

We set out early the next morning anticipating a difficult journey because of swollen creeks and rivers. We could not cross the Perednales near Fredericksburg so we rode upstream, to the West, where we were able to cross it that afternoon. This was about two hours in the wrong direction. We hoped that by the time we reached the Blanco River the flood would have diminished, and we also hoped that it did not begin to rain again. We came upon many smaller creeks and gullies which were hazardous to cross along the way. On the third day we reached the Blanco River which was almost back down to its regular level. We could see that it had been very high the day before. When we crossed the Blanco River I got my boots full of water. They were already wet, but now I was afraid that they would be ruined. It was also very uncomfortable to wear wet boots, but I had no choice.

That night we arrived in New Braunfels and it felt very good to sleep in my warm, dry and soft bed, with my boots next to the fireplace to dry. PaPa said that, even though the Guadalupe River came up very high, there was little serious damage from the storm. The streets of New Braunfels were so muddy that they were nearly impassable and school was canceled.

The fields were too muddy to work. PaPa heard that the towns on the cost were severely flooded by the storm which came from the ocean and I was worried about my friend Harry Knight.

The next day I told Herr Zeller about my worries and he was thinking the same way. He was worried about our warehouse in Carlshaven. Because we needed stoves and other equipment, which could be purchased wholesale in Galveston, we would depart with two wagons and go to Galveston. Once again I told Dorothea and PaPa farewell and set out on the muddy roads. Several times we left the roadway and drove across the grasslands which were less muddy. However we had to watch for large rocks which seemed to pop up out of the ground in unexpected places. We spent the night with Herr Voltz and ate good Chile, coarsely ground beef cooked very slowly with chile peppers. It was good, but my mouth was cooled only by drinking three glasses of milk. My stomach ached that night, but by morning I felt better. We continued to Victoria where we bought hard candy, and on the fifth day we arrived in Carlshaven. It was nearly dark when we arrived at the warehouse where we were delighted to find Harry Knight encamped. Harry's shack was completely washed away by the flood and he actually had to climb on the roof of the warehouse to get away from the flood waters. He stayed on the roof all night and he said that next morning he could not come down because of deep water. He saw many rattlesnakes trying to swim out of the flood. He finally came down from the roof the second day and looked for his house and his few belongings which had all disappeared. He helped to pull a dead body from under an overturned wagon and helped people to get to the sloop to sail to Galveston. We gave him a fine meal of sausage, potatoes and old bread. The next day the three of us drove the wagon to the ferry and went into Galveston. The streets were still muddy but the town was not severely damaged. We bought 15 small wood stoves, rakes, hoes and plows. The horses could hardly pull the wagon it was so heavy. With Herr Zeller's permission I asked Harry to accompany us to Fredericksburg because we would need help with the surveys. Harry readily agreed, for he had no reason to stay in

Carlshaven. I wrote a note for Harry's uncle which we put in a tobacco tin and placed on a tree next to where their shack used to sit. If Harry's uncle came home from sailing hopefully he would find the note saying that Harry was in Fredericksburg.

It was a slow trip back to New Braunfels and we had to take turns walking and guarding at night. Harry was very impressed with New Braunfels and he was even more impressed by our cozy home with its soft beds. We visited and ate breakfast with the Nagel family before taking off for Fredericksburg. I tied the gray horse to the wagon that Harry and I took turns driving and guarding. Herr Zeller rode ahead acting as scout. We arrived at Fredericksburg within four days to find the place looking more like a town. There were several buildings and a fort on Main Street, and most families had completed their houses and were now trying to plow nearby fields for spring planting. Harry and I worked with Herr Zink to survey the farm lands for the settlers. This required camping out every night with our horses, and a wagon filled with supplies and equipment. We had small tents in which to sleep which was good, for the dew was heavy and the ground was still damp. We took turns guarding our camp at night because we were sure that Indians had been watching us from a distance. One day I actually saw three Indians riding up the side of a distant hill. I was sure that, if I saw them, that they also saw me. Each family was to get 350 acres. Each day we scouted to find the lay of the land as well as available water. Herr Zink considered carefully each property line so that the settlers would have access to a creek or river on their property. Also the hills and valleys had to be taken into consideration. 350 acres, all on the sides of a rocky hill, would be impossible to farm. We included some farm land as well as hills, valleys and creeks in each 350 acre survey. At night we studied the stars and used the sextant to plot our location. Herr Zink was drawing a detailed map showing approximate elevations as we did the survey. This was quite time consuming and could become very boring except for the threat of Indians.

One night we put out our fire and Herr Zink and Harry both went to bed. I was on guard duty and stood and walked between the tents and the horses with my loaded rifle. About midnight the horses all raised their heads and stood at attention. The next second there was a loud scream to my right. I shouted, "Help!" and dove to the ground while pointing my rifle in the direction of the scream. I was sure that Indians were going to jump from the nearby rocks. There was another scream and the horses began to jump and try to break away from their ropes. My eyes kept searching the rocks and then I saw a large tan object crouched close to the ground. I had a sick feeling about pulling the trigger to shoot a person. But I did pull the trigger and, as soon as the smoke cleared, I saw the object laying in the same position and very still. By this time Herr Zink and Harry were beside me with their rifles to their shoulders looking for something to shoot. But now all was quiet even though the horses were still moving about and stomping their feet. I quickly pulled my loaded pistol from my belt and began to creep slowly toward the object. When I got near it I realized that it was dead and it was a very large wild cat with very big paws. The wild cat, or panther, had been stalking our horses and was in position to pounce on the gray horse. I immediately reloaded and we sat quietly for about an hour just in case someone had heard the gun shot and was coming to our camp. All was still so I lit two candles and began to carefully skin the lion. I wrapped the hide in salt and then in a blanket to keep it clean. I could not sleep the rest of the night, so I volunteered to guard all night. I looked at the stars, at the gray horse, at the dead lion and at Harry, and thought about my life here in Texas and what a great adventure it has become. I was also thankful to God that I had not killed an Indian, for I believed it is a sin to commit murder unless it was in self defense.

Very gradually we had been able to survey the 17 first farms which would be owned by the people in Fredericksburg. The drawing was held after church services and I drew #8. I quickly looked at the map and remembered this piece of property. It had a spring bubbling up out of the ground which then flowed into a small creek. I took my rifle and an ax and immediately rode out to this property which was about eight miles from town. It was heavily treed near the creek, and had several large, flat areas which would make into fields. There was a high hill behind the spring. I tied my horse and took my canteen and rifle with me as I climbed to the top of the hill. I stood there looking over this magnificent land and then I kneeled down and thanked God for this good fortune. I asked God to guide me in my future. I wished that PaPa was there with me to see the place, but he seemed content to remain in New Braunfels. I went down the hill and chopped down three trees which I would eventually use for my small house. I decided to build a small room where I could stay until I got my larger house built. The small room would later be used for a smokehouse. I would build it out of sturdy logs so that I could lock the doors at night and feel safe inside, for this was a very isolated place and it would be a while before I had any neighbors.

The next weeks were spent in working for Herr Zink and chopping more logs in my spare time. Harry and I were still living in a tent on my town lot. It was fine for now because the weather is mild, but we would have to have better quarters before winter.

Harry and I accompanied Herr Zeller to New Braunfels to pick up more supplies and visit. We had supper with the Nagel family and I described Fredericksburg and the surrounding countryside. Herr Nagel was also entitled to 350 acres near Fredericksburg, but he was not yet prepared to move his family there, for his children were content living in New Braunfels and attending school with their friends. Fritz was still working at the store and wished to open his own store soon. I told him that stores were greatly needed in Fredericksburg, and he should open a store there. We all began to get excited about this prospect and began to figure how much money would be required to begin this endeavor. Fritz would need a wagon and horses and enough building material to build the store. He would then have to have goods to put in the store as soon as it opened. We wrote a list of items on paper and decided that he needed at least $200 to start. Fritz has $90, Herr Nagel could loan $50, PaPa could loan $30. I quickly took all my animal skins to the dealer and was able to raise $50 more. Harry and I borrowed Herr Nagel's wagon and horses and went to a saw mill on the Guadalupe River to buy long, smooth boards to be used for the floor of the new store. We also bought shingles for the roof. The next day Fritz quit his job at Schulenberg's Store and we packed up and departed for Fredericksburg. This was truly an exciting adventure, but it was also very scary, for we did not know for sure that Fritz would make money. As soon as we got to Fredericksburg, we set up another tent for Fritz, and then began to cut logs and build on the town lot on Main Street which Fritz purchased for $25.00.

The building would be 30' x 30' with a lean-too on the back to be used for living quarters. We chopped logs for four days and then began to build the walls. Within 25 days we had the walls and roof completed. While Fritz continued to work on installing the floor, Harry and I took the wagon and went all the way to Galveston to pick up supplies. We drove very far each day to try to get the goods as quickly as possible. After the long and difficult trip, Harry and I spent the night at the Carlshaven warehouse. The note I had written to his brother was still in the tin box on the tree. It was still readable so we left it there. We loaded the wagon with a variety of goods, but tried not to make it so heavy as to slow us down. It was important to have some goods in the store as soon as possible. We went back to Fredericksburg as quickly as possible and found Fritz waiting on the front porch of the store. When I told Herr Zeller about this venture he asked why we used only one wagon. My reply was that was all we could afford. Herr Zeller then proposed to loan me $100 to buy another wagon and horses. At first I had difficulty in accepting this offer, but I realized that we must get more goods to Nagel's Store as quickly as possible. I decided to take the loan from Herr Zeller.

Harry and I set out on another journey to Galveston. This time we stopped in Victoria where I was able to purchase my wagon, 2 horses and harness for $100. We filled both wagons with goods and continued back to Fredericksburg as quickly as possible. When we arrived in Fredericksburg, Fritz was again sitting on the front porch of the store waiting for us. The store was completely empty, for he had sold every item which we had brought on the first load. Harry and I spent the entire summer going back and forth to Galveston and bringing goods to the store. By the end of the summer Fritz had paid all of his debts and was making a profit. Harry, Fritz and I lived in the lean-too on the back of the store and Fritz paid Harry and I for each wagon load of goods.

Our next venture was to bring large loads of sawed lumber to Fredericksburg to sell to settlers who wanted to build a floor in their cabins. I was able to repay Herr Zeller the $100, and I gave him $10 extra because I was so grateful for the loan. Herr Zeller laughed and immediately ordered lumber for his floor. I eventually bought 2 more wagons and 4 more horses, and Harry and I established the Star Shipping Company. We made monthly trips to Galveston and brought goods to various stores along the way back to Fredericksburg. Harry was able to gain many regular customers because of his friendly manner. He seemed to be accepted in Fredericksburg even though he was not a German.

August 21, 1846 finally came and I was to celebrate my 16th Birthday that evening in Fredericksburg with Herr Zeller, Fritz and Harry. Fritz had ordered a cake from Mrs. Hitzfelder for us to eat. I accompanied Herr Zeller, Herr Zink, and six other men on yet another surveying expedition. It was a very hot day and we had to clear brush for Herr Zink. We had axes in our hands to clear the brush, and we had our rifles leaning against the wagon. We were all thirsty and so we sent a boy to the creek to fill the bucket with cool water. A short time later we heard a scream, and saw the boy running from the trees followed closely by an Indian on horseback. The boy ran to the right and the Indian kept coming directly towards us as we stood in bewilderment. The Indian, who was followed by several others on horseback, ran towards Herr Zeller and I, and when he came upon us he hit Herr Zeller with a large stick that had a rock tied on the end of it. Herr Zeller fell to the ground and I jumped back away from the horse.

The Indian turned and came towards me. I raised my ax just as he approached and the ax slashed his arm. He fell from the horse with a heavy thud. I picked up the ax and hit the Indian in the head. He fell to the ground with blood pouring from his black hair. There was shooting and shouting all around me. I turned around and saw another Indian coming at me on foot. I used the ax once again and he fell before me. In just a moment the battle was over and three Indians were running their horses through the creek and fleeing to the west. There was shouting and screaming and immediately I looked for Herr Zeller. I found him lying in the green grass with blood running down his face from a large cut on his forehead. The men were grabbing the rifles and shot an Indian that was wrestling with Herr Bruner. Two men stood guard while the rest of us looked to see who was alive and who was dead. I held Herr Zeller in my arms screaming for help. Herr Zink brought a wet rag and tried to clean some of the blood from Herr Zeller's face. Herr Zeller was restless and tried to get up. We told him to lie still until the bleeding stopped. He grabbed my shirt and then told Herr Zink, "Give all I have to Nicholas". Then Herr Zeller's head fell back and he was dead. I continued to hold him and screamed for a while until Herr Zink pulled me to my feet. He led me to the creek and told me to put cold water on my face, for I was covered with blood and Herr Zink thought that I was also injured. After inspecting me, Herr Zink realized that I had been covered with the blood of others, the blood of Herr Zeller and the two Indians I killed. I staggered back to Herr Zeller's body and fell to my knees crying and finally fell to the grass. After a while I was able to control myself and I sat up and looked around. Herr Burger was hurt and was being loaded into the wagon. Herr Schwarz was sitting under a tree with blood all over his shirt. There were five dead Indians lying on the ground, as well as the body of Herr Zeller. I looked at the faces of the two Indians that I had killed, and I said a prayer over each one. I asked God to forgive me for taking these lives and I told God that I killed them only in self defense. I then picked up the stick with the rock tied on the end which had the blood of Herr Zeller on it. I put it into my saddle bag and I would have it forever to remind me of this terrible Birthday in which I lost my friend and killed two Indians. Herr Zink and I picked up Herr Zeller's body and carefully placed him in the wagon with the two injured men. We then started back for Fredericksburg and left the dead Indians lying where they fell. Herr Zink said that their comrades would return later to bury them in their own tradition.

It was a very sad trip back to Fredericksburg, and as we drove the wagon down Main Street the people began to realize that something had gone wrong. When people looked into the wagon they were astounded by the site of the two bleeding men and the dead body of Herr Zeller, one of the most respected men in the community. Soon, Fritz was at my side helping me down from the gray horse and steadying me as I staggered to the porch of the store. I tried to tell Fritz what had happened, but instead I put my face into my hands and cried. Herr Zink came to me with a bottle of whiskey and said that I should take three big swallows. I did as he said and then I fell back on the porch and slept. I woke up at about sundown. I went to the nearby hill where we had earlier erected a large cross which could be seen for many miles. I sat at the foot of the cross and begged God to forgive me for my sins and to keep Herr Zeller in his tender care. At the foot of the hill I pulled off my blood soaked shirt and burned it. After that I was able to control myself and I even gave a short speech at Herr Zeller's funeral the next day. Herr Zeller was the first person to be buried in the Fredericksburg Cemetery. I will never know why such a man as Herr Zeller was killed and I, a mere boy of 16 years of age, was spared. I believe that it was purely by accident that Herr Zeller happened to be in the path of the murdering Indian, and God did not want this bad thing to happen. After this terrible tragedy, I retreated to my farm for a week where I spent all my time building the small house. It was peaceful and quiet, and there was no sign of Indians anywhere. Sometimes I thought that the Indian attack was only a dream, but at night when I was lying in the small hut trying to sleep, I could see the Indian coming at me as clear as a painted picture. His black hair was flowing in the wind, his horse was brown with a white face, and he had a single feather tied to the end of his hair. Later I had noticed that the feather was covered with blood. The bloody feather stayed with me in my dreams for many years after the incident.

Soon it was time to make another trip to the Gulf Coast and Harry and I stopped off in New Braunfels to visit. I brought a turkey which we roasted. We had great fun with Dorothea, PaPa and the Nagel family. As we were going to bed that night PaPa told me that he had heard about the terrible Indian attack and that he was sorry that I had been involved. He said that he hoped that he had done the right thing by bringing his family to Texas. I assured him that, event though it was a terrible incident, I could never be sorry for coming to Texas. I described our beautiful farm in the Texas hills and I told him about the clear spring which bubbles up out of the ground in back of the small hut that I built.

When Harry and I returned to Fredericksburg, Fritz told me that Herr Zink was looking for me. I went to his office and he escorted me next door to the office of Herr Musbach. Herr Zink recalled that when Herr Zeller was about to die, he said to give all of his belongings to me. Since Herr Zeller was never married and had no heirs, it was therefore decided by Herr Musbach that all of Herr Zeller's belongings and property would be given to me. This included his house in Fredericksburg, as well as his 350 acre farm nearby. He had $100 in cash under his mattress and his estate also included the gray horse, a fine rifle and pistol. Herr Musbach said that I should feel proud to inherit these possessions just as if Herr Zeller were my own father leaving me his inheritance. I shock their hands and then I hurried to tell Fritz and Harry. That very night I slept in Herr Zeller's bed, and I felt as though he was still protecting me. Soon after this, I looked into a mirror, and to my surprise, I looked much older and I even needed to shave my face for the first time. I realized that much had already happened to me, but that my adult life had just begun.

Chapter 5

A Time for Adjustment

Now that I was officially of age to join the local militia I proudly wear the gray coated uniform and I took my turn watching over the community of Fredericksburg. The people could work faster if they felt protected from Indian attack. On Main Street was the Verinskirche building which served as a school, a church, meeting room and fortress. If a cannon shot was fired the people knew to get to the Verinskirche as quickly as possible because of some emergency. We had several practice drills in which everyone dropped whatever they were doing and ran to the Verinskirche. Once we had a practice drill in the middle of the night and Fritz slept right through it. There was a roll call inside the Verinskirche in which every family was accounted for except Fritz. We ran to the store and found Fritz soundly asleep. I shook him and told him to get up at once. It reminded me of the many times when I had to pull on the string which was tied to his big toe in order to awaken him to go hunting.

The area was becoming more dangerous as settlers began to move to their 350 acre farms. The farmers were isolated from the town and had to provide their own protection. Herr Rosenklein had 8 horses stolen from the pen near his house and he did not hear any noise, or see anyone lurking about his farm. Baron von Musbach asked me to accompany Herr Brandt and several other militia members to investigate. We found many horse tracks but no boot tracks. We made a wide circle around the barn and found a place where four or five horses had been held in a small area. This was probably where the Indian's horses were held while they sneaked into the pen and drove Herr Rosenklein's horses away. We eventually found tracks where the Indians had departed the farm. We followed the tracks for four or five miles where we found a dead mare whose stomach had been cut open and nearby was the carcass of her foal. Why would the Indians perform such a vile act against a poor animal? Perhaps they had intended to eat the tender foal meat and something interrupted their plans. Or, perhaps this deed was meant to scare anyone who might follow their trail. We continued for another day when we discovered that the group had joined a large band of Indians and had gone in a northerly direction. We knew that, even if we found the Indians, we had not enough men or rifles to fight with them. We reluctantly returned to Fredericksburg and gave Herr Rosenklein our regrets.

The hills were beginning to turn golden and red as Fall approached. Harry and I had made several trips to Galveston and had begun to make some money. I hoped to eventually have enough money saved to buy cattle to graze on my farms. Herr Zeller's farm, which I inherited, was about 9 miles east of Fredericksburg. It had much pasture land which would be good for raising cattle or sheep.

I arrived in New Braunfels for a visit with PaPa and Dorothea. When PaPa came home from work he was happy to see me, but I could tell that all was not right. He handed me a letter to read. It was from Tante Gretchen in Germany informing PaPa about the death of Opa 2 months ago. I immediately reached for my pocket to make sure that my pocket knife, which Opa had given to me, was safe. I pulled it from my pocket and sat on a stump in the front yard and looked at it. I remembered the last time we had seen Oma and Opa before we left Germany, and the first time I had used the knife to skin a rabbit. Gretchen said that Opa was very proud of PaPa for going to Texas and that things were only getting worse in Germany. Oma was very elderly but still alert. PaPa and I called Dorothea from the Nagel's house across the street and we had a reunion. We ate ham, biscuits and green beans, and then PaPa bought an Appfelkuchen at the bakery and we ate it that night and finished it all the next morning for breakfast. I took Dorothea shopping and I bought a ready made dress and a pair of shoes for her to wear to the dance which would be held on Saturday night. I actually got a haircut and polished my boots. When Saturday night came I escorted Dorothea to the dance. PaPa surprised us by coming to the dance after his work was done. PaPa and I drank beer and Dorothea stood in a corner with her friends. PaPa seemed to know almost everyone at the dance, but I only knew a few people. I felt like an outsider in my own home town. I guess that my home town was now Fredericksburg where I know everyone. PaPa introduced me to many people including Matilda Heske, a stout woman with rosy cheeks who laughed easily. After the dance, as we were walking home, PaPa asked Dorothea and I how we would feel if he got married again. Both Dorothea and I were very surprised and there was a long silence. Then I cleared my throat and told PaPa that I thought it would be good for him because he seemed so lonely. Dorothea said that it would be all right with her but that she intended to continue living with the Nagel family. PaPa said that, with our permission, he planed to begin to court Matilda Heske. Her husband died on the ship as they sailed from Germany and she arrived in New Braunfels all alone with no children. She worked at one of the bakeries. I was happy but also sad inside, and the next day I visited MaMa's grave and prayed. I asked God to lead me into the next phase of my life, for I did not know what I should be doing. Should I become a full time farmer, or continue the Star Shipping Company, should I continue to help with the surveying, or should I be just a member of the militia? Maybe God wanted me to continue to do all of these things, and eventually one of them would become the most important for me. The next day I walked along the Comal River and picked up pecans which were falling from the trees. I remembered when Dorothea and I used to pick pecans to feed our pig and smiled to myself. Using a rock I cracked open a pecan and began to eat the delicious meat inside. Suddenly one of my jaw teeth began to hurt. I chewed on the other side and thought no more about it. But that evening I was eating fried potatoes and once again my tooth began to hurt. By the next day I was in terrible pain and could hardly get out of bed. I told PaPa about it and he suggested soaking it in rags dipped in the cold Comal River. I put the cold rag to my cheek and also put cold water in my mouth but nothing helped. After three days of pain and hardly any sleep I was getting desperate for relief. I asked several people about what could be done and no one had any good advise. The fur buyer came to town and when I could hardly open my mouth to talk to him, I explained that I had the toothache. He suggested that I go to San Antonio where there is a barber who can pull the tooth out. I shuddered at the thought of this, but by the next day I was willing to do anything. By this time Harry was back from a hauling trip to the coast and he was willing to take me to San Antonio. After about 5 miles of riding in the bumpy wagon I was in great pain and had to stop for a while. We stopped at the house of a friend who said the only cure that he knew of was to drink some whiskey. I drank three large gulps of the terrible tasting brew which burned my throat as it went down. In about an hour I was somewhat better and I laid in the back of the wagon while Harry continued the trip to San Antonio. When we arrived it was nearly dark and we camped behind a general store there. I continued to lay in the wagon all night writhing in pain. The next morning Harry departed the camp site and scouted for the famous barber who pulls teeth. By noon he was back at the camp to walk me to the nearby barber. When we walked into the barbershop everyone turned and stared at me. Some of them began to talk quietly about me. "Who is that?" "He must be from the country". "Just another German boy." One man laughed aloud and asked me if I was drunk or sick. Harry asked the barber to please help me as soon as possible. I sat down and grabbed hold of the arms of the barber chair as the dirty barber brought a pair of silver pliers from the drawer. I opened my mouth and he began to tap on each tooth until I moaned. He then knew which tooth to pull. He clasped the pliers onto my tooth and began to pull. I held on to the arms of the chair and, as everyone laughed and watched, he eventually pulled the tooth and blood filled my mouth. I spit into a pan which held my large, ugly tooth with very long roots still attached. I sat in the chair as Harry paid the man $5.00. Harry then helped me back to the camp site and I laid in the wagon all afternoon.

By the next morning I felt like a new man. I was no longer in severe pain and Harry and I walked into San Antonio. It was dusty and dirty, but as I began to look around I saw beautiful old buildings including a large cathedral where I walked inside and kneeled to pray. Harry and I then went to the hay market where we ate chile at a table out in the open air. There was a man with a real live monkey that was tied with a rope around its neck. The monkey wore pants and a shirt and had a hat on its head. If you held out money the monkey would come to you and take it from your hand. We also visited the old Alamo church where Texas patriots died in 1836 for Texas freedom. We looked inside the old building which was now used for storage by the army. That night we saw guitarists playing while beautiful dark haired girls danced to the music. They were wearing brightly colored skirts which they twirled. Harry stayed there the rest of the evening. I spoke to a gentleman wearing a large sombrero who was dressed in a suit and wore silver spurs. I saw two rough looking men begin to fight and, to my astonishment, no one became excited. The other men began to take money from their pockets and bet as to who would win. I did not linger to see, for I thought this manner of behavior was very rude. I walked along the San Antonio River and stood on a bridge called Commerce Street.

The next morning we went back to New Braunfels, loaded our goods, and set off for Fredericksburg. Returning to Fredericksburg felt good—this was home to me. I had named my house in town "Zeller Haus", and the farm to the east "Zeller Farm". My first farm was named "Silverbrook". This was a word I gleaned from reading English newspapers from Galveston. The small stream on my farm shone like silver in the moonlight. This is why I chose the name "Silverbrook".

As more people occupied their farms, Indian raids became more of a problem. A terrible event occurred upon my return to Fredericksburg. Two boys from the Oelke family, Wilhelm and Louis, went to the nearby pasture on their farm about 8 miles from town, to bring in the two milk cows. They were running and playing and suddenly were surrounded by a band of Indians on horseback. They plucked up the younger boy, Louis, who was only 9 years old. Wilhelm, who was 12 years old, began to run and scream. Just as his mother ran to the front door and looked out she saw an Indian pick up Wilhelm and then ride away. Herr Oelke immediately rode his horse bareback at a fast gallop to town. The cannon at the Verinskirche was shot as an emergency signal. I ran there quickly to become a member of the militia sent out to look for the boys. We immediately headed to the Oelke farm and searched for tracks. They were not hard to find since there were at least six horses involved in the raid. We found one of the milk cows with an arrow in her neck. She was bleeding a great deal and died after we left. We followed the trail and found where the six Indians joined another group. It then became dark and, because there was no moon, we could no longer follow the trail. We made camp and kept 3 guards on watch all night. Herr Oelke was very upset and kept pacing back and forth all night and from time to time he would break down and cry and moan. It was very difficult for anyone to sleep and when I took my turn at sleeping I wrapped a shirt around my ears to keep down the noise. We awoke just before dawn and had coffee with hard sausage. We departed as soon as there was enough light to see the ground. The trail led in a northwesterly direction and we went through many steep canyons. As we approached each canyon a 4 member scouting party was sent ahead to determine if there was an Indian trap waiting for us. Since I was now known as an "Indian fighter" because I had to kill two Indians, I was usually a member of the scouting party. The four of us rode slowly into the canyon with rifle in one hand and pistol in the other (along with the reins). The first man looked straight ahead, the next man looked to the left, the third man looked to the right and the last man tried to look back behind us. We were all ready in an instant to drop from our horses and head for the nearest rock. We had bullets, powder and a canteen of water hanging from our necks and belts. When we got to the end of the canyon the first man remained alone, the second and third man took up positions inside the canyon. The fourth man led the group into the canyon and caught up with the other three guards. When I was a guard, left in the canyon all alone, I was listening very carefully and holding my horse very still, usually behind a bush or a tree. Soon I began to hear horses approaching and I prayed that they were Germans and not Indians. They arrived and I silently waved to them as I joined the group near the back to guard their flank. As expected, even though we tried to hurry, this process was time consuming and we knew that the Indians were probably getting even further ahead of us as a result. We rested for a short time at noon as the horses drank water and ate grass. The gray horse was still very handsome and when I looked at him eating the grass it reminded me of my early days in caring for him on the trip from the boat to New Braunfels. I also fondly remember the day that we arrived in New Braunfels and Herr Zeller let me ride the gray. I can still see the look of surprise and happiness on my parent's faces. Soon we remounted and rode all afternoon until it was again too dark to travel. I had to stand watch from 8:00 until 11:00 o'clock and I kept walking in order not to fall asleep. All was quiet and it was difficult to awaken ourselves the next morning. The countryside was changing from hills to flat lands with scattered trees and high grass. We saw deer bounding through the grass and wished that we had time to get one for dinner that night. But we continued on and hoped that we could find water. At about 3:00 o'clock we saw a flock of buzzards circling about one mile ahead. The four scouts, me included, were sent by Herr Brandt to investigate. We crept slowly with our arms at the ready. All was quiet, the sky was clear and very blue. The grass was green on the bottom and light brown on the top of the blades. I was the forward guard and looking straight ahead I saw something lying on the ground. I motioned to the others by making a clicking noise with my tongue. As I got closer I slowly realized that I was looking at a body on the ground. It was 12 year old Wilhelm and he had been dead for a while. His body was cold and he was dirty and very bruised. There were blue marks on his wrists which were tied with a rawhide string, his arms and face. His shoes were gone. There were no arrows in his body. I got off my horse and stood over him in disbelief. He was lying on his side and looked as though he were taking a nap. I knelt beside him and said the 23 Psalm silently. One rider stayed with me as the other two went back to the group. We did not move the body but began to look for clues as to what had happened. We saw many horse tracks scattered about the area and we saw where the ground was really marked around Wilhelm's body as though the group had paused there with their horses. Upon closer inspection we saw that Wilhelm's head was against a rock. About that time the two guards and Herr Brandt arrived and they looked over the crime scene carefully. We together determined that Wilhelm had been roughly treated by his captors as evidenced by the many bruises on his body, torn clothing, no shoes and tied hands. We all agreed that Wilhelm died from a fall against a rock. Either he jumped from a running horse or was thrown down by his captors.

Herr Braun gave us his blanket in which to wrap the boy and then he went back to the group to give Herr Oelke the sad news. Soon Herr Oelke came riding up and jumped from his horse before it was halted. He bent over his son's body, which we had wrapped in the blanket, and he wept. We turned our heads aside during this private moment and Herr Brandt stood beside the grieving father with his hand on the man's shoulder. After a while the body was put onto a pack horse and Herr Oelke and 3 other men began the journey back to Fredericksburg to bury Wilhelm at home. The remainder of the militia continued to follow the trail.

Our next challenge was to find water. By 6:00 o'clock we could see a line of trees extending quite far in the distance. We went to the trees and found a small stream of water.

By the next day we could hardly mount our horses because our bodies were stiff and painful. That afternoon we saw a large billow of smoke coming up in the distance. We continued to ride towards the smoke and by mid-afternoon we were near the fire which was probably set by the Indians to conceal their trail. We saw that the fire had already burned for many miles in the distance and realized that it would be impossible to rediscover the Indians trail. We went back to the small stream, and the next morning we began the journey back to Fredericksburg with heavy hearts and tired bodies.

As we entered the town I remembered that time not long ago when we brought Herr Zeller's body back to town. The people looked at us hoping to see Louis. They were saddened when they realized that he was not to be found. The Oelke family, who had already been grieving for nearly a week, now renewed their grief. For where is their boy, what is happening to him, and will they ever see him again?

That evening I sat at Herr Zeller's grave and thought about our times together. I also thought about MaMa, Opa and Oma. Then, after a few prayers, I went home to Zeller Haus and fell on the bed and slept. I dreamed of the Indian coming towards me on a brown horse with a white face. He had a single feather tied to the end of his long flowing hair. The feather was covered with blood.

The winter was very cold in Fredericksburg and I spent much time guarding a group of men who gathered fire wood for the people in town. The good thing is that there were no Indian raids during the cold weather. At night I liked to read the books which I inherited from Herr Zeller and I sometimes played cards with Fritz and Harry at the store. Fritz was now taller than me and he was growing a thin beard which was a quarter inch in length. Fritz was making money and would soon build a house on his town lot. Harry was known for spending his money foolishly when he went to Galveston or San Antonio.

Four days before Christmas I accompanied a group of 23 people who wanted to visit New Braunfels for the Holiday. We took tents and camped for two nights in the cold weather. Crossing several rivers and streams was no easy task and getting my feet wet was very uncomfortable. Fritz and I were able to shoot nine turkeys for the Holiday feast. When we finally arrived in New Braunfels I enjoyed pulling off my boots and drying them while I sat by the fireplace and read an English newspaper from Galveston. Soon PaPa came home and we talked all evening about any news in New Braunfels and in Fredericksburg. Dorothea came over and spent several days at our house. We cooked biscuits for breakfast every morning and enjoyed delicious peach jelly made by Frau Nagel. Matilda Heske came to our house every evening for dinner and she made delicious food, including chicken and noodle soup and sweet cakes. Mati, as PaPa called her, lived and worked at the bakery. On Christmas Eve PaPa, Dorothea, the Nagel family and I all went to the Christmas Eve service at the First Protestant Church where we sat on real benches. This was much more pleasant than standing as we had done in the past. PaPa smiled broadly when he spotted Mati seated across the isle on the women's side of the church. She wore a red bonnet which made her rosy cheeks shine. After the service PaPa, Dorothea and I walked with Mati back to the bakery. When we arrived there we all told Mati good night and then, as we were about to depart, PaPa said, "Just a moment please." He once again turned to Mati who was going through the door. PaPa walked back to her and, in a strong voice, he said, "Mati, will you marry me tomorrow?" Dorothea and I stared at each other with big eyes and then heard Mati say "Yes, yes, if your children approve." They both looked at Dorothea and me as we silently nodded our heads in consent. PaPa kissed Mati's hand and the three of us began to walk silently back to the house. We looked up at the bright stars and we all remembered our first Christmas here in Texas when our MaMa died of the "red" fever. PaPa said that he hoped we would all be happy for him to marry Mati. I cleared my throat and told PaPa that we were very happy for him and that we knew that Mati would make a good wife. Dorothea said that she liked Mati but restated that she intended to remain with the Nagel family. When we got home PaPa brought out his bottle of wine which he kept for special occasions. We each drank a small glass of wine while we ate a cookie from our gift bags which we received at church.

The next morning I accompanied PaPa to the Preacher's house where PaPa asked him to perform the wedding ceremony that afternoon at the Nagel's house. The Preacher agreed and PaPa gave him a $5.00 bill. We went to the bakery and PaPa and I carried Mati's trunk to our house and she accompanied us to the Nagel's home for Christmas dinner. We ate the turkey, potatoes, green beans, canned tomatoes, with fresh bread, and pie for dessert. That afternoon the Preacher and his wife came to the Nagel's house and PaPa and Mati were married. Dorothea and I both stayed with the Nagels so that PaPa and Mati could be alone.

Chapter 6

The Treaty

The next week Harry and I went to Galveston to pick up a load of goods for the store. We caught five large fish. After eating as much as we could, we gave the fish to Harry's friends in Carlshaven.

We left Carlshaven with our two wagons packed heavily. A cold wind came from the north and it was slow traveling and rain began to pour. It reminded me of a trip long ago when Herr Zeller and I were bringing the sick immigrants to New Braunfels. Harry and I went to the home of Herr Zeller's friend, Herr Voltz, who lived near Victoria. He let us stay there for two days until the storm blew over and we continued our journey back to Fredericksburg.

As spring was approaching I was called to Herr Musbach's office. Herr Musbach had dropped his title of Baron. In this meeting we discussed the fact that, since spring was approaching, the Indians would probably come back and begin to raid the farms. Herr Musbach said that we could either mount a large army to face the Indians and defeat them, or we could make a treaty with the Indians and give them food and clothing if in return they would quit raiding in our community. We all agreed that a treaty would be in the best interest of the community, but wondered how this could be accomplished. Herr Musbach then assigned Harry and I the task of going to San Angelo to Fort Concho to speak to the head of the army there to find out how to go about making a treaty with the Indians. We had never been to San Angelo, but we knew that it was about a 3 days ride to the northwest. Harry and I packed our mule and polished and cleaned our rifles and pistols. We had many bullets which we kept in small pouches on our belts. We each carried two canteens of water as well as two more canteens on the pack mule. The next morning we set out on this journey into unknown country.

We rode through steep canyons and then got to higher ground. We saw four houses that day. We talked to a teenaged boy who was herding sheep in a meadow. He was holding his rifle but did not raise it when he saw that we were friendly. He said that there had been several Indian raids in the area and that he was taking the sheep back to the barn where they would be guarded all night. We offered to accompany him and he took us up on the offer. The log house was near the Llano River which was lined with beautiful trees. There were 5 people in the family living in the one room house. Harry and I enjoyed having a meal with them including fresh milk, butter, biscuits, deer meat, and potatoes with pie for dessert. Harry and I slept in the hay loft of the barn with the sheep, horses and a cow below us locked inside. We took turns guarding and sleeping and all was quiet. After a breakfast of biscuits, eggs and bacon with milk we told the Johnson family goodbye. They invited us to stay with them on our return trip.

As we continued, the sky became cloudy and a spring rain began to fall. We sat under a tree and waited for the storm to pass. Within an hour the rain stopped and we began to get ready to mount our horses. Just as I put my foot into the stirrup there was a loud shout behind me. Harry was already in the saddle and began to run forward leading the pack mule. I leaped into the saddle and followed Harry at a dead run. There was continued shouting behind us and I soon saw arrows fly past me and landing on the ground. Harry and I then began to turn to the left and to dodge behind trees. I shouted to Harry to let the mule go since he could not run as fast and he was holding us up. Harry dropped the rope and we ran towards a group of trees in the distance. While riding I put my canteen around my neck, and tied my food pouch to my belt. As we neared the trees I yelled to Harry to get his canteen and jump. We both scrambled to our feet and rushed to the nearest, biggest trees. The Indians were only about 30 yards behind us and they kept on coming at a fast pace. We both raised our loaded rifles, and as soon as they were within 20 yards from us we both fired. Two Indians fell from their horses. The other 5 Indians veered to the right and ran out of rifle range. We reloaded quickly and watched as they turned around and ran towards us again. My heart was bouncing practically out of my chest when they came near and once more we fired. When the smoke cleared we saw two more Indians lying on the ground and the 3 others running to the west. One of the Indians on the ground stood up and staggered toward us. Harry and I ran towards our horses about 20 feet away. Thank goodness they both stood still while we mounted and began to run back towards the Johnson house on the Llano River. I felt sorry for the gray horse because he was panting heavily and had sweat all over his body from running so hard. After about a half hour we saw the Johnson house and we began to shout for Mr. Johnson. He immediately came out on the porch with a rifle pulled up to his shoulder. He recognized us as we came to a halt in the yard. We quickly explained to him what had happened. We took our horses back into the barn where Harry and I stared out through cracks in the walls. I looked out the front and Harry out the back. The Johnsons were well armed and were in their house with the door and wooden shutters closed and locked. We all stood, with fast-beating hearts, on guard for over half an hour. Then Harry and I began to whisper and talk excitedly about the Indian attack that we had just survived. We gave the horses small sips of water and they were recovering from their hard run. We drank from our canteens and ate a piece of sausage. All remained very still and quiet except for the chickens walking around outside the barn who occasionally made clucking sounds. Late in the day the boy, Joe, came to the barn and brought deer meat and milk. Mr. Johnson stood on the porch with a rifle in hand. We continued to take turns standing guard all night. Once I was able to go to sleep and soon I dreamed of the Indian coming at Herr Zeller and I on a brown horse with a white face. There was a bloody feather hanging from the Indian's black hair. I awoke with a start and realized it was only a dream.

By the next morning all was quiet and Mr. Johnson invited us into the house for breakfast. Mrs. Johnson gave us a bag of food including a loaf of bread and dried deer meat to take on our trip. Harry and I reluctantly left the Johnson farm and proceeded like scared rabbits from tree to tree as fast as we could go without tiring our horses. By that night we were to the river called San Saba. We found grass for our horses and then camped in a dense thicket of brush. We took turns guarding and sleeping. At dawn we set out again and by mid afternoon we saw several houses in the distance. Eventually we saw a man in a field near his house and his wife was in the garden. We walked our horses slowly to their house and called hello. The man grabbed his rifle and held it to his shoulder while we introduced ourselves and explained our mission. Soon we were inside their house where we were met by a five year old girl and a baby boy. We had dinner with the Ackerman family and then Harry and I took turns holding the baby and playing with the five year old girl. The family came here from East Texas six months ago and had not yet seen an Indian. They were surprised when we told them of our great adventure. Mrs. Ackerman fed us roasted meat, beets, potatoes, and cornbread with blackberry jelly. We slept in the barn with our horses and Mr. Ackerman's animals. I slept soundly and it was difficult to get up at 1:00 a.m. when it was my time to take guard duty.

The next morning, after a breakfast of cornbread and bacon, we continued on our journey. Thanks to Mr. Ackerman's directions we arrived at Fort Concho before nightfall. We were met at the entrance to the fort by a guard who asked what we wanted and told us to put our horses in a pen and camp in the barn. We saw guards walking around patrolling the area and for the first time in several days we got a good nights sleep.

I was startled awake by a loud bugle noise and I jumped to my feet and looked outside. About 50 or 60 men were standing at attention as the beautiful American flag was being raised up the flagpole. When the ceremony ended the men marched to a nearby building where they were eating breakfast. In about an hour a sergeant escorted us to the commander's office where we were introduced to Captain Millard Lancaster. He was a tall man in his late thirties with a large brown mustache and short hair. We introduced ourselves and I gave him a letter of introduction from Herr Musbach. We explained where we were from and what we wanted, and we told him about the Indian attack that we had withstood. We discussed the situation all morning and we pointed out Fredericksburg and New Braunfels on a large map of Texas.

Captain Lancaster was impressed with the quick development of the town of Fredericksburg and told us that it was deep in the area where the Comanche Indians were known to raid. He said that no one had ever been successful in making a treaty with the Comanches. I asked Captain Lancaster how we could go about trying to make contact with the Comanche chief. Captain Lancaster called his sergeant who left for a few minutes and then returned accompanied by two Indian men who were dressed in deerskin pants and shirts and wore boots. Their long hair was pulled back and tied together with string. Captain Lancaster introduced us to these Indian scouts, Anka and Joe. They nodded and shook our hands. I told them about the town of Fredericksburg and about the trouble we had with raids, kidnapping, and murder. They listened carefully and then we showed them where Fredericksburg was located on the map. Again it was stated that a treaty with the Comanche was unlikely. I again stated that our leaders would like to try to make a treaty. The negotiations went on all morning. We accompanied Captain Lancaster to dinner in the mess hall where we were served fried beef, pinto beans, and cornbread. Again in the afternoon I said all of the same things that I had said to them in the morning.

Finally, near the end of the day, Anka said that he would try to make contact with the Comanche chief. It was decided that Harry and I would return to Fredericksburg and that our peace delegation would proceed to the San Saba River directly south from Fort Concho where there were twin mountains and a rock bottom where a ford passes through the river. The peace delegation should arrive at the San Saba River on May 8, the next full moon. We were to remain there for five days waiting for the Comanche Chief to arrive. If he had not arrived in five days we should return to Fredericksburg and try again at a later date. I thanked the Captain, the Sergeant, and the Indian scouts for their cooperation and shook their hands.

Harry and I again spent the night in the barn. We left early the next morning with our rifles ready to fire. We traveled to the San Saba River and camped there. The next day we rode along the San Saba until we were sure that we had found the site described to us. There was the twin mountains, and the rock bottom crossing was heavily traveled with wide trails leading to it. We felt very uncomfortable there knowing that Indians could spot us at any time. As soon as we determined that this was the site for the possible future treaty meeting, we quickly went southeast and arrived back in Fredericksburg in two days without incident. I was very happy to lay on my soft bed in Zeller Haus and I slept until noon the next day. I put on fresh clothes and then reported to Herr Musbach about the excitement of our trip and the outcome of the meeting with Captain Lancaster. We talked all afternoon, and the next day several leaders in the militia came for another meeting.

That very night there were three raids on local farms where horses and cows were stolen. We tried tracking the robbers, but eventually all trails led into one large trail where there were about a hundred horses involved. There was no reason to pursue such a large group without an army. On April 2 Herr Lentz was murdered as he was returning to his farm from a shopping trip into Fredericksburg. His body had three arrows in it and his head had been scalped. On April 3 an American by the name of Mr. Farr came running into town on foot saying that his partner had been killed by Indians and their horses stolen. The militia was on full alert and we kept a large contingency of guards patrolling the perimeters of Fredericksburg both day and night. Many families came to Fredericksburg from their farms and stayed with friends or made camps in the town square. I was busy with guard duty, and Harry and a hired man took two wagons to Galveston to buy supplies for Fritz's store.

As Good Friday came all of us were nervous and very mindful of the fact that we, and the very existence of our town, were in danger. We went to church in the Verinskirche on the night of Good Friday and prayed for God's protection. On Saturday 2 more farms were raided and some people were talking about the possibility of taking the women and children back to New Braunfels. On Saturday night, the eve before Easter, I was on guard duty on the North side of town. I noticed smoke billowing up about 2 miles from town. I called to the next guard who went to Herr Musbach to report the fire. Before long there were several other guards from other sides of town also reporting fires. By nightfall it became apparent that Fredericksburg was surrounded by fires on all sides. The sky was very clear and the stars were shining brightly. There was a chill in the night air. Everyone gathered at the Verineskirche and the women and children locked themselves inside. All the men and bigger boys armed themselves and were stationed at the edge of the town. They hid behind barrels, tree trunks, wood piles, and outhouses. They all had their rifles loaded and were prepared to defend themselves and their families even if it meant death. The women tried to remain calm, and it was later said that they told some of the crying children that the fires were merely that of Easter bunnies who were boiling eggs for Easter Sunday. As we all sat and stared out at the darkness beyond the town, we prayed to God for his protection. I found myself looking at the stars and wondering where Captain Kerr was. Maybe he was in a German harbor loading more immigrants aboard the "Angelina". Maybe I would see him again someday. I hoped that PaPa and Mati were still happy and that Dorothea was adapting to the new situation. I thought about Tante Gretchen and Oma back in Germany. I pictured MaMa wiping her hands on her apron. The night went on and on and all of our eyes were wide with fear. But nothing happened! By daylight the fires were no longer burning and the men were taking turns going to the Verineskirche to drink coffee and to see their families. By noon only half of the guards were still on duty. I remained on duty all day and in the afternoon I heard singing from the Verienskirche proclaiming that Jesus had risen! Indeed we had all risen from the brink of disaster! I rested in the afternoon and then we were all on guard duty on Easter night. Again it was very quiet and nothing happened. Gradually, when there were no signs of Indians, things returned to normal and most people even went back to their farms.

On May 4 I accompanied Herr Musbach and 30 other men to the San Saba River. It took 3 days to get there and then we camped openly where we could be seen about a mile from the river. I discovered a bee hive and passed some time robbing it of its honey. We waited for 4 days and there was no sign of Indians. Finally on May 10 a guard shouted that a lone Indian was nearing our camp. I quickly ran to look and, sure enough, it was Anka the Indian scout. When he arrived I gladly shook his hand and led him to Herr Musbach to be introduced. He met with Herr Musbach, Herr Brandt and me and told us that the Comanche Chief, Red Hawk, was willing to speak to our leader about a possible truce, if our leader was willing to give something in return. We had already discussed possible terms of a treaty agreement. Herr Musbach suggested that we were willing to give the Indians food and other basic goods every 6 months in return for our safety. Anka suggested that Herr Musbach arrive at the Indian camp across the river at noon the next day.

At 11:30 on May 11 we all gathered together and kneeled to pray that we would be successful and that we would be safe. We said the Lord's Prayer in unison. All the men prepared for battle and saddled their horses. Then Herr Brandt, Herr Musebach and I departed from the group and proceeded across the San Saba. When we passed through the trees on the other side our eyes were astonished to see an encampment of approximately 300 Comanche Indians with a herd of at least 500 horses. Anka and two Comanches rode toward us and stopped nearby. At this time Herr Musebach turned to Herr Brandt and I and said, "From here I must go alone". I protested to Herr Musebach but he seemed not to listen as he handed me his rifle, his pistol and his knife. Total alone and unarmed Herr Musbach followed Anka and the other two Comanches into the camp. Herr Brandt and I stood staring at them and pleading in our hearts for God's kindness in this matter. A large crowd of Comanches met Herr Musebach and soon they closed around him so that he was no longer visible. Herr Brandt and I glanced at each other in silence and returned our stare to the place where we had last seen our leader, Herr Musbach.

The Comanche Camp was very quiet with only a few boys moving around keeping the horses together. After some time I noticed the gray horse was shifting his feet from one side to the other. He was getting tired of standing in one position. Herr Brandt and I then dismounted with rifles in hand and stood by the horses for another long period of time. We kept staring at the Indian camp, for as long as the camp was quiet there was little danger for us. Eventually I took a drink from my canteen and kneeled on the ground with rifle in hand. Herr Brandt looked at his pocket watch and it was now 3:00 o'clock in the afternoon. Another half hour passed and then suddenly there was a great deal of movement in the Comanche camp. We mounted our horses and motioned to our men across the San Saba to be ready. In a few minutes the crowd of Comanches began to move in our direction, and, when they were a half-mile away, a lone figure began to emerge walking toward us at a slow pace. As the lone figure came nearer, with great relief, we realized that it was Herr Musbach walking all alone. When he came to us he said in a low voice to follow him slowly across the San Saba. He waded across the river with us following on horseback. As we entered our camp there were cries of "Ser Gute!" from the men and we all shook hands and slapped the back of Herr Musebach. Then Herr Musebach feel to his knees in silent prayer, and we all did likewise. After a minute of prayer Herr Musebach stood and directed us to break camp to depart immediately. In just a few minutes we were on our way back to Fredericksburg, our home in the mountains of the great new world called Texas.

We traveled quickly until dark and then made camp with plenty of guards on duty. We gathered together and Herr Musbach told us about his experience in the Comanche camp. He said that he felt just like the martyrs of old who showed no fear as they were lead to their death. He had totally placed his life into the hands of God. As he entered the camp he continued walking until it became apparent that he was standing before Chief Red Hawk. The Chief motioned for Herr Musbach and Anka to sit and many braves joined them in a circle. The Chief asked many questions through the interpreter Anka. The questions where such things as "What is your name?", "Where are you from?" "Why are you here?" When the Chief asked, "How many guns?" Herr Musbach replied "As many as there are days from one spring to the next spring." We all laughed, for this was a very astute answer. Then the Chief offered Herr Musebach a cup of water which he drank, and then a meal was served to all of those people sitting in the circle. It was beef cut into small pieces. After the meal was finished a long pipe was passed from person to person and then given to Herr Musebach who smoked it readily, for pipe smoking is one of his favorite past times. The Chief seemed to appreciate the fact that Herr Musebach did not choke on the powerful tobacco which most likely was mixed with wild tobacco leaves as well as tree bark. There were many discussions between the Chief and the braves none of which Herr Musebach could understand. The interpreter stared straight ahead and did not give explanation. The Chief then announced that many gifts would have to be given in order to prevent raiding in the area of Fredericksburg. Herr Musebach proposed that twice a year, in the spring and in the fall, the Comanches would be given one beef cow for each family living in Fredericksburg. The Chief said that this was not enough. Herr Musbach said that in the fall they would also provide a blanket from each family living in Fredericksburg. After much discussion among the braves, the Chief said that this still was not enough. Then Herr Musebach said that in the spring he would give pots and pans along with the beef. The Chief said that was still not enough. Herr Musebach replied, "If the Comanches have too many material goods to carry with them each time they want to move, it will be a great burden. Be satisfied with what I have offered you and we will not shoot you with our bullets." After more discussion the Chief said that this treaty was dependent upon the people of Fredericksburg to give them what they have promised. Herr Musebach reminded the Chief that the people of Fredericksburg would only give the gifts in the fall and in the spring and that they would only be given to the Chief. Small groups of raiders will not be tolerated and the people of Fredericksburg would ask the U. S. Army for help if raids did occur. The Chief then stood up and Herr Musebach assumed that the meeting must be over. He got up and slowly walked out of the camp without looking to see if anyone was following him. He said the sight of Herr Brandt and I in the distance made him want to run towards us, but he held himself back to a slow walk.

We talked about the experience for most of the night and ate all the honey our stomachs could hold.

We arrived in Fredericksburg three days later and to everyone's surprise we were all alive and well. Fritz slapped me on the back and then bought me a loaf of fresh bread and gave me a large glass of cold milk. I continued to guard every night for 3 weeks, and then I had to make a trip to the gulf coast to pick up supplies for the store.

One month later Anka came to Fredericksburg to organize the first spring payment of 56 live beef cattle with 56 pots and pans which I helped to deliver to a group of braves about five miles from town. Anka told me that day that the only reason that the treaty was accepted was because Herr Musebach walked into the Indian camp alone and unarmed. His great bravery, along with his flowing long bright red hair and beard, led the Comanche Chief to deem Herr Musebach some sort of god-man. The Chief therefore felt compelled to deal with him.

When I told Herr Musbach what Anka had said, he replied that the only reason he could do it was because he was walking with God, and after all of the hardships that the immigrants had endured he could not stand by and watch their dreams of a better life taken away by the Comanches. He said that the true test of courage would come in the next months and years in keeping the treaty in tact.

Chapter 7

Fritz and Katherine

That summer I spent much time working on my farms. I built a small house on the Zeller Farm and rented it to a young couple from New Braunfels who wanted a place to live while they worked on their own farm house. I bought a herd of twenty cattle and one bull to be put on my Silverbrook Farm. When I went to the farm I always took a bag of corn. When the cattle saw me coming they ran to meet me and to get their delicious treat. In this way I could keep up with them and make sure that they were well.

Harry had made many trips to the coast with a hired hand because I was too busy with other work. Fritz was very busy at his store but he always has time to go to the dance on Saturday night and sometimes I accompanied him. We had also been invited to several evenings of games and singing at various houses. This was a fun way for young people to get to know each other.

It just so happened that my 17th Birthday, August 21, 1846, was one of the best days of my life. Herr Musbach had organized a shooting club and the very first annual shooting competition was on my birthday. I cleaned and polished Herr Zeller's rifle for the big event. The competition was very tough because the men of Fredericksburg were excellent marksmen. However, when the competition was over, I was declared the winner and I was given a pouch of gun powder. Many people shook my hand, congratulated me, and thanked me for helping to make the town a safer place. I ate half of an Apple Pie, and that night Fritz and I went to the dance where I danced with almost every girl in town. I did not drink beer, but I was almost drunk with excitement because I had finally won a shooting contest, one of my dreams of many years. That night, as I laid in Herr Zeller's bed, I thought about him and what an influence he had on my life. I could not believe that a whole year had passed since he was killed by the Indian. Unfortunately that night I dreamed about the Indian on a brown horse with a white face, and I saw the bloody feather in his black hair.

I continue to spend most of my days in hunting and most nights in guarding the town. There had been several Indian incidents which had made us all question the validity of our treaty with the Comanches. Herr Schmidt's horses were stolen, and an American by the name of Adams was attacked. His horse was stolen and he was shot with an arrow. However, there had never been a raid on the town of Fredericksburg itself. In the fall of 1847, Mr. Clark came riding into town and ran into Fritz's store shouting that his house was burning. Fritz called to me to come in and talk to the man. I gave him a cup of coffee and tried to calm his nerves with quiet talk. He said that he lived about 30 miles to the northwest of Fredericksburg. He had left his family right after breakfast and had gone on a hunting expedition. When he arrived home that evening, the house was on fire. He rode close to the house and shouted for his wife, but there was no reply. He immediately turned his horse and began to run towards Fredericksburg where he knew he could find assistance. I escorted the man to Herr Musbach where he repeated the same story. Herr Musbach then called a meeting of the militia to determine what to do. During the meeting several men questioned whether we should help someone from outside our own community who lives 30 miles away. Several people said that he should be sent to Ft. Concho to gain their assistance. I brought up the fact that it would take time to ride all the way to Ft. Concho and I pointed out the importance of finding out if any of the family survived. After much discussion it was determined that 5 of us would ride with the man back to his house and inspect the scene. Herr Musebach said that, if we volunteered, Harry and I would be allowed to accompany the man to Ft. Concho to report the crime. We packed quickly and within an hour we departed with Mr. Clark leading the way. We camped overnight and arrived at the house at about noon the next day. All that remained were a few burned logs and the stone fireplace still standing. It was a very depressing sight, and there was only the sound of a mocking bird in a nearby tree. We dismounted and began to search through the ruins. Soon we found the scorched body of the man's wife who had been shot in the forehead. There was a pistol laying beside the body. We urged Mr. Clark to leave her body lie while we continued to search for their 3 month old baby girl. We formed a circle around the house and then began walking away from the house looking for clues. I soon saw the foot prints of many horses. We kept searching, and then Herr Brandt whistled from the other side of the house. We all went there to find Herr Brandt staring into a large cactus bush. Inside the cactus was lying the body of the baby. Mr. Clark began to scream loudly and he reached into the cactus and pulled the baby out, filling his hands with cactus thorns. He held the dead baby in his arms and wept. We persuaded Mr. Clark to allow us to inspect the baby and we found only dirt, bruises, and many cactus thorns in the arms and legs. There were no wounds from arrows or any other weapon. We looked back into the cactus bush and could see where there were many broken thorns around where the baby had lain. We dug a grave and placed the wife's burned body into it. Mr. Clark tenderly placed the baby on the mother's chest. We covered the grave as we all said the Lord's Prayer in unison. We then had a meeting to get everyone's opinion about what we had discovered. We all agreed that probably the Indians took the baby from the mother and threw the baby into the cactus. The mother was so distraught, and was so scared at the prospect of either being burned alive or being at the mercy of the Indians, that she shot herself. Mr. Clark agreed with this assessment. Harry and I volunteered to accompany Mr. Clark to Ft. Concho to report the crime and the others returned to Fredericksburg. We mounted our horses a rode to the home of Mr. & Mrs. Ackerman whom we had met on our previous trip to Ft. Concho. We camped in their barn and then arrived at the Fort the next evening. On the following morning I accompanied Mr. Clark to the office of Capt. Millard Lancaster. The Captain immediately recognized me and began to talk about the famous peace treaty between the town of Fredericksburg and the Comanche Chief Red Hawk. After discussing this in great detail, I related to him the tragedy which had befallen Mr. Clark's family. Captain Lancaster was very sorry to hear about this incident and he filled out papers asking Mr. Clark many questions. Mr. Clark said that he could not go back to the farm, and he decided that he would make his way back to his parent's home in Kentucky. The next morning Mr. Clark shook our hands and thanked us, mounted his horse and departed. Harry and I had dinner with Captain Lancaster and then departed that afternoon. By that night we were back at Mr. Ackerman's farm. The next day we continued our journey and arrived back in Fredericksburg seven nights after the incident had begun. I made a complete report to Herr Musebach and I told him how terrible it was to see the results of the Indian attack, and to think about the poor woman seeing her baby killed and then making the decision to end her own life. Herr Musebach expressed his gratitude for assisting Mr. Clark and he said that he was sorry that I had to witness such dramas at my early age in life.

After this I spent a whole week in New Braunfels visiting with PaPa, Mati, and Dorothea and my friends there. Harry and I took side trips to San Antonio and to Seguin. We then went to Galveston and returned with two wagon loads of goods for Fritz's store.

All winter I worked on my farm and began to cut rocks from the nearby rock beds with which to build Fritz's house in town. Fritz needed a house because he had become engaged to Katherine Weil, the sixteen year old daughter of a farmer. Katherine was tall, slender and had long brown hair. Her most outstanding feature was her dark brown eyes which seem to sparkle when she spoke. Katherine had an outstanding singing voice and was often asked to sing at church and at the young people's gatherings at various homes. Yes, I must say that Katherine was an outstanding catch for Fritz and I was not sure why she would want to marry him. But after thinking this through, I realized that Fritz was a very successful businessman and was highly regarded in Fredericksburg. I hoped she would be able to wake him up in the mornings to get to the store, for he loved to sleep. It was my duty to see that the house Fritz was building for Katherine would be of fine quality.

I scouted the river beds to find large slabs of limestone. I measured the stones and scratched straight lines on them. I used a hand bore to make deep holes at 6 inch intervals along the line. I boiled water in a big kettle and poured it into each hole. The next day I again poured boiling water into the holes, and by the third day the boiling water had softened the limestone so that I could begin to saw between each of the holes. I used a pry bar to lift the large blocks of stone from the creek bed. I tied ropes around the stones and attached the ropes to an oxen to heave the stones out of the creek bed and up the bank. There I began to saw the limestone into large blocks 3 feet long and 2 feet wide. All of this is a very slow process and it took all winter. By spring everyone was joking with Fritz and I that the marriage could not take place until I had the house built, and I was a very slow house builder. Fritz made sure that I had plenty to eat, and from time to time he gave me money. He sent Harry to San Antonio to buy large beams which had been cut in a saw mill to be used for the roof. Harry also bought ready-made doors which are the first ever seen in Fredericksburg. By mid April Fritz hired three men to assist me in heaving the large stones one upon another to form the walls, and to lift the beams into place to form the roof which was covered with shingles. The house had two bedrooms, a kitchen and a sitting room with a fireplace.

There was a large wood stove in the kitchen which Harry brought from Galveston. None of us would allow Katherine to see the house, although we are sure that she has been there in the middle of the night. Finally the wedding was set for July 1, 1848 which was right after Fritz's 18th birthday.

During the third week of June, Harry and I went to New Braunfels with our wagons and picked up PaPa, Mati, Dorothea and all of the Nagel family. We brought tents for camping on the journey to Fredericksburg. We had great fun on the trip, although Harry and I had to take turns guarding each night. When we reached Fredericksburg my family stayed at Zeller Haus and the Nagels stayed at Fritz's store. Everyone in town was delighted to have visitors and they all invited us to afternoon teas, and evening parties. Mati was greatly admired for her rosy cheeks and happy disposition, and PaPa just sat beside her and smiled. PaPa has gained weight and is very content. Dorothea even admitted that she liked Mati. The Nagels were amazed at the new found wealth of their son Fritz, and they keep complimenting him on his wonderful new house. One day we all went to my farm, Silverbrook, where we had a picnic and counted the cows, 35 in all. PaPa was very proud of our beautiful farm, but he said that seeing men carrying rifles with them, even on a picnic, was not the kind of life that he wanted for Mati and Dorothea. PaPa had heard about the Indian attacks and the uncertainty of life in the Texas Hill Country.

On the afternoon of July 1 we all gathered in Fritz's new house to witness the wedding. Fritz looked very handsome in his new suit which we purchased in Galveston. Katherine wore a beautiful dress covered with lace. After the ceremony we ate sandwiches, desserts, coffee and fruit punch. The men gathered on the porch and smoked cigars which Fritz provided. I held the cigar in my hand most of the time and took only three puffs. This was because, once while Harry and I visited San Antonio, I tried to smoke a cigar, and I became very ill at my stomach. I will never truly smoke a cigar again. As darkness came everyone, except the bride and groom, continued the party at the home of the bride where her parents served roasted pork, beets, green beans, potato salad, fresh bread with butter and jelly, and cake. Later we drank beer and wine and danced till early morning. By then breakfast was served including bacon, eggs, biscuits, and coffee. By daylight we all boarded our wagons and proceeded back to Fredericksburg where we slept most of the day. In the late afternoon preparations began for the third and final part of the festival. At about ten o'clock in the evening everyone met at Fritz's store where we organized and then quietly surrounded the new home of Fritz and Katherine. When everyone was in place I whistled a signal and we all began to shout, and to bang together pots and pans, and to ring cattle bells. In a very short time Fritz was standing on the porch wearing his pants with his suspenders still hanging down around his waist. He was shouting for us to "Halt, Halt!" Shortly Katherine appeared dressed in a pretty robe. Food, which we had prepared that afternoon, was taken onto the front porch and the party began again. We ate sandwiches, pickles, kraut, beets, and cakes, and drank beer and coffee. At about midnight we gathered up all of our food, dishes, and other items and departed for home. Needless to say, everyone slept late the next day.

After another week Harry and I took the families back to New Braunfels and continued on to Galveston to pick up a load of supplies for the store. This time when we visited Carlshaven and looked in the tobacco tin we had left there, the note to Harry's uncle was missing. We began to inquire as to his uncle's where bouts and were told that he had been there but that he had left again on a voyage to Europe. Harry never heard from his Uncle again after that.

On our way back, we stopped in New Braunfels to celebrate my 18th birthday with my family and friends. Mati made a large bowl of noodles and we had delicious lettuce and tomatoes from her garden. Frau Nagel baked Pecan Pie. PaPa gave me a new hat and Dorothea gave me a handkerchief. As I was chewing my last bite of pie, PaPa announced to all of us that by Easter Mati would be having their first child. I gulped and almost choked on the pie as I quickly took a large swallow of milk. Everyone began to clap, except for Dorothea who just stood there in stunned silence. As we departed I motioned for Dorothea to follow me out the door. We stood in the Nagel's yard and had a nice conversation about the importance of PaPa's happiness, about how Mati was a good wife, and we also agreed that MaMa was probably smiling down from heaven and was happy for PaPa too. We talked about how we missed Oma and Aunt Gretchen. I suggested that we write them a letter which we did the next day.

As soon as I arrived in Fredericksburg there was news of more Indian raids in the Hill Country, but none near town. Herr Musbach appointed me to oversee the gathering of 62 cattle and blankets which would be given to the Comanche Chief Red Hawk in October. The cows would be purchased from the town treasury and it seemed that the price of cattle had suddenly gone up. A cow that used to be worth $8 was now worth $12. I scouted the many farms in the area trying to buy cattle. I ended up selling most of my own cattle for $8 each in order to simplify the matter and to jolt the market back into its usual $8 price range. Herr Musebach enjoyed watching me and then sent me to Galveston to buy the blankets.

There was an unfortunate incident on our trip to Galveston. As usual Harry and I stopped at the home of Herr Voltz, the old friend of Herr Zeller. Upon our arrival Frau Voltz met us on the porch and said that Herr Voltz was very ill with fever and a stomach ache since yesterday. We went in to him and he sat up in bed to talk, but we could see that he was in great pain and his face was very white. We suggested that we take him to the Doctor in Victoria who had helped us years ago when we had the epidemic among the immigrants. Herr Voltz refused since he thought he would be better by the next day. But by morning he was worse. We made a bed in one of the wagons and gently carried him to the wagon. Frau Voltz stayed at home with their two children, but she had made food to sustain us on our journey which was very slow because at every bump Herr Voltz began to moan and groan. We finally arrived in Victoria and found the Doctor at his hospital. He examined Herr Voltz and said that he had a swelling of the appendix which is located near the stomach. He said that he could give Herr Voltz medicine to help the pain but they would just have to hope that the swelling would go down and he would feel better soon. As Harry and I were leaving to find a place to spend the night, the Doctor followed us onto the front porch and said that Herr Voltz was in very bad condition and may not live through the night. I immediately went to church to pray and Harry went to the bar to forget his troubles in beer. We spent the night in a stable and when we returned to the hospital the next morning Herr Voltz was dead. Harry and I were both scared and did not know what to do. We finally decided to return Herr Voltz to his home. We wrapped him in a blanket and placed him back into the wagon. When we arrived Frau Voltz came quickly out the door, but she could tell by the look on our faces that the news was not good. I got down from the wagon and put my arm around her shoulder. I described our trip and told her what the doctor had said. She asked, "Did you leave him there at the hospital to get well?" I had to tell her that he was dead and that we had his body in the wagon. She ran to the wagon and fell upon his wrapped up body and began to cry. Their two children came running from the barn and I had to tell them and they too were crying. Harry and I immediately dug a grave under a beautiful tree about 50 yards from the house and buried Herr Voltz that afternoon. We stayed for two more days hunting for meat, cutting fire wood, plowing up the garden, and doing other chores to help out the family during this terrible time for them. We continued to Galveston and bought the blankets. We returned to Frau Voltz four days later and stayed another day helping out. We then returned to Fredericksburg with heavy hearts.

It was good to return to Zeller Haus and my comfortable bed. The next morning I made a report to Herr Musbach and showed him the blankets. We were now prepared and would wait to hear from the Indians. That night I had the pleasure of dinner with Fritz and Katherine. Their house was very nice (I must remember that it was a sin to have too much pride in the house that I built), they had real furniture, and to top it all off, Katherine was a good cook. We all laughed a lot and then sat on the front porch and talked to several people as they passed by. After it became dark

I thanked them for the supper and excused myself. Fritz followed me into the street and said that he needed to talk to me. At first this scared me because I thought that maybe something was wrong, for Fritz hardly ever became serious. Fritz asked if I remembered our days in Bicken where we talked about our future in Texas. I told him that I did remember and that, even though we both had a house, we did not have carriages with matching prancing horses pulling them. We both laughed and then Fritz thanked me for being his best friend, for helping him to start his store, for building his house, and for making his wedding a success. We ended up hugging each other, maybe for the first time in our lives, and then we began to laugh and push each other back and forth. He ended up throwing a handful of tree moss at me and I took off running for home.

All week I helped to make bricks to build the new Catholic Church. I was not Catholic, but it was every town member's duty to assist in this endeavor.

On Saturday I was sitting on the front porch of the store and saw Anka riding into town all alone. I immediately invited him into the store and gave him a drink of water and some sausage to eat. We visited most of the afternoon. I asked him many questions and he was willing to talk to me for the first time. He was an Apache Indian who grew up in Mexico. His father left the family in Mexico near the Texas border, and came to visit there from time to time. His mother was part Spanish and he had 6 brothers and 2 sisters, some of whom were older than him. He spoke the Apache language at home, but his mother also spoke Spanish to the children. Near their home was a Spanish padre who started a Catholic Mission Church where Anka went to school from time to time. The padre taught him to speak some English. When Anka was a teenager his father was killed during a raid, and his grandfather called Anka to take his father's place. Anka then became a member of the tribe, but was always treated as an outsider because he did not grow up with them. He also found out that his father had another wife and children who lived with the tribe. This made Anka very angry and, after about 3 years, he wandered away from the tribe. He still visited them from time to time, but his real home was in Mexico where his brothers and sisters all lived with their families. A few years ago Anka found out that the U. S. Government would pay him if he would act as a guide and an interpreter for the military. He could then use this money to purchase food and clothing for his poor family. He had no real kinship with the Comanches, but they knew that his ability to speak English was very useful to them, so they treated him with some dignity. The army men treated him poorly, but he endured this treatment to get the money. I was fascinated with this information and actually felt sorry for Anka because he was between the Indian world and the world of the white man. I took him to visit with Herr Musbach and, at Herr Musbach's suggestion, I took Anka all over town and introduced him to many people so that he would be recognized and would be welcomed to our town. We feared that if someone saw him coming into town they might shoot him, thinking that he was a raiding Indian. The next day Anka left town and was gone for 3 days. He returned to tell me that an appointment had been set up to deliver the cattle and blankets to the Comanche braves in 2 days. We rushed to get ready and 8 men took the goods to a meeting place on the Llano River. We took the cattle to the river and unloaded the blankets there and then went to a nearby hill and watched. About an hour later 20 or 25 braves arrived and loaded the blankets into a wagon and herded the cattle in a northerly direction. I gave Anka $20, as instructed by Herr Musbach, and told Anka to keep in touch with us. He mounted his horse and rode south.

I had decided to spend most of the winter building my house at Silverbrook in the same manner in which I built Fritz's house. It was good to do this hard work in the wintertime when it was not so hot. I had the habit of having dinner with Fritz and Katherine every Friday night. I also played cards and went to dances. Katherine kept re-introducing me to every young lady in town, but I was too busy to go courting.

A week before Christmas Harry and I traveled to New Braunfels for the Holiday. As we approached the town I was reminded once again that this was a very beautiful place where the Comal and Guadalupe Rivers converged. There was now a mill on the river and the town had grown. As I rode the gray horse down the road to PaPa's house, I remembered the first time that we saw this place, how PaPa and I walked to Mill Road and found our lot. We were very happy to own such a piece of property. I remembered cutting the logs for building the houses and how hard we worked to build this house where PaPa and Mati lived. At that time I had no idea what the future would bring. As I rode up to the house I whistled and soon Mati was hugging my neck and PaPa was shaking my hand. A short time later Dorothea heard the commotion and came from across the street to greet me. She had grown so tall and looked so much like a young lady! I was just in time for a delicious dinner of fresh sausage, fried potatoes, and bread. The house now had glass in the window with a lacy curtain around it. PaPa showed me a drawing of how he wanted to remodel the house and build two bedrooms in the back. Then the main room, which was used for sleeping and eating, would become the kitchen and parlor. I approved of the plan because soon there would be a baby who would probably cry at night and I did not want to sleep in the same room with a crying baby. We all laughed at this, even Dorothea. On Christmas Eve we went to church along with the Nagel Family, including Fritz and Katherine. After the service we walked in the bright moonlight back to the house and opened gifts. I gave PaPa a pouch of tobacco, Mati a new apron, and Dorothea a new hat. PaPa and Mati gave me a new shirt that Mati had made, and Dorothea gave me a book of English literature. PaPa went to get something from the woodshed. Dorothea and I smiled and laughed, and Mati cried, as PaPa entered the house carrying a beautiful baby crib which he had made. Just think, by next year we would have another new member in our family.

On Christmas Day all of the Nagel family came to our house and we ate fresh turkey which I had killed on Christmas Eve, boiled potatoes, canned tomatoes, canned green beans (all from Mati's garden), fresh bread, butter, milk and Applekuchen for dessert. We played chess and tossed horse shoes all afternoon.

After Christmas I stayed on to help PaPa build the new bedrooms while Harry went to Galveston. Just as before we took a wagon into the woods, only this time it was our own wagon and the woods were much further from town. We built the bedrooms in the same fashion as the rest of the house and we put a window in each bedroom to be opened on hot summer nights. We also put a floor of sawed pine which PaPa purchased. It was a great day to move the beds into the new rooms and to spread out the kitchen table and chairs and have more room. PaPa was going to build some comfortable chairs to be used in the sitting room by the window with the lace curtain.

By now it was late in January and Mati was supposed to have her baby in only a few more weeks. I decided to stay in New Braunfels for this big event, as my house at Silverbrook did not have to be finished anytime soon. I went hunting every day and also made trips to Seguin and San Antonio.

On February 6, after Mati washed the dishes, she told me that she was not feeling well and went to her bedroom and laid down. I stayed at home just in case she needed me and sure enough, just before noon, she called me from her bedroom and said to go get PaPa. I ran to the furniture shop and told him to come home right away, and then I continued on to tell Frau Busche, the midwife. When Frau Busche and I arrived back home, Mati was beginning to be in great pain. PaPa and I went to the Nagel's house, ate lunch, and sat on their front porch trying to carry on a conversation about the weather, the price of cattle and hogs, and about my future house at Silverbrook. But all of our eyes were on our house across the street which was very quiet. After Frau Nagel finished the dishes from lunch, she went over to check on Mati. We watched her cross the street and walk into the house. We kept our eyes on the front door for about 15 minutes until it opened and she came out. She slowly walked across the street and said that Mati was fine and that it would be a while longer. More time went by and PaPa and I began to pace back and forth on the

Nagel's front porch. We sat down in silence and got up and paced again. Later Dorothea arrived home from school and she sat with us and paced with us. Finally Frau Nagel went back over to our house and this time she stayed. About a half hour later the front door opened and Frau Nagel motioned for PaPa to come. PaPa was out of the chair and across the street in a few seconds. We stood on the porch of our house with Frau Nagel while PaPa went in. Frau Nagel said that all was well and she did not want to tell us any more. A short time later PaPa opened the door and invited Dorothea and I in to see the baby, and introduced us to our new brother, Wilhelm. He was very tiny in the arms of Mati who looked like she had done a hard days work. Mati had a big smile on her face and PaPa had tears in his eyes. This is truly one of the happiest days in Texas.

Soon I went back to Fredericksburg and continued my house building. Harry and I went to Galveston in the pouring rain and camped at the home of Frau Voltz. I was surprised at her appearance, for she had been an attractive lady before her husband died. Her face was very brown from working in the fields, and when I shook her hand I noticed that it was very rough like a man's hands. The house was in disarray and her 10 year old son was trying to chop fire wood, but he was very slow. It was decided that night that Harry would go on to Galveston for supplies and I would stay and help the Voltz family, for I was sure that this was what Herr Zeller would have me do. I cleaned up the yard and barn and killed a hog to made sausage. I helped scrub the floors and then chopped a large pile of firewood. I taught the boy how to milk the cow, and plow the field, and explained to him that he would have to work harder to support his family in this time of crisis. The next day he quit school so that he could spend more time helping his mother. Frau Voltz was grateful for this help but was also a little embarrassed. I assured her that it was my duty to assist in this time of need. Harry brought back a load of food for the family including flour, salt, cornmeal, and cans of fruit.

Harry and I stopped in New Braunfels to visit the family and to become better acquainted with Wilhelm. He was a big baby who liked to eat. He was very friendly and liked for me to walk him around the room and talk to him on the front porch. His face lighted up when he saw Dorothea, and I had never seen her smile so big as when Wilhelm put his arms to her to be held.

In the spring I was ready to start the process of stacking the large slabs of rock to make the walls of my house. I hired a boy from town to help me with the heavy loads. We also went far into the Hill Country and cut large cedar trees which would be used for the beams in the roof. The house had two bedrooms and one large room which served as the kitchen and sitting room, just like PaPa's house and Fritz's house.

One day as I was working on lifting the large roof beams, a rider from town came to Silverbrook and said that Herr Musbach needed to see me immediately. I quickly saddled the gray horse and went to town. When I arrived at Herr Musbach's office I was surprised to see Anka, the Indian, waiting for me. Anka shook my hand and asked several questions about my new house. Then he announced that he had come to Herr Musbach to ask his permission to invite me to accompany the U. S. Army, under the command of Captain Lancaster, on a long trip. He explained that the United States was going to eventually establish a line of Forts into West Texas in order to encourage exploration, settlement, and commerce there. Before this could be done a road, or trail, would have to be scouted for future use. Captain Lancaster knew that I had experience in traveling, surveying, Indian fighting, and hunting and hoped that I would join in this expedition. I explained that I was in the middle of house building and I would be able to come in about one month. Anka explained that I would have to come immediately. Herr Musbach asked how long this trip would take, and we were both shocked when Anka replied that the trip would be about one year in length. Anka excused himself so that we could discuss the offer in private. Herr Musbach said that it would be good if the people of Fredericksburg sent one of their own on this trip. It would prove that our town supported the U. S. Army in establishing Forts and maybe, one day, a Fort could be established in Fredericksburg. Because Anka helped in making our peace with the Indians, it would be good to repay him in this way. I explained that my house was not yet completed and that Harry and I had our business. Herr Musbach said that Harry could run the business by himself and that I really had no deadline on completing my house. Herr Musbach would give me a horse to ride and make sure that my properties were well taken care of. I went to the store and told Anka that I would be ready to go the next morning. He was happy to hear this news and we both went to dinner with Fritz and Katherine. After Anka excused himself to sleep in the barn, Fritz and I had a long talk about him taking care of my business and my property while I was away. I was especially worried about the upkeep of the gray horse. I was thankful that Herr Musbach had given me another horse to ride, for I did not want to make the gray walk for a whole year. I hugged Katherine and shook Fritz's hand and they both told me to have a safe trip. I went to Zeller Haus and wrote a will, just in case I lost my life on this trip. In case of my death I left all of my property equally between Dorothea and Wilhelm. I wrote a long letter to PaPa and took it to Harry so that he could deliver it next week. Harry was going to start a regular weekly mail run between Fredericksburg and New Braunfels. I went back to Zeller Haus and packed my clothes, cleaned my boots and rubbed oil on them, cleaned my rifle and hand gun, and then read the Bible and prayed.

I was awake by dawn and, after eating some sausage and a few pecans, I took the gray horse to Fritz's barn where I brushed his back and gave him some oats. I put my arms around his neck and told him that this was not going to be a trip that he would enjoy and that he would be more comfortable at home. For just a moment, when I looked into his black eyes, I became very sad and felt sorry that Herr Zeller was no longer with us. I then turned and walked down the street to pick up the horse that Herr Musbach had contributed. He was a fine bay stallion named Schnell, which means fast, for he was taller than the other horses in the pen and was a fast runner. This ability could become very important in dangerous situations. I took him to Zeller Haus and packed my few belongings and then met Anka at Fritz's store. We set out on our trip to San Angelo to begin a new adventure in my life away from my German family.

Chapter 8

The West Texas Adventure

We had an uneventful trip to San Angelo and Fort Concho where I was assigned a bunk with the soldiers. The next morning I was awakened by a bugle and I jumped from my bed to accompany the men to the foot of the flag pole where the beautiful Unites States flag was raised. After breakfast in the mess hall, Anka and I went to Captain Lancaster's office. He greeted me with a handshake and introduced me as a surveyor, hunter and Indian fighter sent from the German settlements. There was a total of 20 soldiers plus Captain Lancaster, Anka and me who would be going on the West Texas Expedition of 1849. Some of the men were seasoned soldiers and about 8 of the men were new recruits who were young and not yet experienced. They were from the Eastern and Southern states. Our mission was to survey and mark the path for a future road between San Antonio and the town of El Paso in far West Texas. This was a territory that was heavily traveled by the raiding Indians and was considered very dangerous. Anka and I would be scouts going before the survey party each day to look for possible routes, to hunt, and to be aware of possible attacks. The survey party would be guarded at all times and there would be night guards as well. A cook would accompany the group and there would be no complaining about the food nor would drunkenness be allowed. Privately I was thinking about Mati's good noodles and that it would be a while before I ate sausage again. As the meeting ended Captain Lancaster told me to remain in his office. When everyone else had gone, he thanked me for accepting the job and explained that my pay of $25 per month would be kept at the Fort and would be given to me upon our return. He explained that I would be treated no better, nor any worse, than the soldiers. We spent the afternoon studying the maps with the surveyor. The maps were inadequate because the Western territory was seldom traveled. We would do extensive surveys and try to improve the maps during our trip.

I had decided that I should make the best of the situation and try to quit worrying about my house, my horse, and business at home in Fredericksburg. I would spend this time as a learning experience, just as if this were a university.

The next morning, after a large breakfast of cornbread, eggs, and fried steak we loaded all of our gear and departed from Fort Concho headed in a Southeastern direction, for we would begin our journey in San Antonio. The area to the south was a sea of grass which was brown, but Spring would be coming soon and the new grass will be bright green. We camped on the San Saba River the second night and on the Llano River the fourth night. In this area the Llano River flowed through a large valley about ten miles in width. It was very beautiful and would one day be a prime farming community. This area was to the West of Fredericksburg. We continued until we came to very steep canyons and it was difficult to bring the three wagons through the rocks. We all took turns chopping trees and moving rocks to make a path for the mules pulling our gear. After another 2 days we found ourselves on the edge of the beautiful Texas Hill Country overlooking the plains below. Texas was vast, wild and beautiful with crystal clear streams of water and large oaks. We descended from the hills and continued down to arrive in San Antonio on the twelfth day. We set up our tents and camped near the San Pedro Springs at the edge of the town. We got fresh vegetables from a farmer including carrots and potatoes. They were so good that Captain Lancaster purchased five more sacks of these vegetables to sustain us for several more days. It was complicated to feed 24 people breakfast and supper each day. At dinner we ate leftovers. We also had 50 horses and 18 mules to feed and water. I spent all afternoon writing letters to PaPa and to Dorothea, for I feared that they would be unhappy with me for departing on this expedition without telling them farewell in person. I also wrote a letter to Fritz re-emphasizing the importance of caring for the gray horse and my properties.

After I had written the letters and taken them to the downtown post office, I would try to quit worrying about these things and begin to think more about the expedition. Captain Lancaster told the soldiers that they must be in bed by midnight and that we would depart at 6:00 o'clock in the morning. He dismissed the men and they ran quickly to town to begin to eat, drink and be merry. San Antonio was a good place for those diversions, for there was a bar on practically every corner and there were many places to eat on the street. I walked along the streets and watched as the Plaza filled with people. A man tried to sell me medicine which he said would save my life if I was bitten by a rattlesnake. I had to decline, for I had no room in my saddlebags. I saw a pair of beautiful shiny black boots that I would like to own, but they were more than a month's wages. Again I went to the bridge called Commerce and stood over the green waters of the San Antonio River. I spoke to an older couple who were on their way to visit their daughter's family on the other side of the plaza. They were Spaniards but spoke very good English. They were interested in why I had left Germany and come to such a place as this. I explained to them that there was much opportunity for economic growth here. They agreed, but pointed out that life was also very dangerous in this new state called Texas. They encouraged me to visit the Eastern part of the United States and highly recommended that I visit New Orleans. I stopped in the large cathedral and kneeled at one of the side alters to pray for our safety and success in accomplishing our mission of leading the way for future development in the West. I also prayed for my family, and especially for Oma back in Germany.

I went to bed at about 10 o'clock, but was rudely awakened when the soldiers began to return to the camp just before midnight. They talked loudly and one came into my tent by accident and began to remove his boots. I said, "Excuse me" and he jumped up to his knees and crawled out of the tent very quickly. About that time there was noise outside as two men began to fight. The others stood and watched until shortly later when Captain Lancaster came from his tent. The fight broke up immediately and everyone went quickly to their tents.

The next morning the cook began to rattle the pans at 5:00 o'clock. The bugle was not used for waking the soldiers when on a mission such as this, because it was too loud and could draw Indians to our camp. Everyone, including me, pulled on their pants and boots and stood at attention near the flag. Captain Lancaster announced that we would eat breakfast and depart at 6:00 o'clock. Anka had begun the task of leading the animals to drink and to graze on the grass near the spring. We ate biscuits and fried potatoes and departed through downtown San Antonio. The few people on the street so early in the morning watched as we passed, and some even removed their hats as the United State flag approached. I felt proud to be a part of the United States Army, even though I was not officially a soldier. Captain Lancaster led the group, followed by the Sergeant, Anka and I, the cavalrymen, the three wagons, and finally the herd of spare horses and mules.

We continued all day and finally ended up at the Medina River near the town of Castroville, which was a French/German community. I went to the bakery and bought a loaf of bread and a coffee cake, and then I purchased 5 links of hard sausage from the store which I would keep in my saddlebags. The town of Castroville reminded me of Fredericksburg and I felt a little home sick. I bought a book about great cities of the world to keep me occupied at night.

The next morning we departed the town at 6:00 o'clock and saw smoke coming from the houses and smelled bacon frying. I waved to a young girl who was standing beside a milk cow, with an empty bucket, getting ready to milk. When I waved she smiled and nodded her head in return. The first day on the trip was uneventful as Anka and I killed two deer for the group to eat that night. The cook said that we did a good job and that he hoped we were able to keep up the good work. The cook was an old man who had been in the army for a long time. He was rough talking, but I could see that he appreciated being treated with respect. Captain Lancaster presented me with a Colt Revolver which would shoot 5 rounds in succession. The gun felt very heavy in my hand and I needed practice. The Captain gave me permission to shoot at targets. I quickly adapted to the new feel of the pistol and was able to beat most of the other men who challenged me to a shooting contest. This pistol would be of great value if we had to fight the Indians. I was also given a heavy belt which had loops all around it filled with extra bullets.

We continued for 3 more days camping at the Sabinal River and then the Frio River. Anka said that the word Frio means cold however, when I soaked my feet in the river, the water was not cold at all. We eventually came to a beautiful spring called Las Maras. We camped by the spring and I spent most of the evening helping to feed and water the horses and mules. I attached a rope to Schnell's halter and led him away from camp to a nice green pasture. I sat on the ground while he chewed very slowly and enjoyed his meal. I then gave him water and brushed his back. As I walked back to the camp, Private Adams asked me if I had fed my horse. When I replied "Ya" instead of "yes", Private Harris began to laugh at me. He said, "German boys should stay in Germany." I could feel my face turning red, but I was able to control my anger and walk past him in silence. This was the first time that anyone in the group has mentioned that I was German. I was proud to be German, and was sorry that Private Harris felt that Germans were not worthy to be in Texas. I stayed in my tent the rest of the night and tried to read my book.

We traveled 4 more days on a fairly good trail and arrived at the town of Del Rio on the Mexican border. The Rio Grande was a large river, by Texas standards, which was brown in color and about 50 yards across. On the other side we could see a small town of huts made from brush. The town of Del Rio was not much better in appearance. It was dusty and dry with a bar located in a well worn tent. There were 3 houses made of brush and a store made of rock. The store keeper was a tall man with a large mustache who laughed at me when I asked if he had a newspaper. He said that I could buy a book which was left there by a traveler. I paid 25 cents for a book about pirates raiding in the oceans and then going to a secret island.

We camped at the San Felipe Springs. Anka and I got up before 5:00 and started to water and feed the animals. Before long everyone was awake and standing before the American flag. We then ate and continued on our journey. I filled my canteen from the clear spring which was near the banks of the Rio Grande. I saw several women on the other side of the river who were bringing their dirty clothes to begin washing. Children were running before them and one was leading a donkey to water. I wondered what life is like in that country called Mexico just to the south of Texas. Anka said that it was a good place, but the people were poor and there was no government protection along the borders. He had heard that Mexico is a very large country and that the capital city was very far away from this border. We continued our journey with Anka and I riding ahead and finding the best route for the wagons. We came upon several small rivers, or creeks, which had to be crossed. This was difficult because the mud was very deep in the creek bed. We used all 18 mules to pull the wagons through the mud which took several hours of work. The next time we came upon a creek we would test the footing carefully before leading the group across. We found a small stream of water coming from large boulders where we camped for the night. As soon as we made camp I walked about two miles away where I was able to kill a deer for the next days meals. It was good that I liked to eat corn bread and biscuits because that is mostly what we had to eat, along with pinto beans and deer meat. The country here was desolate, with no people and mile after mile of rocky ground with little grass.

We came to many steep and rugged canyons. Captain Lancaster halted the group and there was a meeting. It was decided that we would break into 3 groups. One group would continue to survey and draw maps, one group would take care of the animals and try to find grass, and Anka and I would take our gear and move forward to try to find out what lies ahead. We would report back to this camp in 4 days. The surveyor gave me paper and pencil so that I could make notes about the terrain, and he told me to try to draw a map as I traveled.

Anka and I set out alone that afternoon and followed the Rio Grande. We kept an eye on the sun as it made its progress toward the West. That night we pitched our tents behind large rocks and ate some of my hard sausage. I slept from 7:00 until midnight when Anka wakened me to take my guard duty from midnight until 5:00. I sat on a rock and looked at the stars. My thoughts turned to my family and to the gray horse. I looked at Schnell who was standing very still with one foot at rest. He was a good horse, but I missed the gray. I thought of Fritz and Katherine and their warm house and good food. I also thought about Captain Kerr and where he might be now. I thought about traveling to New Orleans and perhaps even to the Eastern United States just to see what it was like.

The next day we traveled slowly and I made notes. We came to a steep canyon and then searched all afternoon for a good place for wagons to make a descent. It was very steep but we found a place that was very wide and could be used as a trail.

Many rocks would have to be moved and the wagons would not be able to go straight down. They would have to switch back and forth and make a gradual descent into the canyon. I had seen this done many times in Germany where the mountains were steep. When we finally reached the banks of the river we saw that there was very little water and it was quite muddy. We later found out that the name of the river was Devils River.

On the fourth day we reported back to the camp where we enjoyed a hot meal of fried deer meat and corn bread. The next morning the entire group moved to make a new camp at the Devils River. Anka and I again set out to search for our future while the others stayed at the camp and built a switchback road down to the river and up the other side.

In three days Anka and I were at the Pecos River which was very well known. We were in a forbidding desert with little water and grass. The ground was a light color with scattered thorny bushes. We drank from our canteens and cut stickers from the bushes so that the horses could eat the leaves. We were greatly relieved when we found the Pecos River even though we had to dismount and lead our horses down the steep animal path to its banks. We did not see a crossing for wagons anywhere in sight.

The next morning we started back to the main camp and eventually found them still working on the road out of the Devils River. We stayed with them for two days. Anka and I had a meeting with Captain Lancaster and the head surveyor where we studied the maps to try to gain information about the Pecos River. It was decided that we would accompany the crew to the Pecos River the next day. We filled all of our barrels with water and loaded them on the wagons, for we knew that there was little to eat or drink between the Devils River and the Pecos River. All during this time Anka was constantly trying to teach me Indian words, both in Comanche and Apache, so that I could have a small conversation in that language. It was a rough trip to the Pecos River. When we finally arrived everyone was amazed at the steep canyon in which the river flowed. We had to carefully make a trail to take the animals to water. One of the mules became over anxious because he was so thirsty. He broke away and started going down the bank at a run. Everyone was shouting and two men tried to catch the mule. Suddenly there was a large cloud of dust and quite a loud noise. As soon as the dust began to clear we saw that the mule had lost his footing and had tumbled down the side of the bank. He was lying near the water's edge kicking and flailing his body. We were all busy holding onto our own horses and mules and could only take our time in getting them down the steep canyon safely. When we arrived at the river the animals and men rushed to the water and began to drink. Soon the men were jumping into the river with their boots on. I yelled to them that the water was deep, but no one seemed to mind. About that time one of the men, by the name of Chester, began to wave his hands and was sinking under the water. Two of the men swam to his rescue. They brought him to the shore where he lay on the ground panting for air and saying that he could not swim. He did not expect the water to be deep since the Devils River had been so shallow. The mule that had fallen was dead by the time we reached it.

During the night we heard coyotes fighting and eating the dead mule below by the river. The next morning we moved up river about two miles, made a new camp, and a crew worked on making a safer trail down to the water. This was where I unpacked my fishing hook and was able to catch several large catfish which was appreciated by everyone that night.

In looking at the map we saw that at the Pecos River the Rio Grande takes a sharp turn to the south. Since we were looking for the fastest route to El Paso we would not continue to follow the Rio Grande. We wanted to go due West, but Anka said that he knew there was a terrible desert there. Also the canyon was too steep to get the wagons across at this point of the Pecos River. Anka and I left the group again and followed the Pecos River to the North looking for a place to cross.

On the second day Anka and I had our first encounter with a group of Apache Indians. We were riding beside the Pecos River at about noon when Anka suddenly motioned to halt. We stood still for a few moments and I followed Anka's gaze to our right where we saw dust in the air. We had previously talked about what to do in case of an attack. We had decided to stay away from the steep canyon and to run across country. If we could find a gully we would ride into it and then dismount to fight the Indians as they approached. It is very strange to say, but this was exactly what happened to us. We started running our horses in hopes of finding a gully. We saw the Indians divert from their path and come after us. As we ran I put my canteen around my neck as well as a small leather bag containing extra bullets.

I had my Colt Revolver in my belt and carried my rifle in my hand. Being a very fast runner, Schnell passed by Anka's horse and soon I saw a gully about 100 yards to our right. I turned and Anka followed. As we approached the gully I dismounted and quickly led Schnell down into the gully with Anka and his horse following. I dropped the reins and carefully looked up from the gully to see a band of about 8 to 10 Indians coming in a mass of dust towards us. Anka was beside me and my heart was bouncing inside my shirt. Anka said to wait until they were near. About that time the lead Indian spotted us and they all began to slow their horses. Three of the Indians continued to come upon us and as they neared I shot the first, Anka shot the second, and I shot the third. The first Indian fell to the ground with a thud, but the second and third slumped on their horses and rode back towards the group. I reloaded my rifle and revolver and waited. The band of Indians stood just out of rifle range and looked at us. It was obvious that they were trying to determine what to do next. About that time Anka stood up and shouted words to them in the Apache language. There was a short conversation between Anka and the lead Indian shouting back and forth. Anka came back down into the gully where I was lying on my stomach trying to peer over the edge. Two of the Indians came towards us and I was ready to shoot, but they stopped and picked up the wounded Indian, put him on his horse, and they all started running away from us. Anka and I stared at them until they were out of sight. We both sank down to the ground and sat down. Anka looked at me and began to laugh loudly. He said, "You brown Indian". I wiped my face on my sleeve and it was covered with brown dirt. I must have been sweating on my face and the brown dirt in the gully had stuck to my skin. I got out my handkerchief and wiped by face and I began to laugh with Anka. He said that we must find a new hiding place for fear that the Indians might return. As we trotted our horses across the barren sand I asked Anka what he had said to the Indians. He said, "I am Anka, the son of Lodbe". The enemy said, "Why do you speak my language?" Anka replied, "Because I grew up in the home of Geronimo." The enemy replied, "We will gather our wounded and depart." And so they did.

We trotted our horses for about 3 miles and found a large gully which ran into the banks of the Pecos River. We watered our horses and hid there that night with each taking a turn at guard. The Indians did not come back.

After many days of riding along the Pecos River the steep canyon finally began to level off and ahead of us was a beautiful creek flowing into the Pecos River. We determined that this was a major Pecos River crossing used by the Indians and that this should be the next camp for the soldiers. In the next 3 days we made our way all the way back to what we called the Dead Mule Camp. We stayed in the camp for two days resting and then the group started the journey to the crossing that we had found.

It was a welcome relief to once again find the beautiful creek that had trees. We named it Live Oak Creek and we named the crossing on the Pecos River for Captain Lancaster. Several years later Fort Lancaster was built there.

Anka and I crossed the Pecos River and went West. This was a very dry dessert and we each took a pack mule carrying kegs of water and food. On the second day we saw fresh tracks of 3 horses. We turned and followed them until we saw a clump of small trees in the distance. We tied the animals and quietly crept closer to the trees where we saw a small hut made of sun dried bricks and 4 goats. We got our animals and led them toward the house rifles in hand. When we got 100 yards from the house, Anka whistled in a certain way. Then we stood still. In a few moments there was a man standing in front of the house with a rifle looking for us. Anka waved and said "I am your Apache brother" (I understood this). The man motioned for us to come near. We again stopped and Anka and the man had a longer conversation. He introduced me to the man using the Comanche language and I replied in that language using most of my Comanche vocabulary in the first 30 seconds. The man invited us into his home where there was a wife and a son of about 12 years of age. We were given goat's milk and a piece of roasted rabbit. The man and his family were nomads who spend the summers in the North and then returned to the South for the winter season. They brought 10 goats with them and they would trap and hunt for food. When they found this well and house they decided to stay there for a while. They had been there for over 20 days and had seen no one but us. Anka talked to the man for hours and the man drew maps in the sand directing us to water West of here. The man had been to El Paso many times to trade goat cheese for corn meal to make tortillas. His name was Barancha and he was of Comanche origin. As he drew the maps in the sand I tried to copy them onto my notebook. That night we camped near the house and I carefully studied the stars to try to chart our location. It got very cold at night and my blanket did not seem to help much. During the day the sun was very hot. In the morning I pulled a bucket of water from the well and when I looked into the water I saw my reflection. I did not recognize myself, for my hair was long and I had a slight beard. Anka laughed and said that I was as brown as a Mexican now, except that my blue eyes were a reminder that I was European. Anka asked if we could bring the survey crew to this area to rest near the water, and the man replied that it would be acceptable. I gave him a package of pinto beans as a gesture of good will.

Within several days Anka and I were back at the Lancaster Crossing and relaxing in camp. We had a meeting to convey our new knowledge to Captain Lancaster and the chief surveyor.

In about 12 days we arrived back at the well and house of sun dried bricks. Anka whistled but no one came out of the house. The soldiers were a mile away waiting for us to signal them to come. Anka whistled again and still there was no answer. I stood guard while Anka walked slowly to the house with his rifle pulled up to his shoulder. He opened the door and went inside, and in a moment he motioned for me to come. We were surprised to find no one in or near the house and there were no goats in sight. Where had the people gone, and why did they go? We would never know the answer to those questions. We searched the ground for signs of other visitors, but all we found was a small trail leading to the North with goat dung along the way. Maybe the people just decided to move along to a cooler climate. We signaled for the soldiers to come, and everyone was quite relieved to find the well and the grove of small trees where we could rest from the hot sun.

Our next trip took Anka and I Westward to try to find a spring called Comanche. It was a good thing that we had taken kegs of water on our pack mules, for we used it all before we finally found the spring 9 days later. There were many horse tracks around the spring and we knew that it was used by many Indians. We approached it carefully and took turns standing guard while the other drank and swam. We camped about 2 miles away in some rocks, and the next day we drank and refilled our kegs and headed back to the well camp. I now had 18 large rattles taken from rattle snakes that I had killed in or near camp. On this trip I had killed at least 50 deer, 70 rabbits, and 2 antelope. There was not much to shoot in this wilderness, but most animals would go to the springs at night and this is when we were able to kill enough for the soldiers to eat.

A week later we moved the camp to the rocks near Comanche Springs. The surveyor had made note that this would be a good place for a future fort, as long as the soldiers could keep the Indians away from the springs. Maybe this would even be a town someday in the future.

We knew from talking to the Indian man that there was another spring to the West called Mescalero. So Anka and I set out on yet another journey to find the new place. We did have some trouble along the way. My pack mule broke his leg by stepping in a hole and, because he was in great pain and we could not help him, I had to shoot him. This was a very difficult thing for me to do. That night I had dreams about the gray horse and I woke up wondering if Fritz was taking proper care of him. We drank all the water that we could from the kegs that had been on the back of the dead mule and let our horses and the other mule drink all they could. We hid the remaining kegs of water in a certain place in case we needed them on our return trip. Two nights later it began to rain. This was the first time we had seen rain on the entire trip. It rained on and off most of the night.

I was on guard duty, and just before daylight I heard a loud noise to our left. Just then Anka jumped from his blanket with his rifle in hand. We continued to stare into the darkness listening and we realized that we heard water running. We packed up our gear and by daylight we rode towards the sound. About 25 yards from our camp was a large gully which was full of water and roaring very loudly. We dismounted to stare in disbelief, and then I knelt down on my knees and thanked God for keeping us safe from this torrent. Anka said that rain in the desert could be very dangerous and we must be aware to make camp on high ground if it rains.

Two days later we saw dust in the distance. We went slowly in that direction trying to remain behind rocks and bushes, and we tried not to make dust. Finally we tied our animals and climbed a small hill where we saw, about a mile away, approximately 100 or more Indians at the large, blue, cold Mescalero Springs. We quickly went back to our horses and found a hiding place in tall bushes where we stayed all afternoon. When it got dark we walked our animals to the same hill and again crept closer to look. There were still many Indians camped at the springs. We needed water badly for our kegs were almost empty and the horses kept putting their noses up to smell the fresh water over the hill. We went back to a different hiding place a little further away and waited all the next day and the next night. In the middle of the night we went back to look at the spring and there was no one in sight. We waited until daylight to be sure no one was nearby and then quickly went to the spring and drank and filled our kegs with water. We started back to the Comanche Springs camp. We eventually used the water in the kegs we had left near the dead mule and were quite relieved when we arrived back in camp. We rested and enjoyed eating the cook's hot food.

All the time that we were away the soldiers had been making a road based on small pieces of rope which we tied along the way to show the trail. The men worked very hard in the hot sun and went back to the springs each night. After two days we moved the group to the Mescalero Springs area. The soldiers hid 3 miles away and Anka and I slowly and quietly approached the spring. There were 3 Indians there so we quietly waited in hopes that they would leave. After about an hour we heard them depart. We watched carefully from our vantage point and saw no one coming to the spring. Then we started back to get the soldiers and bring them to the water. When we got about a mile from the soldiers hiding place we saw a great deal of dust and soon we began to hear shooting guns. We stopped our horses and had a quick discussion about what to do. We decided to tie our horses in a gully and creep closer to see what was happening. Within a few minutes we saw 15 to 20 Indians riding very fast in our direction. We crawled under some bushes and hoped that there were no rattlesnakes there. I got cactus thorns in my arm but laid very still as the horses ran within 30 yards from us. We waited a few minutes and then quickly made our way back to our own horses for fear that the Indians had see us or had discovered our horses. I was greatly relieved to see Schnell still standing where I had tied him. We mounted and made a circle to the West of the soldiers camp. Soon we heard men shouting and saw more dust, but we did not hear any gunfire. I told Anka that this was not a good time to go riding into camp because we might be shot by the soldiers. We dismounted and Anka called out towards the camp shouting "Captain Lancaster this is Anka". The camp suddenly became quiet and someone shouted back, "Who is with you?" I then replied, "This is Nicholas Steubing from Germany". The guard shouted, "You may enter the camp." We walked our horses and kept our pistols in our hands. As we neared the camp we saw many rifles aimed at us, but as soon as we were identified everyone stood up and welcomed us back. They had just repelled an attack by about 30-40 Indians who had come upon them as they were sitting and waiting for us to return. There were 3 wounded men, 2 dead Indians and 1 severely wounded Indian. We broke camp very quickly and moved back to the same gully where we had tied our horses. Anka and I crept closer to the spring and saw no one there. One third of the men encircled the gear, one third of the men encircled the spring with their rifles ready to fight, and the other third of the men led the animals to water and filled the many barrels. Anka and I made a quick ride to find a temporary camping place. We returned about an hour later and led the group 3 miles South to a large outcropping of rocks at the bottom of a large hill. This is where we camped for the next 3 days.

Each day we took the animals to the spring and everyone drank. On the fourth day we again filled all of our barrels and began a new journey West through the Mountains. We knew that over these mountains we would find a mountain shaped like an eagle and that there were springs nearby. Anka and I carefully went approximately one mile ahead of the group to search for a trail and to look for Indians. The going was slow but we were able to make our way through these rugged canyons even with the wagons. We mostly followed game trails left by buffalo and antelope. Finally, on the twelfth day, Anka spotted the Eagle Mountain which he had seen before when traveling with his father. We went to the South of the Mountain and there found the Eagle Spring. It was very quiet there and we found no signs of anyone having been at the water for quite some time. Everyone was very tired so we stayed here for one week to rest. While we were there the head surveyor told me that the date was September 18. I realized that somewhere along the trail I and turned 19 years of age and I did not even know when it was my birthday. This was my fifth birthday in the great state of Texas. I remembered the day in Bicken, Germany when I looked on the teachers globe to try to find the state of Texas. I feared that Oma had now passed away and I wondered about Tante Gretchen. Homesickness had overcome me. I took my German Bible to the edge of the camp and began to read it softly to myself just to hear my mother tongue. Would my family still love me when I returned? Did life go on as usual in Fredericksburg? Would I ever get to know little Wilhelm? I hoped Dorothea did not marry while I was away, for I wanted to be a part of that celebration. Was Mati still smiling and was PaPa still happy? I hoped that Fritz and Katherine were enjoying their beautiful house.

Anka and I left the group to find a way over the Sierra Blanco Mountains. After 4 days we met a group of Indians as we entered a canyon. They were sitting on the ground eating meat and talking loudly. As soon as we heard them there were two armed guards standing before us. Anka began to talk to them in the Comanche language and we were soon in the camp eating with them. Anka knew two of the men in the group and he was a distant cousin of another. They greatly appreciated my attempts to speak their language and they laughed loudly when I choked while smoking a pipe that they insisted I try. We actually spent the night in their camp and, as I was lying there looking at the stars, I could not believe that this was really happening to me. I was amazed at how like us these men were. They laughed and joked and told stories. One told me that he had 4 children in Mexico and he was going there now to see them. He said that his wife was very beautiful and his little daughter would run to him and grab him by the legs when she saw him coming. I felt sorry that the settlers had to fight with these people. I felt sorry that I had killed some Indians and that an Indian killed Herr Zeller. I asked God for guidance to help me to understand life.

The next day we told the Comanches good bye and I was presented with a necklace made from a piece of rawhide which had 3 shells from the Concho River tied in the middle. I placed the necklace around my neck and thanked the men in the Comanche language. Anka and I continued our trip and, with new information gained from the Comanches, we easily made our way through the mountains. We back tracked to the soldiers camp and had a wonderful hot meal of antelope stew with pinto beans and cornbread. In a few days we led the entire group through the Sierra Blanco Mountains and continued West until we met the Rio Grande. We turned in a northwesterly direction and followed the river. We came to two Spanish Mission ruins at San Elizario and then at Socorro. They were built for the Tigua Indians who still resided there and were quite friendly. I was offered a goat for my Concho shell necklace, but I refused. The Tigua Indians treated us to delicious pinto beans and tortillas and I drank my fill of goat's milk. We continued on to Ysleta where we visited more friendly Indians and had more tortillas and goat's milk. This was good for, even though I had grown taller, my pants were very loose and I knew that I had lost much weight. I was sure that warm goat's milk would give me renewed energy.

It was a beautiful day on November 20, 1849 when we finally arrived at our destination in El Paso. Actually we camped at Franklin Village on the North side of the town where a new Fort would be established. Anka and I went to El Paso and I bought a shirt and pants. I needed new boots but I did not have enough money to buy them. I ate many tortillas and drank beer for the first time in a year. I got so lively that I even danced with a beautiful señorita. When I arrived back at the camp I was met by a very drunk Private Harris who pushed me to the ground. He said that Germans should not dance with Mexicans. I got up and pushed him and then he jumped up and came at me with his fists. I ducked and his fist hit me in the shoulder. I lifted my own fists and I hit him in the jaw. Immediately my hand hurt badly and before I could recover he hit me in the jaw. I hit him in the nose and he began to bleed. This startled me and I was unprepared when he kicked me in my ribs on the left side. I fell to the ground writhing in pain. He came upon me and began to hit me in the head. About that time Captain Lancaster took hold of Private Harris' shirt and pulled him off me. He ordered Private Harris to his tent and told me to go to the cook tent where I staggered and fell. The old cook looked at me on the ground and smiled. He said he never thought that I would end up like this. He poked my ribs, which hurt a great deal, and said that I was lucky that none of them were broken. He wrapped a long towel around my ribs, tied it very tight, and to leave it on for about a week. I walked very slowly to my tent where I laid for the next day. I finally went to the river to wash my face and when I saw my reflection I realized that my face was black and blue and that one eye was swollen. Anka asked me how I was doing and I replied, "It only hurts when I breathe." Anka laughed a great deal and said that I was a funny sight. Eventually Anka and I were called to Captain Lancaster's tent. We discussed what would happen next. It was decided that half of the company would stay at Franklin Village and establish a Fort led by Lt. Roberts. The other half of the company, led by Captain Lancaster, would follow our own trail back to civilization and San Antonio. By retracing our steps we could finalize our maps and erect markers showing the way for future travelers.

For the next two weeks I went to El Paso only a few times and I never drank beer. I did drink lots of goat's milk and ate as much meat as I could find. Private Harris ignored me from then on and this was fine with me.

The time finally came for us to depart and it was difficult to leave half of our group behind. Captain Lancaster asked for volunteers to stay in Franklin Village. When almost everyone volunteered he had to decide who would return with us back to San Antonio. Some of the men were unhappy with his choice because they dreaded the long trip through the dessert and mountains.

We back tracked following our own trail and rested on Christmas Day at Eagle Spring. I spent the day reading the German Bible and saying many prayers for my loved ones back home. If my calculations were correct we would arrive in San Antonio by Easter. My mouth watered as I daydreamed about Mati's delicious noodles and Frau Nagel's pecan pie. I thought about walking to the Church in New Braunfels on Christmas, and I could see PaPa bringing into the house the cradle he made for Wilhelm. I wondered if Fritz and Katherine went to New Braunfels for Christmas? I decided that when I got money I would buy all of them Christmas gifts, even if it was not Christmas.

Even though we were in the dessert the wind was very cold on our return trip. I wore three shirts almost every day and I was sorry I did not have a coat. It seemed that the Indians were not traveling much in the cold weather, for we did not see a single Indian on our return trip. It was difficult to find deer or antelope to kill for food and we often ate only beans or cornbread. Eventually we crossed the Pecos River and arrived at the town of Del Rio by Easter. There I attended a Catholic Mass and actually sat on a bench, which seemed odd after having been sitting on the ground or rocks for many months. Anka asked me if I would like to meet his family. I was very eager to meet them for I had often heard about them and I knew some of them by name. With Captain Lancaster's permission, we crossed the Rio Grande and went to the town of Cuidad Acuna where we bought 8 goats and herded them for about 7 miles to a small village on the Rio Grande. There were approximately 12 huts scattered about. We were greeted by many children who happily took over the control of the goats and herded them to a pen made from cactus plants. We rode to a nearby house where Anka was greeted by his sister, Mara, with many hugs. Other people came to see what the noise was all about, and Anka went from hug to hug, to handshake to handshake. Eventually he remembered that I was there and introduced me to the group. Several people shook my hand and welcomed me and I replied, "Gracias". They were all impressed that I spoke some Spanish and they thought it quite strange when I sometimes mixed Spanish and Comanche words all in one sentence. Immediately Anka's brother killed one of the goats and began to cook it over a fire. That night we had a feast of goat meat, tortillas, beans, and boiled cactus cut into small pieces. All that evening I could not keep my eyes away from looking at Mara's daughter, Anna. She was a very beautiful girl of about 14 or 15 years old. He long hair shone in the firelight. Every time I looked at her she was looking at me. If my face was not covered with a beard everyone would see it turning red with embarrassment. The next day I actually talked to Anna as she was looking for eggs that the chickens had laid in the bushes near the house. I only understood a portion of what she said, but it did not matter what she said, but how she said it. She would talk and then look at me and smile. Her dark brown eyes would reflect the light and my heart would melt. Before I knew it the whole day had passed by and all I had done was to follow Anna while she did her chores. That night I sat beside her when we ate out in the yard where it was cool. Anka and I slept in the yard near our horses. I spent half the night thinking about the poor people who were rich in spirit. I thought about Anna and what her life might be like here. Why should she live in a hut made of sticks and grass and have no shoes? A woman as beautiful as Anna deserved a better life. By the next morning I was sure that I was in love with Anna, but I did not know exactly what to do about my feelings. After we ate tortillas and eggs for breakfast, Anna came out of the hut carrying several shirts. She was going to the river to wash the shirts and I immediately got up and started to follow her. Anka grabbed my arm and gently pulled me back beside him. He said in a low voice, "Men do not go to the river to wash clothes." I felt embarrassed and smiled at him. We went to the next village to meet with the constable, or lawman who was in charge of the area. He was a friend to Anka and they talked so fast that I could not keep up with the conversation. I said only a few sentences during the visit. Anka and his friend drank a strong whiskey which I declined. I wanted to hurry and get back to see if Anna was finished washing clothes. I later helped Anna look for eggs and we had fun when a rooster decided that I was an intruder and began to chase me. That night Anka told me that I was a very different person here, for I was running from a rooster and searching for eggs. I admitted that I would do anything in order to be with Anna. Anka became very serious and he told me very sternly that we were not here to play with women and that tomorrow we would be departing. For the first time since I met Anka we had an argument, for I was not about to give up having fun with Anna just because he did not like it. The argument continued and I eventually said that perhaps I would like to take Anna back to Fredericksburg with me. Anka became enraged and he actually slapped me across the face so hard that I fell to the ground. I did not get up to fight him, I just remained seated there and asked Anka why this could not happen. He explained to me in a low voice that Anna would be married in a few months to a man that her parents had already chosen for her. He also explained that, even though the people there respected me, they would kill me if I tried to take one of their daughters away. Anka said that we must leave the next morning before anyone else suspects that I found Anna to be attractive. I was very sad and went quietly to my bedroll where I tossed and turned half the night feeling miserable. The next morning Anna served us eggs and tortillas and she smiled as our eyes met. I was very sad to leave her there for I knew that I would never see her again. Anka and I slowly rode across the Rio Grande and joined the soldiers in camp.

Within a week we were back in the city of San Antonio which looked very large and quite civilized. This was because I had been in the wilderness of West Texas for such a long time. I went to the large cathedral and thanked God for my return to San Antonio, and then I stood on the bridge called Commerce and peered at the river below. I had no money, and the only way to get the money that I had earned was to return to Ft. Concho with Captain Lancaster. It was difficult for me not to jump on Schnell and run all the way to New Braunfels to see my family. However, if I did that, I am sure that they would have been afraid of me, for I looked like a man from the wilderness. My skin had turned brown, my hair was to my shoulders, and I now had a real beard. There were holes in my pants, shirts and the soles of my boots. My hat was dirty and misshapen.

We left San Antonio and in 12 days were back at Ft. Concho. We ate heartily in the mess hall and the next day Anka and I were called to Captain Lancaster's office. He thanked us for our good work and, at the end of our meeting, he gave each of us a bag which contained gold coins totaling $350. We shook his hand and, as we were leaving, he said that he might be calling on us for help again when the Forts are being established. I thought to myself that I hoped I never had to go to the wilderness again. When we got outside Anka and I shook hands and I thanked him for being my teacher. He laughed and told me that he had learned many things from me as well. He said that he was going back to his sister's house to stay for awhile. I told him to give everyone there my regards. He winked at me as he turned away and mounted his horse. As he rode out of the fort I thought that this might be the last time that I would see him. I walked into the nearby town and went to the store to purchase 2 pairs of pants, 2 shirts, underwear, socks, boots, handkerchiefs, and a hat. I went to the barber who painfully removed my beard and cut my hair. I paid 25 cents to take a bath with real soap, and went to the stable and paid a young boy 10 cents to polish my saddle and brush my horse.

The next morning I departed Ft. Concho and spent the night with the Ackerman family bringing them a 5 pound bag of flour. They were doing well and had only 2 horses stolen by the Indians. I had not be alone in quite some time and I enjoyed my trip through the Hill Country. I practiced talking in German by telling Schnell how wonderful it would be to get home. Finally, after 4 days of riding, I could see the lights of Fredericksburg before me. It was too late in the evening to go visiting, so I took Schnell to the pen behind Zeller Haus and had a wonderful feeling of elation as I walked into my own home. I kneeled down beside my bed and thanked God for my safe return. My soft bed afforded me a good night's sleep, and when I awoke it was nearly 8:00 o'clock in the morning. I quickly fed Schnell and went to the stable behind Fritz's house to see the gray. As I neared the barn I became afraid that maybe the gray would not be there. But just then I caught a glimpse of him. He was staring at Fritz's house, looking for Fritz to come to feed him. I made a clicking noise with my teeth and the gray jerked his head around and saw me. He ran to the side of the pen where I grabbed his neck and hugged him and smelled his hair. I petted him on the face and neck and told him how much I had missed him and how glad I was to see him. I fed him several handfulls of oats and pulled out a bundle of hay for his morning snack.

About that time a dog was smelling my boots and there was Fritz coming to feed the gray. When he saw me he ran towards me and grabbed me by the shoulders and we spun around in a circle until we began to stumble. We laughed loudly and Fritz slapped me on the back and welcomed me home. It felt good to be speaking the German language. He said that all was well here at the moment and that there had been no major tragedies during my absence. I asked about my family and he said that they were all well. We walked to the house and into the back door where Katherine was washing dishes. When she saw me she grabbed a dishcloth to dry her hands as she bounded into my arms and hugged me. My throat was very tight and it was a few moments before I could speak. We sat at the table as Katherine fried more eggs and bacon, and poured me a large glass of milk and a cup of coffee. We talked for half an hour before Fritz realized that it was past time to open the store. He got his hat and left quickly. As I helped Katherine put the dishes in the pan to be washed I realized that she was very large with child. She saw the look on my face and smiled. She said the baby was due in about a month. I walked out to the barn, put a saddle on the gray, and then rode up the hill near the town to the large cross. I got off and sat down on the ground and, for some unknown reason, I began to cry. After a while I felt much better and went to Herr Musbach's office to report on the expedition. We talked and drank coffee all morning and then went to Herr Musbach's house for dinner. After that we talked all afternoon on his front porch. He told me that he was very proud of my accomplishment in helping the U.S. Army with this expedition and that now I should work on my house. I said that first I must go to New Braunfels to see my family. As I was departing from his house I said that I would return Schnell to the stable. Herr Musebach replied that by all means I should keep the poor horse and let him rest. We both laughed and I thanked him for the gift. I went by Fritz's store, helped him close, and then went home with him for supper. We all had a jolly time talking about how Fritz became ill at the stomach every time Katherine became ill at her stomach when she was first with child. Katherine said that I must return from visiting in New Braunfels before her baby was born because she thought that Fritz would faint and need help.

The next morning I put Schnell in a nearby pasture where he would have lots of grass and water, mounted the gray and went by Fritz's store to buy gifts for my family. I departed by noon and rode quickly for 3 days to get to New Braunfels. I arrived there at about supper time and I had to hold myself back to keep from running the gray down Mill Street to PaPa's house. I arrived to find PaPa behind the house picking up wood. When I said "Pa Pa" he turned around, dropped the wood, and stood like a frozen statue. I went to him, put my arms around him, and hugged him. He almost began to cry when Mati came dashing out the back door and began hugging me and jumping up and down. On the porch stood Wilhelm with very large eyes wondering what all the excitement was about. He is a handsome boy with blue eyes and light blonde hair. I resisted the temptation to pick him up and hug him for fear that I would scare him. We went into the house and sat down to a delicious meal of ham, green beans and fresh bread. Mati assured me that she would be happy to cook noodles tomorrow. After supper I walked across the street and found Dorothea in the kitchen drying the dishes. We hugged and there was lots of squealing and excitement by all of the Nagel children. Frau Nagel just happened to have a half of a buttermilk pie which I ate in its entirety. Dorothea and I visited on the front porch until it was time for both of us to go tell Wilhelm good night. Dorothea told him to give me a good night kiss and he gently kissed my cheek. My heart melted, for I loved this little boy even though I hardly knew him.

The next day I visited all around town and met many new people as well. PaPa was one of the finest furniture makers in town and he took over the shop when his boss moved on to St. Louis. I played in the mud with Wilhelm and afterwards I put him in a bucket of water to clean him up. We laughed and I had to chase him around the yard to get the towel around him. Indeed Mati did make noodles and I cleaned up all of the bowls so that she had no left overs. That night Dorothea came to the door and invited me outside to meet her fiancee, Gunar Helmke. He had come from Germany only one year ago. He was a farmer with his father and he was 19 years old. I congratulated them and told them that I often wondered if I had missed Dorothea's wedding. I was pleased that I would be able to attend this event in October.

Chapter 9

Silverbrook

After two weeks of fun in New Braunfels it was time for me to go back to Fredericksburg to help Fritz through the crisis of childbirth. In the meantime I began work once again on my house. The day finally came on July 10 when I was called to town. There I found Fritz pacing back and forth on his front porch. I told him that it would be a long wait and we went to the store and made a pot of strong coffee. We both drank a cup and then took a cup with us and went back to the house to check. There was no word from within. We sat on the porch and I told Fritz many stories about West Texas in order to calm his nerves and to try to distract him from his worry. After a while Katherine's mother came outside and told us that the baby would be born very soon, and in a while we heard the baby crying. Fritz rushed through the door and I remained on the porch while he went in to meet his newborn son.

One month later I became the Godfather when Ernst Nicholas Nagel was baptized in the Lutheran Church. When it was time for my 20th birthday I went to New Braunfels to celebrate. We had a dinner with the

Nagel family where I enjoyed Mati's noodles and Frau Nagel's Pecan Pie. I spent a week helping my future brother-in-law, Gunar, with his corn harvest. I also helped shingle the roof of the small house he had built for Dorothea near his parent's house. His parents were older and they were very nice. Gunar was their only surviving son. The family told me many sad stories about Germany having a civil war and them loosing 2 sons in the fighting. I was very happy that I had come to Texas when I did. PaPa certainly made a good decision with God's help. Unfortunately my premonition about Oma's death was true. Tante Gretchen is now living out her old age with her niece. I found Gunar to be an honorable man and I was sure that he would make Dorothea a good husband.

Harry Knight, my dear friend, and I met in New Braunfels and we dissolved the Star Shipping Company. We sold all of the wagons, harnesses, mules and horses and divided the money equally between us. I told Harry to keep all of the profits which he made in my absence. Harry decided to go to New Orleans and do some gambling there. I promised that I would come there to visit in a few months.

Dorothea's wedding was a very exciting time. I took the groom to Victoria where I bought him a nice suit to wear and bought a beautiful veil trimmed in delicate lace for Dorothea. The couple was married on the porch of PaPa's house and the Nagels had a party for the new couple. Three nights later we all sneaked up to Gunar's little house, rattled the pots and pans, and got them out of bed for another party. Gunar's parents were very happy about this union and were hoping for many grandchildren.

I went back to Fredericksburg and continued to work on my house at Silverbrook. I wanted to have it ready by Christmas so that when my family visited they can see it. PaPa wrote me a letter and informed me that he was bringing some furniture. By Christmas the house was completed and I was very proud, but I was also very tired of being a carpenter. I drove a wagon to New Braunfels to pick up PaPa, Mati, Wilhelm, Herr and Frau Nagel and several of their younger children. We brought a second wagon which contained a bed, wardrobe, wash stand, table with four chairs, and two rocking chairs, all of which PaPa had made for my new house. We moved the furniture into Silverbrook and this was where PaPa, Mati and Wilhelm stayed through January. The Nagel family stayed at the Zeller Haus and I slept at Fritz's store. There were many parties since PaPa and the Nagels knew many people there. Mati was very well liked because of her jolly nature. I took Wilhelm horseback riding and we went fishing even though it was cold. I also took him hunting but he kept talking and scaring away the deer.

In late January I visited with Herr Musbach and told him about my intention to return my family to New Braunfels and then to continue on to New Orleans to see Harry Knight. He approved of this adventure and I felt good about going. I left both my horses in Fritz's care. We had one more dinner with Fritz and Katherine before we departed. It was hard to tell them goodbye and I kissed little Ernst on the forehead and hugged my friends.

We had a cold trip back to New Braunfels and one of the Nagel girls fell into the Guadalupe River. I had to jump in to save her and I got very cold and also ruined my boots. I wanted to scold her, but the Nagels were so upset about the incident that I bit my tongue and remained quiet.

Chapter 10

The Vagabond

In mid February I departed New Braunfels and got a ride on a wagon train headed to Galveston. I visited with a few people there and boarded a ship for New Orleans. It was very interesting to be back at sea after so long. I enjoyed looking at the stars and plotting our course with Captain Fromby. He said that he knew Captain Kerr and had seen him in Galveston about a year ago. I asked if Captain Kerr had gray hair yet and his reply was "no".

New Orleans was a big city and was very different from Texas. I had no idea how to find Harry Knight so I went to several bars and gambling houses. Finally a bartender pointed to a back room and said that Harry was there. I quietly opened the door and saw very thick cigar smoke which nearly choked me. There were several tables in the room surrounded by men playing poker. I tried to find Harry through the heavy smoke and finally I spotted him at one of the tables. I hardly recognized him because he was dressed in a black suit and had a fancy bow necktie. I stood near the table where others were standing and observing. It seemed that Harry was a big time player at this table. Finally the game was over and I was glad because my eyes were burning from the smoke. Harry stood up and walked forward and, when he recognized me, he grabbed my hand and shook it in a friendly manner. He invited me to go to breakfast, for it was just before daylight. We went to a fancy hotel dining room and had a large breakfast of eggs, ham, biscuits and a mush called grits. I did not eat this for it reminded me of my former journey in which we subsisted on corn meal mush. After breakfast we went to Harry's rented room in a boarding house and I slept on the floor.

We got up in late afternoon and went to supper in the boarding house. There was an interesting mixture of people at the table including 3 or 4 gamblers, river boat crewmen, a business man, and, believe it or not, there were 4 nuns who just arrived in the city to open a Catholic school. I felt a little embarrassed as the men all sat at a large table and told numerous yarns often using foul language. Sometimes they were reminded of the presence of the nuns and then garbled their curse words and became quiet. The nuns ate at a separate table in an adjoining room but they could surely hear all that was said.

After supper Harry and I walked along the docks where we saw ships and paddle wheelers. The Mississippi River was very impressive and I was thankful that we did not encounter such a river in West Texas. We went to several bars where the "painted ladies" would actually sit on our laps to serve up the drinks. I drank a beer at each bar, and by the fourth one I was getting very full. We went to a fancy place which served food and drinks and then there was a show, on a real stage, which featured dancing girls and beautiful singers. Harry was ready to go to his favorite gambling establishment. I did not think that I could stand the atmosphere full of cigar smoke, so I remained at the club and watched the same dancing show two more times. I finally went to see Harry play poker and put up with the smoke for more than two hours until the game had ended. Harry had won a moderate amount of money. We went to breakfast at the boarding house and I was able to take over a room for one week. This was fine for me because, even though the bed had bumps and lumps in it, it was still better than sleeping on the floor.

The next day I explained to Harry that I could not continue to go to bars and gambling casinos. He understood, and after that we met for supper every evening and had great fun together. I decided that I wanted to see the city from my own viewpoint. I talked to several men in the boarding house and was soon on the banks of the Mississippi River fishing. That night I had the cook fry fresh fish for Harry and I, as well as the nuns.

In conversation with the nuns I learned that their baggage was arriving that day from New York and I offered them my assistance. I rented a wagon and mules and met them at the dock where we claimed the baggage of approximately 5 crates and 14 large kegs. It took two trips to haul the baggage to their new school located in an old house next to the Catholic church. The house was old and dirty and they had been working every day to clean it. I helped with unloading the baggage and cleaning the rooms. We went to the market place and bought 10 chairs which could be used by the students. I suggested that they needed to find a better place to stay than at the boarding house. They all agreed with my assessment. They were spending $10 per week for room and board and we hoped to find another place for them to stay for this same amount of money. We talked to the priest, who talked to the caretaker of the church, who talked to his aunt, who had a neighbor with had a small house at the back of their larger house. We went to look at it and the nuns rented it for less money than they were paying at the boarding house. I helped them move all of their personal belongings from the boarding house to the new accommodations. This pleased them very much and they thanked me over and over again. I knew that the men at the boarding house would be pleased that the nuns were gone so that they could tell their stories and continue to curse without worry.

By the end of the week I had enough of city life and I was ready to move on. One of the workers on a paddle wheeler told me that his Captain was hiring men to do labor on the ship. I went to the Captain and was hired to help load the boat on their trip to St. Louis. I had supper with Harry to tell him farewell, and then went to the nuns and told them goodbye. I wrote a letter to PaPa and to Fritz and told them that I would be in St. Louis in about 4 weeks and that they could write me there in care of the St. Louis Shipping Company. The next morning I reported to my new job at daylight and worked the entire day loading kegs, barrels, bales of cotton, hay and cases of beer aboard the boat. We took off that night with about 12 passengers on board. My bed was a cot below deck in a small room with 5 other men sleeping and snoring very loudly. I eventually put on my clothes, went on the deck, and slept on a bale of cotton. It was very relaxing and the air was fresh. The next day we made 4 stops each time loading more goods and people onto the boat.

On the third day we arrived in the town of Natchez where we stayed overnight. I enjoyed a meal at a little restaurant on the main street, sat on the dock and read the newspaper. The next morning we continued our journey and the countryside was very beautiful. I scrubbed the decks, cleaned the kitchen, and ran coffee to the bridge where I got to talk to the Captain. We had an interesting conversation about coming across the ocean aboard ship because he used to be a seaman from England. Captain O'Toole was a stocky man with a red face. He explained to me that the Mississippi was a very treacherous river and that it took much experience to pilot its waters. Each evening after that I took the Captain a cup of coffee and we talked. Eventually he called upon me to do special errands and jobs for him. By the third week I was considered to be a crewman and no longer had to swab the decks or wash dishes. This was a very fast paced kind of life and I missed my slow rides through the Hill Country and speaking the German language.

When we arrived in St. Louis I immediately asked for my mail, and to my surprise I had 2 letters from PaPa and 1 letter from Fritz. Well, Katherine wrote the letter and Fritz signed it. My horses were doing well and little Ernst was growing. PaPa said that all was well in New Braunfels and, oh no, they would be having another child in the summer!

I bid Captain O'Toole farewell and thanked him for all that he taught me. He suggested that I continue on my journey to see the big city of Chicago. He gave me the name of a man who operates a shipping company who could probably use help with his horses and mules.

I visited the city of St. Louis for 5 days and then I departed on the work crew of Mr. John McGreggor who had 8 wagons filled with merchandise to take to Chicago. Mr. McGreggor was drunk most of the time and there was only moldy bacon and beans to eat. The other men were a crude bunch, except for one 14 year old boy who was very quiet. I eventually took over the duties of killing deer to cook for our meals and my status among the group was greatly improved. I also fished in the Illinois River and we had fried fish. I was greatly relieved to arrive in Chicago where there was real food and friendly people.

I walked along the shoreline of the lake and visited with people in the park. I visited 2 museums and read books in the large public library. I went to many shops and looked at the beautiful clothes and many items that were for sale there.

After one week I purchased a horse with an English style saddle and I rode all the way back to St. Louis. I spent each night with friendly farmers that I met, usually at a store or post office.

When I arrived back in St. Louis I was told that Captain O'Toole was departing the next morning for New Orleans. I sold my horse, making a small profit, and ran to the dock. I was just in time to get a job with Captain O'Toole for the return trip.

We arrived in New Orleans, and after a quick visit with Harry and the nuns, I sailed back to Galveston. There I bought a wagon and two mules and filled the wagon with goods for Fritz's store. I stopped at the former home of Herr Voltz but the house looked as though it had been vacant for some time. I asked about Frau Voltz in the town of Victoria and was told that she married a man who lived somewhere in East Texas.

I continued on for 4 days to New Braunfels where I had a happy reunion with my family in May 1851. After a week I continued on home to Fredericksburg where I was very happy to rest with my new furniture at Silverbrook. I spent all summer being a rancher and raising a large garden with many vegetables which I sold at Fritz's store.

I spent my 21 birthday in New Braunfels getting to know my new baby sister, Ella. I was very happy with this name because it reminded me of my friend Ella Brockoff who died of the fever. I always thought that I would some day marry Ella, but that was never to be. I went to Ella's grave and thought about what it would be like if she was with me at Silverbrook. Maybe we would have our own little girl by now. I also visited MaMa's grave and I knew that she was happy for all of us when she saw our lives here in Texas.

Chapter 11

To Build a Fortress

In the fall I went back to Fredericksburg and, before I got settled in for the winter, I was again called upon by Captain Lancaster. The army needed a guide and they could not find Anka for the last 6 months. I was asked to lead a Cavalry unit to Live Oak Creek on the Pecos River where Ft. Lancaster would be established. Captain Lancaster could not go because he had broken his leg when a horse fell on him.

I agreed, and we set out in October 1851 with a Cavalry unit of 50 men plus 40 more horses, 9 wagons, and 25 mules. Many of the wagons held tools such as saws, hammers and nails with which to build the fort. The trip was uneventful except that we got into a cold rain which lasted for several days.

We arrived at Live Oak Creek and then came the formidable task of building a fort when there was very little wood for construction. We eventually built two barracks, a commanders house, the mess hall, an office, and a barn all of rocks. We dismantled 3 wagons and used the wood to build the doors. We built a waist high rock fence around the buildings and placed large cactus plants on the outside of the fence. We traveled many miles to a cedar grove near the Rio Grande to cut posts to be used for the roofs of the buildings. And then we covered the posts with mud and grass as a temporary cover until shingles could be brought.

This construction took many months. Before Christmas I went to great effort to kill enough turkeys so that everyone could have a good meal. We dug a hole in the ground and built a fire in the hole. When the flames died down we wrapped the turkeys in burlap and placed them in the coals and covered them up with dirt. The next day, on Christmas morning, we uncovered the turkeys and they were cooked with a good flavor. A spent Christmas afternoon in my tent reading the German Bible.

In January I accompanied 10 men back to Ft. Concho where we ordered supplies. During this time I was able to make a quick trip on Schnell back to Fredericksburg for a visit. I had letters from PaPa saying that they were doing well. I wrote PaPa a letter and telling him that I was going back to Ft. Lancaster to continue the construction. I had several happy evenings with Fritz, Katherine and Ernst. The gray horse was doing fine and seems to like his easy life.

In February I went back to Ft. Lancaster with a large load of supplies including windows, lumber, and shingles. I began to lead troops out from the fort daily so that they could get an understanding of the land. We also studied maps and I showed them Indian trails.

We rode all the way to Mescalero Springs. This is where I had a very interesting experience. After we left the springs we accidentally met a group of about 30 Indians. There were only 10 soldiers. We immediately headed for the nearest gully where we dismounted and began to fight. We shot several Indians and 2 of our men were wounded. One wounded Indian got up on his feet and began walking towards me. I was about to shoot him when he fell to the ground and I thought that he was dead. After the battle had ended I saw the Indian and walked towards him carefully. I had noticed that his hair was brown instead of dark black. When I got near him he was groaning and I saw that he had been shot in the leg and in the arm. I got closer to him and saw his blue eyes looking at me. For a moment I was startled and then my mind raced trying to figure out what to do. I told the other men that I thought this was a white man dressed as an Indian. They brought him into camp and bandaged his wounds. He was very sick and the next day we put him on a horse and took him with us. We eventually took him back to Ft. Lancaster where we locked him in chains. I tried to talk to him and he was very defiant. When I gave him good food each day he eventually calmed down and I was able to talk to him in the Comanche language. He said that he was a Comanche, but I argued with him that his eyes were blue and his hair was brown. I kept talking to the man for several weeks and eventually he told me that he remembered that when he was a boy he lived with a white family. In July I took him to Ft. Concho where he tried to learn the ways of the white man. Eventually he said a few words in German and this really got my attention. Who could this man be? I began to question him in German and after about a week he was able to say his name—it was Louis! Could this possibly be Louis Oelke, the boy who was captured by Indians years ago? I was afraid to mention this to anyone but Captain Lancaster who suggested that I go to Fredericksburg and tell Herr Musbach. I did this and Herr Musbach was stunned. He eventually called Herr Oelke to his office and asked me to tell him the story of the capture of the Indian with brown hair and blue eyes. Herr Oelke got tears in his eyes and said that he wanted to see the man. I accompanied Herr Oelke to Ft. Concho where he talked to the man and he concluded that it was indeed his son, for he said that the man looked very much like his own father. Louis Oelke stayed at Fort Concho for 2 more years and several times his mother and father made trips there to see him. He was friendly to them but he said that he did not want to be a farmer or to live in a house. Eventually he went back to Fort Lancaster where he became a scout. He lived there for the rest of his life and was eventually married to a Mexican woman and had several children. The Oelkes continued to visit with him once a year until they became elderly and could no longer travel.

I continued to work on building forts throughout West Texas where I had vowed that I would never return. I was needed there and my salary increased each year. I went back to Fredericksburg about every 3 or 4 months and visited in New Braunfels on my birthday and at Christmas. Life in West Texas was harsh and I looked forward to the wonderful days with my German family and friends.

Chapter 12

The Massacre

Whenever anyone went to New Braunfels or some other larger town they always brought newspapers which I enjoyed reading in both German and English. Every newspaper lately had been talking about the problems brewing between the Northern states and the Southern states. When the men gathered at Fritz's store to drink coffee they discussed the slavery situation. Almost all of us were against slavery, for those of us who came from Germany were well aware of how bad life can be with others making the rules which must be followed. We came to the United States for freedom and economic opportunity, and all of us were scared that the state of Texas would secede from the United States. A vote would be taken to determine the desires of the people. The famous Sam Houston wanted Texas to remain in the Union. If Texas decided to secede, would the men of Fredericksburg, New Braunfels, and other German towns have to join the Rebel army? What would happen to our businesses and farms? How would the families survive? What would the Indians do? What would happen to the forts in West Texas which I had worked so hard to establish?

These were all important questions for which no one seemed to know the answer.

I went for a visit to New Braunfels where I became the Godfather of Dorothea's little daughter Elsie. I went to sleep that night thinking about how life just continues to move forward even though at times we think that it all may end. I asked God to watch over my family and to somehow help us to get out of this coming war.

The next day I visited with many people in New Braunfels. I accompanied three men to the nearby town of Seguin where we went to hear speeches about the upcoming voting. This was a quaint town with a pretty square in the middle and a large court house surrounded by pecan trees. The speeches were held in the cool river bottom. There were all sorts of people in attendance and I could not help but notice several slaves standing by their master's carriages tending to the horses. I had seen many slaves working on the docks along the Mississippi River, but I had seen very few slaves in the New Braunfels and Fredericksburg areas. There were farmers as well as men in business suits in attendance, and there were ladies in fancy dresses carrying umbrellas. Some of them had small children who rode in fancy carriages and were dressed in lace. Many of the men carried pistols on their belts and they wore tall boots. Herr Brendle told us to keep quiet because Germans were not always welcome at such gatherings. The speeches went on and on about the United States government not having the right to tell the states what to do. Some of the speakers were interesting and some were very boring and said the same things over and over again. After about 3 hours of speech making the crowd began to get restless and gradually people began to depart. When we got back to New Braunfels we reported what we had seen and heard and the discussions went on and on. I was not so interested in politics but I was afraid about what the Indians might do in the Hill Country and in the new settlements in West Texas if the men are off fighting in the war.

When I went back to Fort Concho I asked Captain Lancaster about the situation. He said that if Texas seceded from the Union that he, and all of the other men would abandon the forts and go East to join in the war effort against the South. Captain Lancaster was from the state of Pennsylvania and was against slavery. He also said that he could keep his pension if he joined the Union Army. I told him about my worries with the Indians and he suggested that the people of Texas form their own army to guard the frontier from Indian attacks.

It was very unfortunate for the Germans in the Hill Country when the voters in Texas decided to secede from the Union in March 1861. I was in Fredericksburg to cast my vote and I later found out that this was a good thing. At Fort Concho and at Fort Lancaster there was much fighting between the soldiers as they each had to make their decision about which side to give their allegiance. I heard that Captain Lancaster and 200 men immediately left Ft. Concho and went through Oklahoma on up to St. Louis and eventually to Ohio.

As time went by Captain James Duff, who was in charge of the Rebel army in the area, came to Fredericksburg and had a short talk with Herr Musbach. He threatened to burn the town unless the younger men of the community joined the rebel forces. That weekend, when many farmers were coming to town for shopping, dancing and attending church, some of them were stopped and kidnapped by the rebel forces. They were put into the rebel army against their will and they had no recourse but to serve as they were told. Several of them were eventually killed, and two of them escaped from a prison in the East and walked all the way back to Fredericksburg. When they arrived no one recognized them because they were so thin and sick.

I told Fritz to grow a long beard, to wear glasses all the time, and to begin to limp and use a cane for walking. Because of old age PaPa was not in danger, but I wrote Dorothea's husband a letter and told him to stay on the farm as much as possible.

Eventually the Indians made clear what they intended to do now that the soldiers had left the forts in the West. The Comanches, Apaches and

Kiowas went on a robbing and killing spree the likes of which we had never seen before.

As a result of this the State of Texas founded the Texas Militia to fight the Indians. I received a telegram from the Governor of Texas telling me to report to Fort Concho to command a troop of Indian fighters. This is what I did throughout the war.

In West Texas 2 young boys and their father were herding their goats. The father was riding a mule and the boys were walking. Indians suddenly came upon them and shot the father with 3 arrows. The boys ran into the bushes and eventually both of them got back to the house where they prepared for ambush. The Indians did not come to their house. And so the next day they found their father's body and the mule and goats were gone. The word of this came to Fort Concho by messenger and 12 of us set out to find the raiding Indians. Only 5 miles from Fort Concho we saw dust rising in the distance. We made sure our rifles were ready and then we ran to the left and then parallel to the dust. Our aim was to get in front of the Indians and then to attack. But, as we got approximately even with the cloud of dust, the cloud turned and came towards us. We went straight ahead to large rocks we could see in the distance. We were being pursued by this ominous yellow cloud. When we reached the rocks we tied our horses, and got down on our knees behind whatever cover we could find. As usual I had my canteen and extra bullets around my neck. Very soon a mass of pounding hooves came at us and the men were running and diving behind rocks in order not to be trampled. Directly after the herd of horses and mules was a large number of Indians. The dust was so thick that the Indians were hard to spot. I began running from rock to rock and shooting as fast as possible. Very soon I had to reload. An Indian came upon me and threw a spear down at me. I rolled to my side and to my astonishment the spear went through my canteen and into my skin. The Indian thought that he had killed me and he kept on riding. I pulled on the spear and it easily came out of my skin because it had penetrated only about an inch. The canteen was stuck to the spearhead. I took the canteen off my shoulder and dropped it as I ran to the next rock and began shooting again. Blood was coming through my shirt and then to my pants. I remember thinking that I hoped the blood did not reach my boots and ruin them. I continued running and shooting and once an Indian fell from his horse onto me with a knife, but I was saved by Phil Adkinson who was standing nearby and shot the Indian. Finally the Indians were gone and the cloud of yellow dust continued in the distance. The entire episode lasted for perhaps 10 to 15 minutes, but it seemed as though it went on for an hour or more as each movement and event was magnified in my mind.

After sitting still for 5 minutes, we all began to stand up and started looking around for more attacks and to see the condition of our comrades. Two men were dead and 8 of us were injured. One man had broken his arm when he fell against a rock. Only 2 men were without injury. I took off my shirt and held it against the wound on my side, and then someone told my that my back was also bleeding. I had skinned both of my hands badly on the rocks. There were 6 dead Indians lying nearby and one Indian who had a stomach wound. We knew that he would die so we left him behind. We quickly put the dead and injured on their horses and started back to Fort Concho where we arrived at about sundown. The medic began to slowly tend to the injured and I ended up with 8 stitches on my side and 14 stitches on my back. This was much more painful than the original injury and I laid on my bunk for several days feeling very ill with fever.

Another time a rider came to the Fort to report a house on fire several miles away. Eight of us went to investigate. We found no people or animals at the house and many tracks all around. Then we heard moaning from a nearby stream and there we found a 10 year old girl lying on the ground crying. I held her and asked what happened. She said that the Indians came because her father had killed an Indian earlier in the day. They shot both her father and mother with arrows and drug their bodies away. They captured her older sister. I asked the names of her family and wrote them down. The girl had many wounds and she became weaker until about an hour later she died. We buried her on a little hill overlooking the stream bed and then we started looking for her parents. We found her mother about a mile from the house and her father about 3 miles from the house. They were so mutilated that their faces were not recognizable. We buried them back beside their daughter. We followed the Indian trail and saw that it joined another large trail with many footprints. We realized that we would not be able to save the girl. We did follow the trail for 3 days in hopes that the girl had been released or had escaped, but we did not find her. We asked the nearest neighbor if the family had any relatives. Nobody seemed to know where the family had come from. When we got back to Fort Concho I began to make a list of people killed or kidnapped by the Indians. I also begged God to forgive me for killing so many Indians and not being able to save more families.

We divided our unit into 4 groups of about 12 in each group and set out on patrols in 4 directions from the fort. We usually went out for 3 to 5 days and then returned to Fort Concho for 2 days. We made our presence known to the settlers as well as to the raiding Indians. Whenever Indians were spotted we rode to all of the nearby ranches and warned the people to take cover. We also ambushed raiding parties and killed many Indians over a 2 year period. In this way we saved many families from destruction. We lost half of our men because of injury or disease.

On July 15, 1862 I had just finished breakfast at Fort Concho when I received a telegram from Herr Musbach saying that I should come to Fredericksburg immediately because some of the men had been killed. I left within 10 minutes and rode as quickly as Schnell could carry me. I arrived at Herr Musbach's door at midnight and found him still awake sitting on his porch. He explained to me that a very bad thing had happened. Captain Duff had required everyone to take an oath of allegiance to the Confederacy, and those who would not repeat the oath had 30 days in which to leave Texas. Many of the younger men in the area had decided that they could not take the oath or fight for the Rebels. About 80 men met at the head of Turtle Creek to discuss the problem. 61 men decided to leave Texas and go to Mexico. On August 9th they made their camp on the West bank of the Nueces River in South Texas. At about 2:00 a.m. the men were attacked by the Rebel forces while they were sleeping. At least half of the men were killed. Some of them made it to the Rio Grande River where at least 7 of them were killed. Herr Musbach had received a telegram from some unknown person in Victoria telling what had happened. He did not know if the telegram told the truth or not, but he wanted me to go to South Texas and find out. The news had spread through Fredericksburg that the men were killed and everyone was extremely upset. I told Herr Musebach that I would depart at daylight to begin the investigation. As I shook his hand Herr Musebach put his hand on my shoulder and said, "Son, I am sorry to tell you that Fritz was with the group who was attacked." My face turned white and I sat down on the step and tried to catch my breath. Why did Fritz go? Didn't he need to stay here with his family? Does Katherine know? My mind was swamped with questions and I was distraught. I sat there for a while and Herr Musebach sat on the step beside me. He told me how sorry he was that this had happened, that Texas had broken away from the Union, and that he had no control over Capt. Duff. He said that he should have called me to come home sooner, but it all happened so fast and that by the time he had gotten the telegram it was too late. I got up and staggered towards Fritz's house. The house was dark and so I went to my own house and fell on the bed and slept. Before daybreak I gathered money from several different hiding places, packed some food and water onto Schnell and went to Fritz's house. Again the house was dark. I petted the gray horse and then Schnell and I took off and headed for New Braunfels where we arrived in 2 days.

I slept for a few hours and then I left at the same time that PaPa, Mati, the Nagels and all of their children where departing to go to Fredericksburg to be with Katherine and their many friends there.

I rode hard and even found myself sleeping in my saddle a few times. Eventually I got to near the Nueces River and I stopped at several houses and asked the people if they knew anything about a battle. Finally one man told me where he had heard that the battle took place. I rode there and saw a sight which I do not want to describe. There were 19 men lying dead for over a week. I tied my handkerchief around my nose and mouth and looked at the bodies. I wrote down the names of those that I could recognize and I noticed that empty wallets were lying on the ground. None of the men were Fritz. I was sorry that the coyotes and wolves had also found their bodies long before I did. I decided to drag the bodies to the side of a knoll and then to stack them there where I would cover them with dirt. I was afraid to touch the bodies and so I began to tie a rope around their feet and drag one at a time to the burial sight. I had brought 4 bodies to the site when Schnell snorted, lifted his head and pointed his ears. I dropped the rope, jumped on the horse, and started running the opposite way. I ran from tree to tree and in a zig zag motion rather than in a straight line. About 200 yards from the site I stopped and looked back. I saw a group of gray coated soldiers dismount and look at the dead men that I had moved. They began discussing and looking for tracks nearby. Schnell and I took off as fast as he could run and we ran for about half an hour without stopping. We rode through several streams and I rode down stream and then back upstream to throw the trackers off, and then exited the stream in a rocky area.

I continued to ride until I got to the town of Victoria. There I slept with Schnell in the stable. To my advantage I did not look like a German man because West Texas had browned my skin. My hair was long, and I did not look like a farmer. My English was good and I could always throw in a few Spanish words which made me sound like I was from South Texas.

The next morning I went to the Doctor's house in Gonzales. His wife came to the door and said that he had gone to the store and that he would arrive home soon. She told me to wait for him in the barn and not to leave my horse in front of the house. I waited for an hour there and then heard a horse coming around to the back of the house. I recognized the Doctor and I said hello so that I would not surprise him by being in his barn. He stayed on his horse while I explained to him my identity. He said that he well remembered me from the epidemic and from Herr Voltz's death. He asked why I was in his barn. I tried to explain to him about the massacre and about half way through the story my throat began to get very tight and I could not finish. I just sat down on the hay and put my hands over my face. The Doctor got off his horse and put his hand on my shoulder. He expressed his sympathy and said that he had heard about the incident. He asked if anyone had escaped and I said that some of them had gotten to Mexico. He invited me into the house for breakfast and we talked about my time spent fighting the Indians. Eventually I described how I had gotten the telegram from Herr Musebach and that is why I came here. I told him that my best friend, Fritz Nagel, was with the group and that I did not find his body. The Doctor then said that he wanted to tell me something. He said that he had been afraid that I was a spy, but that he must tell me that Fritz survived the massacre and was seriously wounded. He came to the Doctor's house in the middle of the night. The Doctor took him to a small house in the country to hide him from the Rebels. Soon Fritz became very ill with fever and he was lying in that house barely alive. I asked him how to get there and immediately I mounted Schnell and rode in a round about way to the little house on Plum Creek.

I tied Schnell a distance from the house and then quietly walked to the house and opened the door. There was Fritz lying on a bed in the corner. I rushed in to him and called his name, but there was no response. He looked as though he was sleeping. I sat beside him and talked, and bathed his face and body with a wet cloth. I scolded him for what he had done and for getting himself into this problem. I talked about his son and Katherine, and soon I was remembering aloud all the wonderful times we had together. I told him about that day at school when we looked on the teacher's globe and found Texas. I reminded him of our trip on the ship and the wagon train to New Braunfels. I talked about the Four Farmers and reminded him about our first hunting experiences. I talked about the store and how he met Katherine and their wedding, and the house that I built for them. Eventually I laid on the floor and went to sleep.

The next morning Fritz was still breathing and I again talked to him and told him that he must get well very soon so that we could go back to Fredericksburg. Right at noon there was a gasp and then his chest stopped moving and I knew he was dead. I said the Lord's Prayer aloud and prayed for God to take Fritz into heaven very quickly so that he could wait their for Katherine and I to join him later. I wrapped his body in two blankets and tied them with ropes. I then hid his body under the house for fear that someone would discover his body and remove it.

I mounted Schnell and rode to Victoria to the undertaker. I explained that my friend had died and that I needed a casket and a hearse. At first he was very resistant to helping me but after a while he became more at ease. I saw a painting on the wall of his office that pictured tall mountains with tall green trees growing on them. I slowly began to realize that the painting was of Germany. I spoke a few words to him in the German language and he immediately put his finger to his mouth and told me to be quiet. I whispered that my friend had died and that I needed to take his body back to Fredericksburg. I explained that I needed a suit for my friend to wear, I needed to have him embalmed, and I needed a hearse pulled by two black prancing horses. He looked at me as though I was crazy, but he saw that I was very serious about this. He told me to bring the body to the back of his store after dark. He said that he had a hearse that I could rent if I promised to return it within 20 days. He said that he did not have black horses.

That night I did as he said and brought Fritz's body in a rented wagon to the back door of the undertaker. I talked to Fritz as I drove the wagon and I told him not to worry about me being angry with him any more, that all would be fine and that I would take care of him and his family. I returned the rented wagon and asked the stable keeper if he knew where I could get two black horses to pull a wagon. He said to try the stable in Seguin because he had sold them two black horses 6 months ago. I rode all the way to Seguin and there found the two black horses which I bought for twice the normal rate. I led the horses back to Victoria and harnessed them to the hearse. Fritz looked very handsome in a new suit. He looked as though nothing had happened to him, and there was no sign of blood from the three gunshot wounds he had suffered. We put him into the hearse and the undertaker gave me a letter informing anyone who might ask that I was transporting the body of a man who possibly had died of yellow fever. I then set out on the very long journey to Fredericksburg. I was stopped on 3 different occasions by soldiers who wanted to search the hearse. Each time I spoke to them in Spanish and then gave them the letter. As soon as they read the letter they always motioned for me to leave. Other people who saw me took off their hats as the hearse passed by. I stopped only to rest the horses and to eat and I only slept for about 4 hours each night.

Finally I arrived in Fredericksburg at about 10:00 o'clock in the morning on the seventh day. People began to follow me as I went directly to Fritz's house. Soon Katherine came from the house supported by her father on one side and by Herr Nagel on the other. Katherine's mother stood on the porch holding Ernst and Mati was nearby. I seemed to be stuck to the seat of the hearse, for I did not want to get down and face the mourners. But I made myself jump down and Katherine fell into my arms. I said, "He was seriously injured in the battle, but I found him later near the town of Gonzales and he died quietly as I talked to him." Katherine thanked me and immediately I escorted her to the waiting buggy. All the other family members loaded into wagons and I drove the hearse with the fancy prancing black horses down the Main Street of Fredericksburg. People came from the shops and from their homes to walk behind the wagons to the nearby cemetery. We unloaded the coffin and carried it to an open grave which had been dug the day before in case I was able to bring home any of the bodies. I used a hammer to gently lift the lid of the coffin so that Katherine and the Nagel family could see Fritz one last time. I nailed the lid back on and we lowered the coffin into the ground with ropes. The Reverend read the 23 Psalm and led the group in the Lord's Prayer. Herr Nagel and I covered up the grave with dirt.

The family went back to Fritz's house and invited me to come there, but I was too exhausted and too emotional to face Katherine and the Nagel family. I went to Zeller Haus, laid on my bed, cried for a while, and then drifted off to sleep. I dreamed of Fritz and I riding in a fancy carriage, pulled by prancing black horses, down the streets of Bicken, Germany. All of the people of the town were following us to get a look at the two rich men from Texas.

The next morning I had breakfast with Katherine and her family and they were all doing quite well. I explained that I had to return the hearse to the undertaker in Victoria. I accompanied PaPa, Mati, the Nagel family and all of their children back to New Braunfels. I stayed there for one day and then continued on to Victoria without any problems. I returned the hearse and thanked the undertaker for his kindness, and then took the black horses to Seguin to sell them back to the man from whom I had purchased them. He said that he was not interested in buying them back. In order to get back some of my money I needed to sell them. I went all the way to the city of Austin where I was finally able to sell them for $125. I understand that eventually they were used to pull the carriage of the Governor of Texas.

I again went to New Braunfels where I visited with Dorothea and saw her new baby son, John. I was warned to stay away from the main roads as Captain Duff was looking for anyone who might have been involved with the group from the Texas Hill Country. I rode on to Fredericksburg to visit with Katherine and Ernst. Katherine's parents decided to stay with her for a while as their other children could tend their farm. Katherine and I sat on the front porch and I told her the entire story of how I found Fritz. She wanted to know every detail of how he looked, if he ever woke up, and many other questions. She also told me that they had a very big argument because she did not want Fritz to go to the meeting at Turtle Creek. He said that he felt that it was his duty to stand beside his friends.

He told Katherine that he was not going to go with the group to Mexico, but then he went without coming home and telling her goodbye first. I defended Fritz by saying that he thought he was doing the right thing. Katherine then told me that she was with child and that she had not yet told Fritz. Then we both began to cry. I held her and told her that I would see her at Christmas.

The next morning Schnell and I departed for Fort Concho and we went back to our regular duty of chasing Indians and protecting settlers. I tried to stay busy, even cleaning the barracks, for I did not want to have time to think. During the fall I had to write many more names into my book of people who had been killed by the Indians. I also had to kill many Indians during that time, and it weighed heavily upon my heart. I often wondered what would have happened to Fritz and I if we had stayed in Germany. We would have been put into the army and would have had to fight in the civil war there. We came to Texas and we ended up being involved in a civil war here instead. I knew that, as soon as the war ended, I would become a farmer and I would never hunt for Indians again.

Just before Christmas I went home to Fredericksburg and enjoyed being at Silverbrook. I accompanied Katherine and Ernst to church on Christmas Eve and then gave Ernst a rocking horse and Katherine a pretty shawl. They gave me a new canteen which was almost too pretty to use.

On Christmas Day I departed for New Braunfels, arriving there in 2 days to have dinner, with the Nagels, Papa and his family, and Dorothea and her family. Our family has grown from 3 to 9 in only a few years. This was a very happy time for me and I stayed for a week.

There were many Indian raids after Christmas and I spent much time in the cold wind looking for ways to protect the settlers of West Texas.

By early April it was time for me to return to Fredericksburg to support Katherine through childbirth. I was welcomed with open arms by a very tired Katherine. I played with Ernst and took him riding and fishing, and helped Katherine's father with Fritz's store. On April 25 the big day finally arrived and we all welcomed Fritz and Katherine's baby boy, Fritz Nagel Jr.

I stayed on for another 10 days to continue my baby sitting duties. Fritz Jr. had his father's name, but he looked like Katherine. Ernst looked more like PaPa Fritz. I enjoy telling Ernst stories about his father and I intended to keep up this tradition so that he would have a good feeling about his father.

I went back to West Texas until the end of the war. Captain Duff was mustered out of the army and was later convicted of crimes which he had committed before the war. I had the honor of accompanying a group of men from the Texas Hill Country to the Nueces River where we gathered together the bones of the men who had been massacred there. We took the bones to the town of Comfort where they were all buried in one grave with a monument to their honor.

Unfortunately, after the war, there was much trouble with Indians as well as robbers. I moved to Silverbrook but spent most of my time tracking down robbers and marauding Indians. Katherine's parents remained living with her and running the store. By 1867 things had settled down and the Forts in West Texas were reopened. I never saw Captain Lancaster again, but I heard that he had survived the war and was a Colonel stationed in New York.

Once I did ride down to the Rio Grande and found Anka living there with his family. He was married and had 5 children and he rarely came back to Texas. No mention was made of his niece Anna. We talked for several days not using the English language a single time.

Chapter 13

The Happy Years

In the fall of 1867 my life was forever altered. I rode into Fredericksburg to transport Ernst to his first day at school. I arrived just as he finished his breakfast. He kissed Katherine goodbye, slammed the screen door, and I pulled him from the porch to the back of the gray horse. We waved to Katherine as we departed. Arriving at the school, I dismounted and took Ernst down from his perch at the back of the saddle. I straightened his clothes, made sure his shirt was tucked into his pants, and handed him his lunch pail. As he was walking toward the school he turned around and said, "Danke PaPa Nic."

I smiled broadly, watched him enter the school, and then I rode to Katherine's house. We each got a cup of coffee and sat on the front porch where we watched Fritz Jr. play in the dirt. We talked about how we could not believe Ernst was old enough to go to school, and how excited Fritz had been when Ernst was born. I told Katherine that I was sure that she had secretly visited Fritz's house during the construction. She admitted that she had persuaded her younger brother to bring her there on his mule in the dead of night because she could not stand the suspense. Then I said, "Katherine, you know that you are the only woman that I have ever loved." She slowly placed the coffee cup on the saucer and smiled at me. I said, "Katherine will you marry me?" Without hesitation she said "Yes", and that was the beginning of my new life as a family man. We were married at Silverbrook the next Saturday afternoon and that was the first time that I kissed Katherine on the lips instead of the cheek. While my new in-laws baby sat the boys, Katherine and I took a 2 week honeymoon trip to Galveston. On our return we stopped in New Braunfels for 2 days and let everyone there shower us with good wishes. The Nagel family was very happy for us and they said that there could be no better stepfather for their grandchildren. Just before we all started to cry, Mati came from the kitchen with a large white cake to celebrate the occasion.

We returned to Nagel Haus, for this is what I have named Fritz's home, but eventually we lived there only during the school term and on weekends. We spent the rest of our time at Silverbrook where we had cattle, horses, chickens, hogs, 4 large fields, and 3 children of our own-2 boys and a girl.

Katherine's father continued to run Fritz's store until Ernst was old enough to take over at the age of 16, and eventually Fritz Jr. took over the Nagel farm near Fredericksburg.

My life before 1867 was adventurous, challenging, exciting, and full of turmoil. I was constantly in a state of learning and fearing what I had to do. There was never a soft bed, or a good meal, or clean clothes, or someone to talk to privately, and nobody to hug and kiss. My life after 1867 was a life of goodness, happiness, compassion, and love, all because I married my beloved Katherine.

In January 1868 I mailed the black book, in which I had entered the names of the people killed by the Indians, to the office of the Texas Rangers in Austin. I still enjoyed hunting occasionally and making deer meat sausage. I was not allowed to enter the local shooting contests, but on occasion I shot targets just for an exhibition. I also had a hobby of making pictures by shooting into a piece of tin. I could shoot the form of a buffalo, an Indian head, and a heart.

Once I took Katherine all the way to New Orleans and up the Mississippi to St. Louis. In New Orleans I tried to find Harry Knight but I was unsuccessful. We were successful in visiting the nuns who had one of the finest private schools in New Orleans.

On our return trip we took a sloop over to Carlshaven where we found the old warehouse in shambles. We bought a buggy and traveled the road to Victoria where we visited the undertaker, and to the town of Gonzales where we visited the old doctor. Katherine asked many questions about Fritz and he assured her that he cared for him as well as he could, but infection had already set in. Fritz told him that he must contact his family in Fredericksburg because he needed to apologize to them. The doctor was the person who had sent a telegram to Herr Musbach telling about the massacre.

Katherine and I visited San Antonio where we looked at the old Alamo fortress, watched dancers at the market, and prayed in the cathedral. That night I kissed Katherine on the bridge called Commerce.

Postscript

What Happened Later

On June 21, 1888 Nicholas celebrated his 56th birthday with Katherine and the children. Four days later he had a fever and sat on the front porch for most of the week instead of getting out and working with the boys in the fields. By June 30 he had pains in his sides every time he took a breath and the doctor said that he had pneumonia. On July 1 each of his children came to the house and sat with him for a while to say goodbye. On July 2, 1888 Nicholas quietly died while Katherine held his hand. His last words were, "I see the feather".

Nicholas was buried one space over from Fritz so that later Katherine could be buried between her two husbands. Katherine lived for 8 more years and she always told her children and grandchildren that she had a wonderful life because she was married to the best two men in Texas.

On July 16 a very old man with a long white beard and white hair to his shoulders, walked into the general store in New Braunfels, and asked if anyone knew Nicholas Steubing. He was informed that Nicholas had just recently died in Fredericksburg. The man expressed his sympathy and went on to Austin, Texas where he built a magnificent hotel near the Capitol.

The descendants of Fritz, Katherine and Nicholas indeed enjoyed the fruits of the good land called Texas, and many of them still live in the Hill Country. The descendants include teachers, ranchers, construction workers, a county sheriff, a tax consultant, a jet pilot, homemakers, and many others who from time to time visit the Civil War Memorial in Comfort and the cemetery in Fredericksburg. One of Nic's great grandsons will killed fighting the Germans at the Battle of the Bulge during World War II. Most of Nic's descendants know only a few words of the German language, but several of them have visited the town of Bicken, Germany where they found the graves of Oma, Opa and Tante Gretchen. The old house still stands at Silverbrook and is inhabited by a great great grandson. Zeller Haus is a part of a museum complex. Zeller Farm and Nagel Farm we sold years ago, and the Nagel Haus in Fredericksburg is now a Bed and Breakfast. The old houses along Mill Street in New Braunfels were demolished at the turn of the century, about 1900, and new houses were built.

This is in part a work of fiction. Although inspired by actual events, the names, persons, places, and characters are inventions of the author. Any resemblence to people living or deceased is purely coincidental.

Study Guide

CHAPTER ONE

1. From where did the Steubing family originate in Germany?
2. What had been their business for generations?
3. How old was Nic when he departed his homeland?
4. What reason did PaPa give for immigrating to Texas?
5. When Nic and Fritz fantasized about the future, what kind of wagons and horses would they own when they were rich men?
6. What was the name of the ship on which Nic sailed to Texas?
7. On what two rivers was the town of New Braunfels situated?
8. How long did Captain Kerr say he would remain at sea?
9. What language did Nic learn during the voyage?
10. On what date did Nic first arrive in New Braunfels?

CHAPTER TWO

1. Where did the Steubings live while they built a house?
2. What was the first piece of furniture PaPa made?
3. On what street in New Braunfels did they live?
4. How many acres was the farm outside of town?
5. What did MaMa use to stuff the homemade mattresses?

6. How did PaPa acquire a baby pig?
7. What type of fence did they build to protect the crops?
8. Who gave Nic his first hunting lesson?
9. How did Nic awaken Fritz for hunting expeditions?
10. How much did Nic pay for his new boots?

CHAPTER THREE

1. Where did Nic get his first taste of pinto beans?
2. What was the first city in Texas that Nic visited?
3. When Nic thought of home, which home did he think about?
4. What did Herr Zeller say would happen if Nic ate candy?
5. Who taught Nic how to fish?
6. What type of weather caused problems for the new immigrants?
7. What trait could make the difference between life and death, success and failure?
8. In what town did Herr Zeller leave the sick immigrants?
9. What happened to Ella Brockoff?
10. Why did Nic bury his face in the mane of the gray horse and cry?

CHAPTER FOUR

1. What obvious landmark verified that Herr Zeller located the land grant in the Hill Country?
2. Name the new town in the Hill Country that Nic helped found.
3. On what date did the new settlers depart New Braunfels for the new settlement in the Hill Country?
4. What did the group do when they arrived there?
5. What happened on the fortieth day in the new settlement?
6. Who did Nic rescue from the storm in Carlshaven?
7. What was Fritz's new business?
8. What was the name of Nic and Harry's company?
9. What dramatic event took place on Nic's 16th birthday?
10. What did Nic inherit?

CHAPTER FIVE

1. To what city did Nic go to have his tooth pulled?
2. On what bridge did Nic view the river there?
3. What was the name of Nic's town house in Fredericksburg?
4. Why did Nic name his farm Silverbrook?
5. What happened to Wilhelm Oelke?
6. How did the Indians conceal their trail?
7. What did Nic dream about when he returned home?
8. Did the Indians raid during the winter?
9. Where did Nic spend Christmas?
10. What happened on Christmas Day?

CHAPTER SIX

1. What exciting event took place when Nic and Harry rode to Ft. Concho?
2. Name the family that gave Nic and Harry refuge.
3. Name the second family where Nic and Harry stayed and played with the baby.
4. Who was the Captain of Fort Concho?
5. What was the purpose of Nic and Harry's visit with the Captain?
6. On what holiday did the Indians build fires around the town of Fredericksburg?
7. What did the mothers tell the children about the fires?
8. On what river did the meeting between the Germans and Indians take place?
9. What was the Comanche Chief's name?
10. Who went into the Comanche camp all alone?

CHAPTER SEVEN

1. How did Nic get the cattle to come to him at Silverbrook?
2. What happened to Nic on his 17th birthday?
3. Name the man whose home was burned by Indians?

4. To who was Fritz engaged?
5. What was this young woman known for in the community?
6. Where did Nic get the rocks to build Fritz's house?
7. Why was Mati so popular with PaPa's friends and family?
8. On what date did Fritz get married?
9. Name Nic's new half-brother.
10. Name the horse given to Nic by Herr Musebach?

CHAPTER EIGHT

1. Name the expedition in which Nic participated in 1849?
2. In what city did the expedition officially begin?
3. Did the Frio River feel cold?
4. What happened to a mule at the Pecos River?
5. How did Anka stop an Indian attack?
6. What did Nic say to the Captain when he wanted to enter the camp?
7. Where was Nic on his 19th birthday?
8. How did Nic get a concho shell necklace?
9. Name the young woman that Nic found attractive in Mexico.
10. To whom did Dorothea become engaged?

CHAPTER NINE

1. How long did Nic remain in New Braunfels to visit?
2. Name Fritz and Katherine's firstborn son.
3. On what date was the baby born?
4. Who was the baby's Godfather?
5. Where did Nic celebrate his 20th birthday?
6. After the shipping company was dissolved where did Harry go?
7. Where did Nic buy a wedding suit for Gunar?
8. By what holiday did Nic want to complete his house at Silverbrook?
9. What did PaPa give Nic for his new house?
10. How did Nic's boots get wet on the return to New Braunfels?

CHAPTER TEN

1. How did Nic get from Galveston to New Orleans?
2. Where did Nic find Harry Knight in New Orleans?
3. Where did Harry and Nic stay in New Orleans?
4. What women stayed in the same establishment?
5. Did Nic like to watch Harry play poker?
6. Who was the Captain of the paddlewheeler on which Nic worked?
7. Where did Nic prefer to sleep while on the paddlewheeler?
8. Name the wagonmaster for whom Nic worked from St. Louis to Chicago?
9. How did Nic travel back from Chicago to St. Louis?
10. Where did Nic spend his 21st birthday?

CHAPTER ELEVEN

1. Why did Captain Lancaster call on Nic to help build the forts?
2. Where was Fort Lancaster established?
3. When did Nic set out to help build the fort?
4. Why didn't Captain Lancaster go to establish the fort?
5. What was the primary building material used to build the fort?
6. What special treat did Nic provide for Christmas dinner?
7. Name the spring where Nic participated in an Indian fight?
8. Who did Nic discover after the Indian fight?
9. How was this person identified by his father?
10. Where did this man live out his life?

CHAPTER TWELVE

1. Was Nic in favor of slavery?
2. Did Sam Houston want Texas to secede from the Union?
3. What was Dorothea's daughter named?
4. Where did Nic go to hear political speeches?
5. Where there many slaves in New Braunfels and Fredericksburg?
6. What would Captain Lancaster do if Texas seceded from the Union?

7. What was Nic's job during the Civil War?
8. Where were the German men from the Hill Country attacked?
9. Where did Nic finally sell the pair of black horses?
10. Did Nic like to kill Indians?

CHAPTER THIRTEEN

1. In what year did Nic say that his life was "altered forever"?
2. How did Ernst Nagel address Nic on his first day of school?
3. Where were Nic and Katherine sitting when he proposed to her?
4. Where did Nic and Katherine get married?
5. Where did Nic and Katherine go on their honeymoon?
6. Where did Nic and Katherine live most of the time?
7. How many children did Nic and Katherine have of their own?
8. Who ran Fritz's store until Ernst was old enough?
9. What did Nic mail to the Texas Rangers in Austin in 1868?
10. On what bridge in San Antonio did Nic kiss Katherine?

POSTSCRIPT

1. On what date did Nic die?
2. Why did Nic die?
3. What were Nic's last words?
4. Where was Nic buried?
5. How many more years did Katherine live?
6. Who asked about Nic in New Braunfels a few days later?
7. Did any of Nic's descendants remain in the Hill Country?
8. Did Nic's descendants continue to use German as their primary language?
9. What happened to Silverbrook?
10. When were the old houses on Mill Street in New Braunfels demolished?

FOR A DEEPER UNDERSTANDING

1. Describe Nic's physical features and his personality.
2. Would you consider Nic to be a generous person? Give examples.
3. Would you consider Nic to be intelligent? Give examples.
4. Did Nic hold a grudge against all Indians?
5. Contrast the personalities and appearances of MaMa and Mati.
6. Why did Dorothea prefer to live with the Nagel family?
7. Describe the relationship between Nic and Herr Zeller.
8. What was the significance of Captain Kerr in this story?
9. How did PaPa change?
10. Do you think that Nic's life may have been different if Ella Brockoff had not died?
11. Describe Nic's relationship with Fritz.
12. Was Nic always in love with Katherine, or did their love develop later?
13. Why was the gray horse so important to Nic?
14. Did Nic love to kill animals?
15. Why did Nic go to New Orleans and Chicago?
16. Was Nic too young to be a leader and a scout? Explain your answer.
17. What did Anka provide for Nic?
18. Why was Chief Red Hawk willing to make a treaty with Herr Musbach?
19. Describe the character of Harry Knight.
20. What did you learn from this book? Please explain.

ANSWERS TO THE STUDY QUESTIONS

CHAPTER ONE

1. Bicken, Germany
2. the freighting business
3. 14 years old
4. freedom and opportunity
5. surrey pulled by a pair of matching black horses
6. "Angelina"

7. Comal and Guadalupe
8. until his hair turned gray
9. English
10. June 8, 1845

CHAPTER TWO

1. a tent
2. a bench
3. Mill Street
4. ten acres
5. tree moss
6. by making 5 beds
7. rock
8. Herr Zeller
9. by tugging a string tied to Fritz's toe
10. $2.00

CHAPTER THREE

1. house of Herr Voltz
2. Victoria
3. his new home in New Braunfels
4. it was bad for your heart and teeth
5. Harry Knight
6. rain and cold
7. experience
8. Castell
9. died of fever
10. MaMa died

CHAPTER FOUR

1. the domed granite rock, the rock of enchantment
2. Fredericksburg
3. April 23, 1846

4. prayed
5. flood
6. Harry Knight
7. store in Fredericksburg
8. Star Shipping Co.
9. Herr Zeller killed by an Indian
10. house, farm, $100, gray horse, rifle, pistol

CHAPTER FIVE

1. San Antonio to a barber
2. Commerce
3. Zeller Haus
4. reflection of moonlight in the creek
5. captured and killed by Indians
6. by setting a grass fire
7. the Indian killing Herr Zeller and the feather covered with blood
8. no
9. New Braunfels
10. PaPa married Mati

CHAPTER SIX

1. Indian attack
2. Johnson
3. Ackerman
4. Captain Lancaster
5. to make contact with the Comanche Indians in order to enact a peace treaty
6. Easter
7. that Easter bunnies were boiling eggs
8. San Saba
9. Red Hawk
10. Herr Musbach

CHAPTER SEVEN

1. he fed them corn
2. won the shooting contest
3. Mr. Clark
4. Katherine Weil
5. her fine singing voice
6. from the river beds
7. rosy cheeks and happy disposition
8. July 1, 1848
9. Wilhelm
10. Schnell

CHAPTER EIGHT

1. West Texas Expedition
2. San Antonio
3. no, even though the word Frio means cold in Spanish
4. the mule fell down the rugged cliff and died
5. by calling out to the Indians in their own language
6. "This is Nicholas Steubing from Germany"
7. on the desert of West Texas
8. from an Indian
9. Anna
10. Gunar Helmke

CHAPTER NINE

1. 2 weeks
2. Ernst Nicholas Nagel
3. July 10
4. Nic
5. in New Braunfels
6. New Orleans
7. Victoria

8. by Christmas
9. bed, wardrobe, wash stand, table with 4 chairs, and 2 rocking chairs
10. when he rescued the Nagel girl from the Guadalupe River

CHAPTER TEN

1. by ship
2. at a gambling house
3. at a boarding house
4. Catholic nuns
5. no
6. Captain O'Toole
7. on a bale of cotton on deck
8. John McGreggor
9. purchased a horse
10. in New Braunfels

CHAPTER ELEVEN

1. could not find Anka
2. on Live Oak Creek on the Pecos River
3. October 1851
4. broken leg
5. rocks
6. turkey
7. Mescalero Springs
8. Louis Oelke-white man dressed as an Indian
9. looked very much like his grandfather
10. Fort Lancaster as a scout

CHAPTER TWELVE

1. no
2. no
3. Elsie
4. Seguin

5. no
6. abandon the fort and head east
7. command State Militia
8. on the Nueces River
9. Austin
10. no

CHAPTER THIRTEEN

1. in 1867
2. “PaPa Nic”
3. on the front porch of Nagel Haus
4. Silverbrook
5. Galveston and New Braunfels
6. Silverbrook
7. 2 boys and a girl
8. Katherine’s father
9. the black book in which he had listed the names of people killed by Indians
10. Commerce

POSTSCRIPT

1. July 2, 1888
2. pneumonia
3. “I see a feather”
4. in Fredericksburg one space over from Fritz
5. 8 years
6. Captain Kerr
7. yes
8. not much
9. a great great gandson lives there
10. about 1900

ANSWERS FOR A DEEPER UNDERSTANDING

1. brown hair, blue eyes, tanned skin, friendly, liked to read, liked to laugh, tried to please others
2. Yes, helped PaPa and Captain Kerr, bought clothes for Dorothea, bought Fritz and Gunar suits, helped the nuns in New Orleans
3. yes-he went to school in Germany, learned languages easily, liked to read, was good at business, worked hard to become a good marksman and hunter, and worked hard at all jobs he was given
4. no, he did not enjoy killing Indians and viewed them as real people
5. MaMa was sickly, quiet and worried, Mati was plump, had a rosy complexion, and was happy and popular
6. When her mother died PaPa worked all the time and Nic was usually gone, and she liked to be with the Nagel girls
7. Herr Zeller was Nic's mentor, was a good family friend, and Nic became his heir
8. Captain Kerr was the first person that Nic met on the trip to Texas and Nic saw him as a bridge between his old world and the new life in Texas. Captain Kerr continued to make the trip across the Atlantic and did not come to Texas to stay until the end of the story. Maybe he took over the idea of coming to Texas for Nic when Nic was gone.
9. PaPa was following the family traditions in Germany but when he came to Texas he set out on his own to provide for his family. He became a carpenter which he had never dreamed of before. He was able to remarry and have a happy life. He made the right decision in bringing his family to Texas even though he never saw his parents or his homeland again.
10. Maybe Nic would have married Ella and remained in New Braunfels to be a farmer.
11. Nic and Fritz were best friends. Nic always took care of Fritz, even when he died, and Nic took care of Fritz's family.
12. Nic and Katherine loved each other as friends and later gradually fell in love. Nic's love was an extension of Fritz's love.

13. The gray horse was an fine animal and was the symbol of growing up in Texas. They gray was a link to Herr Zeller.
14. Nic killed animals only to provide meat. He turned his head when he saw the deer suffering and said that he would never kill for sport.
15. He was upset by Fritz's death and needed to get away. He was also curious about other places in the United States.
16. The young immigrant had to grow up very fast in order to survive. Nic changed from a boy to a man rapidly after he came to Texas. As Nic said "a little experience could mean the difference between life and death, success and failure". Nic's PaPa was not able to provide much for his family and Nic had to go out on his own at an early age.
17. Anka gave Nic an education in the ways of the frontier. He taught him how to speak Spanish, Comanche and Apache, how to hunt, scout and fight the enemy. Nic said that Anka gave him and "university education". Anka helped Nic realize that Indians were also human.
18. Chief Red Hawk said that it was because Herr Musbach came to the camp alone and unarmed. The Indians had never seen anyone with long flowing red and beard.
19. Harry had a poor upbringing and no education. Nic taught him and helped him to earn money. Nic considered Harry to be reckless with his money because he spent it on gambling and alcohol.
20. Determination and a kind heart will help a person to succeed in life. Obstacles will get in the way but the person must keep trying to meet life's goals. Problems and sorrows are as much a part of life's experiences as are the good and easy times. Nic became stronger because of adversity and he did not give up.

About This Book

Each day became a quest for survival for Nicholas, a 14 year old German immigrant who came to New Braunfels, Texas in 1846 and grew into a man very quickly. Based on the author's ancestors, *Silverbrook* is about the adventures in Nic's early years and his reactions to these events. Nicholas Steubing will leave a lasting impression in your heart and mind. Use the study guide questions for a deeper understanding of this historically accurate epic adventure.

Author's Note

A school was named for my great grandfather, Henry Steubing Jr., and I supplied family information for the dedication. I began to wonder what life had been like for my great great grandfather, Heinrich Steubing Sr., who came from Bicken, Germany to New Braunfels, Texas with his family at the age of 16 aboard the ship "Angelina". This led me to write an account of a boy becoming a man and building a new life in Texas.

About the Author

After extensive research, Karen Petersen has written many articles for newspapers and prepared the thesis for two Texas State Historical Markers. Because of her love of local history, Karen has been a professional tour guide in San Antonio for many years and designed tours and events for convention groups. She authored "Owning and Operating a Destination Management Company" published by Haworth Press, Inc., and a short story about her horses is included in *Saddle Pals* published by Country Books. Karen is a graduate of Trinity University and is a former teacher.

Printed in the United States
3625